Also by Robert A. Heinlein

FOR US, THE LIVING

A Comedy of Customs

By

Robert A. Heinlein

With an Introduction by SPIDER ROBINSON
and an Afterword by ROBERT JAMES, PH.D.

SCRIBNER
New York   London   Toronto   Sydney   Singapore

for Heinlein's Children

"It is for us, the living, rather, to be dedicated to the unfinished work . . . that this nation, under God, shall have a new birth of freedom . . ."

—Lincoln at Gettysburg

EDITOR'S NOTE

This novel was written by Robert Heinlein between 1938 and 1939 and was never edited while Heinlein was alive. While the novel is presented in its original form, minor editorial changes have been made for clarity and style.

INTRODUCTION

RAH DNA

"Any map of the world that does not include Utopia is not even worth glancing at."

—OSCAR WILDE

Most authorities are calling this book Robert A. Heinlein's first novel. I avoid arguing with authorities—it's usually simpler to shoot them—but I think it is something far more important than that, myself, and infinitely more interesting.

But my disagreement is respectful, and I'm not prepared to dispute the point with sidearms, or even ripe fruit. Robert himself called *For Us, The Living* a novel, repudiating that label only once that I know of, in private correspondence, and the book clearly has at least as much right to be called a novel as, say, H. G. Wells's *When the Sleeper Wakes* (Robert's favorite novel, he once told me) or *The Shape of Things to Come*.

But no more right. And those two volumes are from the last stage of Wells's illustrious career, at the point when, in Theodore Sturgeon's memorable phrase, the master had "sold his birthright for a pot of message." They are not the books to give to a reader unfamiliar with H. G. Wells, and this is not the book to give to the hypothetical blind Martian hermit unfamiliar with Robert A. Heinlein's work. Like the Wells titles, or Edward Bellamy's *Looking Backward*, this book is essentially a series of Utopian lectures, whose fictional component is a lovely but thin and translucent negligee, only half-concealing an urgent desire to seduce. At age thirty-two, Robert was already trying to save the world—and perfectly aware that the world was largely disinclined to be saved.

If this were really a novel in the same sense as any of Robert's other long works, one would be forced to call at least its fictional aspect deficient, for many of its characters—*quite* uncharacteristically—achieve little depth and behave oddly. Even in his most exotic settings, Robert's characters—even, or perhaps especially, his aliens—were always, always *real*. And in real life, the standard response to a man who tells you he was born 150 years ago in a different body is not, we may as well admit, simply to nod and begin explaining to him how keen everything is nowadays, as do all the people that Perry Nelson meets in 2086.

If one supposes, however, that none of these characters was ever intended—or needed—to be any more real than their colleague Mr. A Square of Flatland, then one cannot help but be struck by how surprisingly much humanity, personality, and appeal they do manage to acquire for us, without ever shirking their lecturing duties. There is no question that by book's end, Perry and his Diana are as real and alive as any other Heinlein couple, if more lightly sketched.

Nonetheless, I submit that there was never a day in his life when Robert Anson Heinlein *the fiction writer* would have written a two-page footnote—and certainly not to introduce *character development*. To me, that detail alone is sufficient proof that he simply was not thinking in story terms when he sat down to compose *For Us, The Living*.

That is why I say that it is so immensely much more than just his first novel. It is *all* of them, dormant.

It seems clear to me, as he himself admitted, that Robert began this book with the perfectly honorable artistic intention of lying through his teeth: of disguising a series of lectures as fiction, purely in order to bring them to the attention of those who, finding the implication of their own imperfection upsetting, would not knowingly consent to be lectured. He succeeded brilliantly; one may agree or disagree with any of the theories and ideas he puts forth here, but one will most certainly and emphatically do one or the other: I defy anyone to lose interest in the middle of the argument—this despite the extreme complexity and, in some cases, sheer profundity of the ideas discussed. Perry is easily as good at his job as Mr. A Square, and does it at much greater length and (ahem) depth.

As thinly fictionalized lecture series, the book failed, for much the same reasons Robert himself had failed of election the previous year: in 1939, most of his ideas were—one is quite unsurprised to learn—wildly ahead of their time, radical, and opposed by powerful societal institutions. Nonetheless, though unpublishable then, its completion was an event of almost inexpressible importance in twentieth century English letters.

Because here, *I* think, is what happened:

On some unknown day in the first four months of 1939, Robert Anson Heinlein sat looking gloomily at a carbon of the manuscript that had just been rejected a second time and found himself thinking back over the whole long, painful period of its creation—the endless hours hunched over a typewriter, staring at a blank piece of paper until beads of blood formed on his forehead. And as he did so, two revelations came to him, in this order:

First, he realized, with surprise and warm pleasure, that the most enjoyable, almost effortless part of the entire experience had *not* been the world-saving he'd set out to accomplish, not the logical theories, mathematical proofs, or clever arguments of which he was so proud . . . but the storytelling part, that he had intended only as a come-on for the crowd. All at once, I think, it came to him that the lecturer must remain standing in the square, on a rickety soapbox, and speak at the top of his lungs, and be heckled by boobs . . . but the storyteller sits in cross-legged comfort in the shade, and *his* listeners crowd round to hear him whisper, offering beer for his sore throat. And when he is done, they give him money, without him even asking.

Second, he looked back over the lengthy and detailed imaginary future he had just thrown together as a set decoration, and saw the ideas stacked all round its empty stage . . . and realized it offered him a canvas so broad that, given enough time, he might contrive to spend all the rest of his working days in the sheer joy of telling stories, creating friends and heroes out of nothing, leaping across galaxies and inside hearts—and still end up putting across every insight and opinion he felt the world needed to hear.

In that moment, he understood for the first time that he wanted to be a storyteller. That he wanted to be a science fiction writer. No, I'm wrong: he realized that he *was* a science fiction writer—and accepted his doom. In the terminology of Roger Zelazny's immortal novel *Lord of Light*, he took on his Aspect, and raised up his Attribute, and was born a god. In that moment, he ceased being Bob Heinlein, shipwrecked sailor and unemployed engineer, and became RAH, the Dean of Modern Science Fiction—the Man Who Sold The Moon—Lazarus Long, who cannot die. In my dreams, I can almost imagine what it must have felt like.

When he was good and ready, he announced the news to the rest of us, by sitting down in April and producing, first crack out of the box, one of the most unforgettable pieces of short fiction in the English language, "Lifeline." *Two years later,* he was the Pro Writer Guest of Honor at Denvention, the Third World Science Fiction Convention in Denver, and everyone in that banquet hall already knew he owned the field. Five months after he gave his famous Guest of Honor speech on time-binding, "The Discovery of the Future," Japan blindsided Pearl Harbor. But once that pesky distraction had been dispensed with, Robert turned his attention to the *non*–science fiction literary world, and conquered that, too, with an ease, elegance, and speed that Hitler and Tojo could have learned from.

But everything began on that unknown day or night sometime in early 1939, when Robert had his own personal equivalent of the blinding flash in which Nikola Tesla suddenly saw in his head a complete 3-D working model of the first-ever AC electric motor, correctly tuned and broken in, ready to be manufactured without delay for testing.

The seeds of *many* of Robert's major novels are clearly visible, here, needing only room and time to grow. The essential core of his entire career is implicit as DNA code buried in the pages of *For Us, The Living:* it constitutes an overflowing treasure chest of themes, ideas, theories, concepts, characters, and preoccupations he would draw on again and again for the next half century to inform his stories. Time travel; multiple identity; transcendence of physical death; personal privacy; personal liberty; personal and political pragmatism; using good technology for personal hedonistic comfort; balancing of privilege and responsibility; the arts, and especially new future artforms like dance in variable gravity; the metric system; rolling roads; then-unconventional loathing of racism, sexism, and anti-Semitism; Alfred Korzybski's general semantics; alternate histories; the nature of sexual love; alternatives to monogamy and conventional marriage; spirituality; the pseudospirituality of the loathsome Nehemiah Cheney—excuse me, Scudder; The Crazy Years; space travel, the Moon, and Diaspora to the stars . . . it's all here, nascent, in thumbnail view. So is that splendid, unmistakable voice.

Robert's ideas and opinions certainly evolved over time, particularly after he met his last wife, and this book is far from his last word on Utopia. But the differences themselves are fascinating and illuminating to any serious student of his work. It's clear that, from the moment it finally dawned on him he was a storyteller, all Robert Heinlein really needed to produce that towering body of work that changed the world and put footprints on the Moon was time, typing paper, Virginia Gerstenfeld Heinlein, and a series of publishers' royalty checks sufficient to keep them both smiling. He may not have consciously known, himself, just where his work would take him, in anything like the kind of detail this book prefigures. I rather hope not. But the work already knew.

And now, thanks to Robert James—may he be as lucky in love as Lazarus, for as Long!—and thanks to Michael Hunter, Eleanor Wood, and Sarah Knight, we all do.

We are deeply in their debt.

This may not (or may—I repeat: I won't argue) be a novel in the classic sense, but to me it's something more interesting. It's a career in a box . . . a freeze-dried feast . . . a lifetime, latent in a raindrop . . . a lifework seed, waiting to be watered by our tears and laughter—RAH's literary DNA . . .

. . . or half of it, at any rate. It's worth remembering that this is one of the very few examples we'll ever see of the writing of one of the century's great lovers, the man who literally defined the word* . . . *before* he met the love of his life. The difference is

---

*love: the condition in which the welfare and happiness of another become essential to your own.

palpable; I'm not trying to offer a Zen koan when I say that it is in her very absence in this book that Ginny is perhaps even more present than in any other. One senses him yearning for her, straining to imagine her. The Portuguese word for "the presence of absence," *saudade,* is the heart of *fado*—reading this book was an emotional as well as intellectual experience for me, is all I'm trying to say: I kept hearing Django play a bittersweet guitar as I turned the pages. To read this book is to know both Robert Heinlein and the late Virginia Heinlein much better—and that is something I've wanted to do all my adult life.

Fate has brought an unexpected gift from beyond the grave, for us, the living.

Spider Robinson
Bowen Island, British Columbia
5 September 2003
www.spiderrobinson.com

FOR US,
THE LIVING

"FOR US, THE LIVING—

A Comedy of Customs

by
Robert Heinlein

2 words

"Look out!" The cry broke involuntarily from Perry
Nelson's lips as he twisted the steering wheel. But the
driver of the green sedan either did not hear him or
did not act. The next few seconds of action flickered
through his mind like slow motion. He saw the left
front wheel of the green car float past his own, then the
right wheel of his car crawled over the guard rail, his
car slid after it and hung poised on the edge of the
palisade. He stared over the hood and saw facing him
the beach a hundred and thirty feet below. A blonde
girl in a green bathing suit was catching a beach
ball. She had jumped in the air to do it, both arms
outstretched, one leg pointed. She was very graceful.
Beyond her a wave broke on the sand. The crest hung
and dripped whipped cream. He glanced back at the
girl. She was still catching the beach ball. As she
settled back on her feet, he drifted clear of the car
and turned in the air away from her. Facing him were
the rocks at the foot of the bluff. They approached

I

"Look out!" The cry broke involuntarily from Perry Nelson's lips as he twisted the steering wheel. But the driver of the green sedan either did not hear him or did not act. The next few seconds of action floated through his mind like slow motion. He saw the left front wheel of the green car float past his own, then the right wheel of his car crawled over the guard rail, his car slid after it and hung poised on the edge of the palisade. He stared over the hood and saw facing him the beach a hundred and thirty feet below. A blonde girl in a green bathing suit was catching a beach ball. She had jumped in the air to do it, both arms outstretched, one leg pointed. She was very graceful. Beyond her a wave broke on the sand. The crest hung and dripped whipped cream. He glanced back at the girl. She was still catching the beach ball. As she settled back on her feet, he drifted clear of the car and turned in the air away from her. Facing him were the rocks at the foot of the bluff. They approached as he watched them, separated and became individuals. One rock selected him and came straight toward him. It was a handsome rock, flat on one side and brilliant while in the sunshine. A sharp edge faced him and grew and grew and grew until it encompassed the whole world.

• • •

Perry got up, shook his head, and blinked his eyes. Then he recalled the last few seconds with startling clarity and threw up his hands in convulsive reflex. But the rock was not in front of his face. There was nothing in front of his face but whirling snow flakes. The beach was gone and the bluff and the rest of his world. Nothing but snow and wind surrounded him—wind that cut through his light clothing. A gnawing pain in the midriff resolved into acute hunger. "Hell!" said Perry. Hell. Yes, hell it must be, cold instead of hot. He commenced to walk but his legs were weak under him and a giddiness assailed him. He staggered a few steps and fell on his face. He attempted to rise, but was too weak and decided to rest a moment. He lay still, trying not to think, but his confused brain still struggled with the problem. He was beginning to feel warmer when he found a solution. Of course! The girl in the green bathing suit caught him and threw him into the snow bank—soft snow bank—nice warm snow bank—nice—warm—

"Get up" the girl in the green bathing suit was shaking him. "Get up! Hear me? *Get up!*" What did she want—to hell with games—just because she wanted to play games was no reason to slap a fellow's face. He struggled to his knees, then fell heavily. The figure beside him slapped him again and nagged him until he rose to his knees, then steadied him and helped him to his feet. "Easy now. One arm over my shoulders. It's not far."

"I'm all right."

"Don't be a fool. Lean on me." He looked down at the face of his companion and tried to focus his eyes. It *was* the girl in the green bathing suit, but what in hell was she doing dressed up like Admiral Byrd? Complete to the parka. But his tired brain refused to worry and he focused all of his attention on putting one icy leaden foot in front of another.

"Mind the steps. Easy. Now hold still." The girl sang one clear note and a door opened in front of them. He stumbled inside and the door closed. She guided him to a couch, made him lie down, and slipped away. Presently she returned with a cup of liquid. "Here. Drink this." He reached for it, but his numbed fingers refused to grasp, and he spilled a little. She took the cup, lifted his head with her free arm, and held it to his lips. He drank slowly. It was warm and spicy. He fell asleep watching her anxious face.

He awoke slowly, becoming aware of a deep sense of comfort and well-being almost before he was aware of his own ego. He lay on his back on a cushion as soft as a feather bed. A light cover was over him and as he stretched he became aware that he was 'sleeping raw'. He opened his eyes. He was alone in a room of ample proportions possibly thirty feet long and oval in shape. Opposite him was a fireplace of quaint but pleasing pattern. It consisted of a vertical hyperboloid, like half a sugar loaf some ten feet high, which sprang out from the wall. In the base a mighty yawning mouth had been carved out, the floor of which was level and perhaps ten inches above the floor of the room. The roof of the mouth was another hyperboloid, hollow and eccentric to the first. On the floor of this gargantuan gape a coal fire crackled cheerfully and threw its reflections around the room. The room appeared almost bare of furniture except for the couch which ran two thirds of the way around the wall.

He turned his head at a slight noise and saw her coming in the door. She smiled and hurried to him. "Oh, so you are awake. How do you feel?" One hand sought his pulse.

"I feel grand."

"Hungry?"

"I could eat a horse."

She giggled. "Sorry—no horses. I'll soon have something better for you. But you mustn't eat too much at first." She straightened up. "Let me get out of these furs." She walked away while fumbling with a zipper at her throat. The furs were all one garment which slipped off her shoulders and fell to the floor. Perry felt a shock like an icy shower and then a warm tingle. The fur coverall was her only garment and she emerged as naked as a dryad. But she took no note of it, simply picked up the coverall and glided to a cupboard, which opened as she approached, and hung it up. Then she proceeded to a section of the wall covered with a mural of Demeter holding a horn of plenty. It slid up, exposing an incomprehensible aggregation of valves, doors, and shiny gadgets. She kept very busy for some ten minutes, humming as she worked. Perry watched her in fascination. His amazement gave way to hearty appreciation for she was young, nubile, and in every way desirable. Her quick movements were graceful and in some way very cheerful and reassuring. Her humming stopped. "There!" she exclaimed, "All ready, if the invalid is ready to eat." She picked up a laden tray and walked toward the far end of the room. The mural slid back into place and the shiny gadgets were gone. She set the tray on the couch, then pulled a countersunk handle. The handle came out in her hand, dragging with it a shelf perhaps two feet wide and four long. She turned back towards Perry and called, "Come, eat while it's hot."

Perry started to get up, then stopped. She noticed his hesitation and a troubled look clouded her face. "What is the matter? Are you still too weak?"

"No."

"Sprain anything?"

"No."

"Then come, please. Whatever is the matter?"

"Well, I—uh—you—see I—" How the hell do you tell a pretty girl who is naked as a jaybird that you can't eat with her because you are naked too? Especially when she doesn't seem to know what modesty is?

She bent over him with obvious concern. Oh, the hell with it, said Perry to himself, and climbed out of bed. He swayed a little.

"Shall I help you?"

"No, thanks. I'm OK."

They sat down on opposite sides of the shelf table. She touched a button and a large section of the wall beside them slid up, exposing through glass a magnificent view. Across a canyon tall pines marched up a rugged mountainside. Up the canyon to the right some seven or eight hundred yards a waterfall hung a curtain of gauze in the breeze. Then Perry looked down—down a direct drop from the window. Vertigo shook him and again he hung poised on the palisade and stared over the hood of his car at the beach. He heard himself cry out. In an instant her arms were about him, consoling him. He steadied himself. "I'm all right," he muttered, "But please close the shutters."

She neither argued nor answered, but closed them at once. "Now can you eat?"

"Yes, I think so."

"Then do so and we will talk later."

They ate in silence. He examined his food with interest. A clear soup; some jelly with a meaty flavor; a glass of milk; light rolls spread with sweet butter; and several kinds of fruit, oranges, sugar-sweet and large as grapefruit, with a skin that peeled easily like a tangerine, some yellow fruit that he did not recognize, and black-flecked bananas. The dishes were light as paper but covered with a hard shiny lacquer. The fork and spoon were of the same material. Finally he dropped the last piece of rind and ate the last crumb of roll. She had finished first and had been leaning on her elbows, watching him.

"Feel better?"

"Immensely."

She transferred the dishes to the tray, walked over to the fireplace, dumped the load on the fire, and returned the tray to its rack among the shiny gadgets. (Demeter swung obligingly out of the way.)

When she returned, she shoved the shelf-table back in its slot and extended a slender white tube.

"Smoke?"

"Thanks." It was about four inches long and looked like some Russian atrocity. Probably scented, he thought. He inhaled gingerly, then drew one to the bottom of his lungs. Honest Virginia tobacco. The only thing in the house that seemed absolutely homey and normal. She inhaled deeply and then spoke.

"Now then, who are you and how did you get onto this mountainside? And first, your name?"

"Perry. What's yours?"

"Perry? A nice name. Mine's Diana."

"Diana? I should think so. Perfect."

"I'm a little too cursive for Diana,"—she patted her thigh—"but I'm glad you like it. Now how did you get lost out in that storm yesterday without proper clothes and no food?"

"I don't know."

"You don't know?"

"No. You see, it was this way. I was driving down the palisade when a car tried to pass a truck on a hill coming towards me. I swung out to miss it and my right front wheel jumped the curb and over I went, car and all—the last I remember was staring down at the beach as I fell—until I woke up in the snow storm."

"That's all you remember?"

"Yes, and then you helping me, of course. Only I thought it was a girl in a green bathing suit."

"In a what?"

"In a green bathing suit."

"Oh." She thought for a moment. "What did you say made you go over the palisade?"

"I had a blowout, I guess, when my wheel hit the curb."

"What's a blowout?"

He stared at her. "I mean that my tire blew out—when it struck the curb."

"But why would it blow out?"

"Listen—do you drive a car?"

"Well—no."

"Well, if a pneumatic rubber tire strikes a sharp edge when you are going pretty fast, it's likely to explode—blowout. In that case anything can happen. In my case I went over the edge."

She looked frightened, and her eyes grew wide. Perry added, "Don't take it so hard. I'm not hurt."

"Perry, when did this happen?"

"Happen? Why, yester—No, maybe—"

"No, Perry, the date, the date!"

"July twelfth. That reminds me, does it often snow here—"

"What *year*, Perry?"

"What year? Why, this year!"

"What *year*, Perry—tell me the number."

"Don't you know?—Nineteen-thirty-nine."

"Nineteen-thirty-nine—" She repeated the words slowly.

"Nineteen-thirty-nine. But what the devil is wrong?"

She stood up and paced nervously back and forth, then stopped and faced him. "Perry, prepare yourself for a shock."

"OK, shoot."

"Perry, you told me that yesterday was July twelfth, nineteen-thirty-nine."

"Yes."

"Well, today is January seventh, twenty-eighty-six."

II

Perry sat very still for a long moment.

"Say that again."

"Today is January seventh, twenty-eighty-six."

"January—seventh,—twenty—eighty—six—It can't be—I'm dreaming—pretty soon I'll wake up." He looked up at her. "Then you're not real after all. Just a dream. Just a dream." He put his head in his hands and stared down at the floor.

He was recalled to his surroundings by a touch on his arm. "Look at me, Perry. Take my hand." She grasped his hand and squeezed it. "There. Am I real? Perry, you must realize it. I don't know who you are or what strange thing happened to you but here you are in my house in January twenty-eighty-six. And everything is going to be all right." She placed a hand under his chin and turned his face up to hers. "Everything is going to be all right. Place that in your mind." He stared at her with the frightened eyes of a man who fears he is going crazy. "Now calm yourself and tell me about it. Why do you think that yesterday you were in nineteen-thirty-nine?"

"Well, I *was*, I tell you—It had to be nineteen-thirty-nine, because it *was*—it couldn't be anything else."

"Hmm—That's no help. Tell me about yourself. Your full name, where you live, where you were born, what you do and so forth."

"Well, my name is Perry Vance Nelson. I was born in Girard, Kansas in nineteen-fourteen. I'm a ballistics engineer and a pilot. You see I'm an officer in the navy. Up until today I was on duty at Coronado, California. Yesterday—or whenever it was— I was driving from Los Angeles to San Diego on my way back from a weekend when this guy in the green sedan crowds me and I crack up on the beach."

She smoked and considered this. "That's clear enough. Except of course that it would make you one hundred and seventy-two years old and doesn't explain how you got here. Perry, You don't look that old."

"Well, what's the answer?"

"I don't know. Did you ever hear of schizophrenia, Perry?"

"Schizophrenia? Split personality." He considered, then exploded. "Nuts! If I'm crazy it's only in this dream. I tell you I *am* Perry Nelson. I don't know anything about twenty-eighty-six and I know all about nineteen-thirty-nine."

"That gives me a notion. I want to ask you some questions. Who was president in nineteen-thirty-nine?"

"Franklin Roosevelt."

"How many states in the union?"

"Forty-eight."

"How many terms did La Guardia serve?"

"How many? He was in his second term."

"But you just told me that Roosevelt was president."

"Sure. Sure. Roosevelt was president. La Guardia was Mayor of New York."

"Oh."

"Why did you ask that? Did La Guardia become president?"

"Yes. Two terms. Who were the most popular television actors in nineteen-thirty-nine?"

"Why, there weren't any. Television wasn't yet available. But listen, you are quizzing me about nineteen-thirty-nine. How do I know it's twenty-eighty-six?"

"Come here, Perry." She walked over the wall beside the fireplace and another section of the wall slid out of view. (—disconcerting, thought Perry, everything slips and slides—) Several rows of books were exposed. She handed him a slim volume. Perry read *Astronomikal Almanak and Efmerides 2086*. Then she dug out an old volume whose pages were brown with age. She opened it and pointed to the title page: *The Gallion of God—Sinclair Lewis, 1st printing, 1947*.

"Convinced?"

"I guess I'll have to be.—Oh, God!" he threw his cigarette in the fire and paced nervously up and down. Presently he stopped. "Look, is there any liquor here? Could I have a drink?"

"A drink—of what?"

"Whiskey, brandy, rum.—Anything with a jolt in it."

"I think I can take care of you." She disturbed Demeter again and returned presently holding a square bottle filled with an amber liquid. She poured him three fingers in a cup and added a small yellow pill.

"What's that?"

"Jamaica rum surrogate and a mild sedative. Help yourself. I've got an idea." She left him and went to the far end of the room where she seated herself on the couch and pulled out a small panel set in the wall. It appeared to be the front of a drawer. She lifted up a screen approximately a foot square and pressed a series of buttons below. Then she spoke: "Los Angeles Archives? Diana 160–398–400–48A speaking. I request search of Los Angeles and Coronado newspapers of July 12, 1939 for report of automobile accident involving Perry Nelson, naval officer. Expedited rate authorized. Bonus on thirty minutes. Report back. Thank you, clearing line." She left the drawer out and returned to Perry. "We will have to wait a while. Do you mind if I open the view now?"

"Not at all. I'd like to see it."

They seated themselves at the west end of the room where they had eaten and the shutters peeled back. It was late afternoon and the sun was nearing the shoulder of the mountain. Snow lay in the canyon and the thin amber sunlight streamed through the pines. They sat quietly and smoked. Diana poured herself a cup of surrogate, and sipped it. Presently a green light flashed from the open drawer and a single deep gong note sounded. Diana pressed a button nearby and spoke, "Diana 400–48 answering."

"Archives reporting. Positive. Disposition request."

"Televuestat Reno station with tube delivery, destination G610L-400–48, expedite rate throughout, bonus on ten minutes. Thank you. Clearing."

"You mentioned Reno. Are we near there?"

"Yes, we are about thirty kilometers south of Lake Tahoe."

"Tell me, is Reno still a divorce mill?"

"A divorce mill? Oh, no, Reno is not, as you call it, a divorce mill. There are no such things as divorces anymore."

"There aren't? What do a man and his wife do if they can't get along together?"

"They don't live together."

"Rather awkward in case one of them should fall in love again, isn't it?"

"No, you see—Good heavens, Perry, what a lot there is to teach you. I don't know where to start. However, I'll just plunge in and try to answer your questions. In the first place, there isn't any legal contract to be broken, not in your sense of the word. There are domestic contracts but they don't involve marriage in the religious or sexual aspects. And any of these contracts can be dealt with like any other secular contract."

"But doesn't that make a rather confusing situation, homes broken up, children around loose—what about children? Who supports them?"

"Why they support themselves on their heritage."

"On their heritage? They can't all be heirs."

"But they are—Oh, it's too confusing. I'll have to get some histories for you and a code of customs. These things are all bound up in major changes in the economic and social structure. Let me ask you a question. In your day what was marriage?"

"Well, it was a civil contract between a man and a woman usually sealed by a religious ceremony."

"And what did this contract stipulate?"

"It stipulated a lot of things not specifically mentioned, but under it the two lived together, she worked for him, more or less, and he supported her financially. They slept together and neither one was supposed to have love affairs with anybody else. If they had children they supported them until they were grown up."

"And what were the objects of this arrangement?"

"Well, principally for the benefit of the children, I guess. The children were protected and given a name. Also women were protected and supported and looked out for when they were bearing children."

"And what did the man get out of it."

"He got—well—a family and home life, and someone to do his cooking, and a thousand other little services, and if you will pardon me mentioning it, he had a woman to sleep with any time he needed one."

"Let's take the last first; was she necessarily the woman he wanted to 'sleep' with as you so quaintly put it?"

"Yes, I suppose so, else he probably wouldn't have asked her to marry him. No, by God, I know that is not true. It may be true when they first marry, but I know damn well that most married men see women every day that they would rather have than their own wives. I've watched 'em in every port."

"How about yourself. Perry?"

"Me? I'm not—I wasn't married."

"Didn't you ever see a woman you wanted to enjoy physically?"

"Of course. Many of them."

"Then why didn't you marry?"

"Oh, I don't know. I guess I didn't want to be tied down."

"If a man didn't have children to support and a wife to support would he be tied down by marriage?"

"Why yes, in a way. She would expect him to do everything with her and would raise Cain if he stepped out with other women and would expect him to entertain her sisters and her cousins and her aunts, and would be sore if he had to work on their anniversary."

"Good Lord! What a picture you paint. I don't understand all of your expressions but it sounds unbearable."

"Of course not all women are like that, some of them are good sports—man to man, but you can't tell when you marry them."

"It sounds from your description as if men had nothing to gain by marriage but an available mistress. And tell me, weren't there women for hire then at a lower cost than supporting one woman for life?"

"Oh yes, certainly. But they weren't satisfactory to most men. You see, a man doesn't like to feel that a woman goes to bed with him just for the money in his pocket."

"But you just said that women married to be supported."

"That's not quite what I meant. Or that's not all—at least not usually. Anyhow it's different. Besides men don't always play the game. You see a man marries partially to have exclusive right to a woman's attention, especially her body. But lots of them carry it to extremes. Marriage is no excuse for a man to slap his wife's face for dancing twice with another man—as I've seen happen."

"But why should a man want to have exclusive possession of a woman?"

"Well, he just naturally does. It's in his nature. Besides a man wants to be sure his children aren't bastards."

"We are no longer so sure, Perry, that such traits are 'nature' as you call them. And bastard is an obsolete term."

At this moment an amber light flashed at the other end of the room. Diana arose and returned shortly with a roll of papers. "They have arrived. Here, look." She unrolled them and spread them on the shelf-table. Perry saw that they were photostatic copies of pages of the *Los Angeles Times*, *Harold-Express*, and *Daily News* for July 13, 1939. She pointed to a headline:

NAVAL FLIER KILLED IN CAR CRASH

Torrey Fines, Calif., July 12. Lieutenant Perry V. Nelson, Navy pilot of Coronado, was killed today when he lost control of the car he was driving and plunged over the palisade here to his death on the rock below. Lieut. Nelson jumped or was thrown clear of the car but landed head first in a pile of loose rock at the foot of the cliff, splitting his skull. Death was instantaneous. Miss Diana Burwood of Pasadena was bathing on the beach below and narrowly escaped injury. She attempted to give first aid, then scaled the bluff and reported the accident with aid of a passing motorist.

There were similar stories in the other papers. The *Daily News* included a column cut of Perry in uniform. Diana examined this with interest. "The story checks perfectly, Perry. This is just a fair likeness of you, however." Perry glanced at it.

"I should say that it wasn't bad, considering the limitations of a half-tone reproduction."

"The surprising thing is that it looks like you at all."

"Why do you say that, Diana? Don't you believe me?" His hurt showed plainly in his face.

"Oh, no, no. I believe that you are telling the literal truth—insofar as you know it. But think, Perry. The head that was photographed to take this picture has—if this newspaper account is true—been dust for more than a century."

Perry stared at her and a look of horror crept into his eyes. He closed his eyes and clasped his head between his palms. He remained thus, face averted and body tensed for several minutes until he felt a gentle touch on his hair. Diana bent over him, pity and compassion in her eyes. "Perry, please. Listen to me. I didn't mean to distress you. I wouldn't hurt you intentionally. I want to be your friend if you will let me."

Gently she removed his hands from his temples. "It is a strange and marvelous thing that has happened to you, Perry, and I don't understand it at all. In some ways it is horrible and certainly terrifying. But it could be much worse—much worse. This is not a bad world in which you have landed. I think it is a rather kindly world. I like it and I am sure it must be better than being crushed and broken at the foot of the palisades. Please, Perry, I'd like to help you."

He patted her hand. "You're a good kid, Dian', I'll be all right. It's the shock more than anything. The realization that all that world I know is dead and gone. I knew it of course when you told me what year it was, but I didn't realize it until you pointed out to me that I'm dead, too—or at least that my body died." He jumped to his feet. "But say!—if my body is dead, where in God's name did I get this!"—and he slapped his side.

"I don't know, Perry, but I have an idea."

"What is it?"

"Not just yet. But we can start a little action toward finding out. Come with me." She opened out the drawer containing the communication instrument, and pushed one button. A pretty red-headed girl appeared on the screen and smiled. Diana spoke. "Reno, please relay Washington, Bureau of records, Identification Sector."

"Check, Diana." The red head faded out.

"Does she know you?"

"Probably recognized me. You will understand."

Shortly another face appeared, that of an iron grey studious man. Diana spoke. "Identification requested."

"Which one of you?"

"Him."

"Check. Take position." The face turned away and a camera-like apparatus appeared.

"Put up your right hand, Perry," whispered Diana. Perry did so. The grey haired man re-appeared.

"Listen, how can I analyze if you don't hold position? Haven't you ever used a phone before?"

"I—I guess not." Perry looked confused.

The slight irritation vanished from the man's voice. "What's the trouble, friend? Lost your continuity?"

"I guess you'd call it that."

"That's different. I'll fix you up in no time. Then you'll probably have no trouble to orient. Now do just as I tell you. Right hand, palm toward me about twenty centimeters from the screen. Down a little. Now just a hair closer. Your palm is tilted. Get it parallel to the screen. There. Hold it steady." A soft shirring and a click. "That's all. Do you want a full dossier or just name and number?"

Diana cut in. "Brief of dossier, please, with last entry in full.

Televuestat Reno station, tube delivery G610L-400–48, expedited rate."

"Charge to him when I get his number?"

"No, to me, Diana, 160–398–400–48A."

"Oooh! I *thought* I recognized you."

"This is private action." Diana's voice was cool and crisp.

The man looked indignant, then his face became impassive. "Madam, I am an official clerk of the Bureau of Records. I thoroughly understand the spheres of public and private action, and my oath and charge."

Diana melted at once. "I'm sorry. I truly am. Please forgive me."

He relaxed and smiled. "Of course, Miss Diana. You probably have to insist on the spheres. But, if you will permit, it would be an honor to provide this service for you."

"No, please, make the routine charge. But may I do you some service?" She inclined her head. The clerk bowed in return. "A picture perhaps?"

"If madam permits."

"My latest stereo. Face or full?"

He bowed without speaking.

"I'll send both. They shall cross your brief in the tubes."

"You are very kind."

"Thank you. Clearing." The screen went blank. "Well, Perry, we'll know soon. But I must get the poor chap his pictures. I didn't mean to offend him, but he was too touchy." She returned in a moment with two thin sheets and started to roll them up. Noticing Perry's interest, she paused. "Would you care to see them?"

"Yes, of course." The first picture was Diana's face in natural colors with a half smile warming it. But Perry was startled almost into dropping it. For the portrait was completely stereoscopic. It was as if he were looking through a window of cellophane at Diana herself posed stationary three feet back of the frame.

"How in the world are these done?"

"I'm neither an optics student nor a photographer, but I know the picture really does have some depth to it. It's a colloid about a half centimeter thick. It is done with two cameras, so it works only on one axis. Turn it around sideways." He did so. The picture went perfectly flat although remaining a fine photograph. "Now tilt it about forty-five degrees." He did so and had the upsetting sensation of watching Diana's beautiful features melt and run until no picture was visible, but just an iridescense like oil on water. "You have to look at it along the right axis and within a narrow view angle, but when you do the two images blend in the stereo illusion. The brain interprets the confused double image given by two separated eyes as depth and by duplicating that confusion, they achieve the illusion."

Perry stared at the picture a moment more and tilted and twisted it. Diana watched with interest and sympathetic amusement. "May I see the other picture?"

"Here it is." Perry glanced at it, then swallowed. He had grown accustomed to Diana's nudity, more or less, and had been too much occupied mentally to think much about it, but nevertheless he had been aware of it in one corner of his mind all the time. Still, he was startled to discover that the second picture portrayed all of Diana in her own sweet simplicity, nothing more, and that it was as amazingly lifelike as the first, real enough to pinch. He swallowed again.

"You intend to send this, er—uh, these pictures to a man you've just met on the phone."

"Oh, yes, he wants them and I can afford it. And I was a bit rude. Of course some people would think it a bit brash for me to give him anything as intimate as a facial portrait but I don't mind."

"But,—uh—"

"Yes, Perry?"

"Oh, well, nothing I guess. Never mind."

III

Later while Diana monkeyed with the gadgets in the Demeter niche, the green light and gong note announced a tube delivery. "Get it, will you, Perry?" she called. "I've got both hands full." Perry puzzled with the controls, then found a small lever that opened the receptacle. He brought over the roll to Diana. "Read it aloud, Perry, while I finish dinner." He unrolled it and first noticed a picture of a young man who resembled his own memory of himself. He commenced to read. "Gordon 932–016–755–82A, Genes class JM, born 2057 July 7. Qualified and matriculated Arlington Health School 2075, transferred (approved) Adler Memorial Institute of Psychology 2077. Selected for research when Extra-sensory station was established by Master Fifield in 2080. Author of *A Study of Deviant Data in Extra-Sensory Perception.* Co-author (with Pandit Kalimohan Chandra Roy) of *Proteus: a History of the Ego.* Address Sanctuary (F-2), California. Unofficially reported in voluntary corporal abdication in 2083 August and transferred at the request of Sanctuary Council to inactive status 2085 August, body to remain in Sanctuary. Credit account on transfer to inactive $11,018.32 less depreciation $9,803.09, credit account re-entered with service deduction $9802.09 less $500 credit convenience book $9,302.09 (enclosed)."

Attached to the end of the roll was a small wallet or notebook. Inside Perry found that the leaves were money, conventional money, differing only slightly in size and design from money in 1939. In the back of the book was a pad of blank credit drafts, a check book.

"What do I do with this stuff, Diana?"

"Do with it? Anything you like, use it, spend it, live on it."

"But it doesn't belong to me. It belongs to this fellow Gordon something-or-other."

"You are Gordon 755–82."

"Me? The hell I am."

"You *are*, though. The Bureau of Records has already acknowledged it and has your account re-entered. You have the body listed as 932–016–755–82A. You can use any name you like, Perry, or Gordon, or George Washington, and the Bureau will gladly note the change in the record, but that number goes with that body and that credit account and they won't change it. Of course you don't have to spend it but if you don't, nobody will, and it will just get bigger."

"Can't I give it away?"

"Certainly—but not to Gordon."

Perry scratched his head. "No, I guess not. Say, what is this voluntary abdication stuff?"

"I'm not able to give a scientific account of it, but so far as anyone else is concerned it amounts to suicide by willing not to live."

"Then Gordon is dead?"

"No. Not according to the ideas of the people who monkey with these things. He simply was not interested in living here and chose to live elsewhere."

"How come his body is here okay?"

"According to this report Gordon's body—this body—" She

pinched his cheeks. "—has been lying quietly in a state of arrested animation in the Sanctuary on the other side of this mountain. And so the mystery is partially cleared up."

His wrinkled brow showed no satisfaction. "Yes, I suppose so. But each mystery is explained with another mystery."

"There is just one mystery left that worries me, Perry, and that is why in the world you didn't break a leg and maybe your brand-new neck in getting over here. But I'm glad you didn't."

"So am I. Lord!"

"But now I must get to work." She stacked the supper dishes as she spoke.

"What work?"

"My paid work. I am not one of the ascetic souls that are content with their heritage checks. I've got to have money for ribbons and geegaws."

"What do you do?"

"I'm a televue actress, Perry. I dance and sing a little, and occasionally take part in stories."

"Are you about to rehearse?"

"No, I go on the waves in about twenty minutes."

"Goodness, the studio must be close by or you'll be late."

"Oh, no. It will be picked up from here. But you will have to be a good boy and sit still and not ask questions for a while or I *shall* be late. Come. Sit over here. Now face the receiver so." Another section of the wall flew up and Perry faced a flat screen. "There you can see the whole performance and watch me dance directly too." She opened the communicator drawer and raised the small screen. A rather homely debonair young man appeared. He wore a helmet with bulges over his ears. A cigarette drooped from one corner of his sardonic mouth.

"Hi, Dian'."

"Hello, Larry. Where j'a get the circles under your eyes?"

"That from you—and you so huffy about the private sphere of action. I had a blonde paint 'em on."

"She got the left one crooked."

"Cut out the arcing and get down to work, wench. Got your setup made?"

"Yeah."

"OK, testing." Lights sprang out from the near end of the room. Diana walked to the center of the room, turned around twice, and walked back and forth and up and down, then returned to the communicator.

"OK, Larry?"

"There's a halo in the lower left and it's not in my side, I don't believe."

"I'll take a look." She returned with the tube that had contained the Gordon dossier in her hand. "Gone now, Larry?"

"Yeah, what was it?"

"This." She held up the tube.

"Just like a female. Can't integrate. Sloppy minds, unable to—"

"Larry, one more crack out of you and I'll report you for atavism—probably Neanderthal."

"Cool down, small one. You have a super-magnificent brain. I love you for your intellect. Time's running short. Want some music?"

"Give it a blast.—Okay, turn it off."

"What are you giving the mob tonight, Dian'?"

"Highbrow stuff. Watch it—you might get an idea."

He glanced down at his controls. "Take your place, kid. I'm clearing."

Diana went quickly to the middle of the room and the lights went out. The larger screen facing Perry came suddenly to life. Facing him in stereo and color was a brisk young man, who bowed and smiled and commenced to speak: "Friends, we are again in the studios of the Magic Carpet in the tower of the Edison Memorial overlooking Lake Michigan. We bring you tonight your favorite interpreter of the modern theme in dance, lovely Diana, who will present another stanza in the Poem of Life."

The colors on the screen melted together, then faded to a light blue and a single high clear crystal note impinged on Perry's ears. The note trembled, then pursued a minor melody. Perry felt a mood of sadness and nostalgia creep over him. Gradually the orchestra picked up the theme and embroidered it while on the screen the colors shifted, blended, and ranged in patterns. Finally the colors faded and the screen went dark as the harmony wafted out of the music leaving a violin alone carrying the theme in the darkness. A dim finger of light appeared and picked out a small figure far back. The figure was prone, limp, helpless. The music conveyed a feeling of pain and despair and over-powering fatigue. But another theme encouraged, called for effort, and the figure stirred gently. Perry glanced over his shoulder and had to exert self control to refrain from going to the poor forlorn creature's assistance. Diana needed help, his heart told him, go to her! But he sat quietly and watched and listened. Perry knew little about dancing and nothing about it as a high art. Ballroom dancing for himself and tap dancing to watch were about his level. He watched with intent appreciation the graceful, apparently effortless movements of the girl, without any realization of the training, study and genius that had gone before. But gradually he realized that he was being told a story of the human spirit, a story of courage, and hope, and love over-coming despair and physical hurt. He came to with a start when the dance ended leaving Diana with arms flung out, face to the sky, eyes shining, and smiling in joy as a single bright warm light poured over her face and breast. He felt happier than he had since his arrival—happy and relieved.

The screen went dark, then the ubiquitous young man re-appeared. Diana cut him off before he spoke, switched on the room lights and turned to Perry. He was surprised to see that she appeared shy and fussed.

"Did you like it, Perry?"

"Like it? Diana, you were glorious, incredible. I—I can't express it."

"I'm glad.

"And now I'm going to eat and we can visit some more."

"But you just had dinner."

"You didn't watch me closely. I don't eat much before dancing. But now watch—I'll probably get it down on the floor and worry it like an animal. Are you hungry?"

"No, not yet."

"Could you drink a cup of chocolate?"

"Yes, thanks."

A few minutes later they were seated on the couch, Diana with her legs curled up under her, a cup of chocolate in one hand, an enormous sandwich in the other. She ate busily and greedily. Perry was amused to think that this hungry little girl was that unearthly glorious creature of a few minutes before. She finished, hiccoughed, looked surprised and murmured, "Excuse me," then wiped up with one finger a blob of mayonnaise which had dropped on her tummy and transferred it to her mouth. "Now, Perry, let's take stock. Where are we?"

"Damned if I know. I know where I am and when I am and you tell me that I know who I am. Gordon zip zip zip and six zeros, but I might as well be a day old baby as for knowing what to do about it."

"Not so bad as that, Perry. In addition to an identity you have acquired a nice credit account, not large but adequate and your heritage check will keep you going, too."

"What is this heritage check business?"

"Let's not go into that now. When you study the economic system you'll understand. Right now it means a hundred and fifty dollars, more or less, every month. You could live comfortably on two-thirds of that, if you wanted to. What I wanted to talk about was the 'what to do about it' aspect."

"Where do we start?"

"I can't decide what you are to do about anything, but it seems to me that the very first thing to do is to bring you up to date so that you will fit in twenty-eighty-six. It is a rather different world. You must learn a lot of new customs and a century-and-a-half of history and a number of new techniques and so forth. When you are up to date, you can decide for yourself what you want to do—and then you can do anything you want."

"It sounds to me as if I'd be too old to want to do anything by that time."

"No, I don't think so. You can start right away. I've got a number of ideas. In the first place, while I haven't very many useful books in this house, I do have a pretty fair history of the United States and a short world history. Yes, and a dictionary and a fairly recent encyclopedia. Oh and I nearly forgot, an abridged code of customs that I had when I was a kid. Then I am going to call Berkeley and ask for a group of records on a number of subjects that you can play on the televue whenever you like. That will really be your most beneficial and easiest way to learn in a hurry."

"How does it work?"

"It's very simple. You saw my act in the televue tonight. Well, it's just as easy to put a record on it and see and hear anything that you want to that has ever been recorded. If you wanted to, you could see President Berzowski open Congress in 2001 January. Or if you like, you could see any of my dances from records."

"I'll do that first. To hell with history!"

"You'll do nothing of the sort. You will study until you are oriented. If you want to see me dance, I'll dance for you."

"OK, right now."

She stuck out her tongue at him. "Be serious. Besides the records, I'll think over who among my friends can help and I'll get them to come talk with you and explain the things that I can't."

"Why do you take all this trouble about me, Dian'?"

"Why, anybody would, Perry. You were sick and cold and needed help."

"Yes, but now you undertake to educate me and set me on my feet."

"Well, I want to do it. Won't you let me?"

"Well, maybe. But look here, oughtn't I to get out of your house and find some other place to stay?"

"Why, Perry? You're welcome here. Aren't you comfortable?"

"Oh, of course. But how about your reputation? What will people say?"

"I don't see how it could affect my reputation; you don't dance. And what does it matter what people think—all they could think is that we were companions, if they bothered to think about it at all. Besides very few people except my friends will know. It is strictly in the private sphere of action. The custom is quite clear."

"What custom?"

"Why, the custom which says that what people do out of public service or private employment is private as long as it doesn't violate the other customs. Where people go, what they eat, or drink, or wear, or how they entertain themselves, or who they love, or how they play are strictly in the private sphere. So one must not print anything about it or broadcast it, or speak about it in a public place, without specific permission."

"Paging Walter Winchell! What in the world is in your newspapers?"

"Lots of things. Political news and ships' movements and public events and announcements of amusements and most anything about public officials—though their private sphere is much narrower. It's an exception in the custom. And new creations in clothing and architecture and food and new scientific discoveries and lists of new televue records and broadcasts, and new commercial projects. Who's Walter Winchell?"

"Walter Winchell, why he was a—Dian', I don't think you will believe it but he made a lot of money talking almost entirely about things in what you call the private sphere of action."

She wrinkled her nose. "How disgusting!"

"People ate it up. But look, how about your friends? Won't they think it strange?"

"Why should they? It isn't strange. I've entertained lots of them."

"But we aren't chaperoned."

"What's 'chaperoned'? Is it something like married?"

"Oh Lord, I give up. Listen, Dian', just pretend like we never said anything about it. I'll be most happy to stay if you want me to."

"Didn't I say I did?"

They were interrupted by the appearance of a large grey cat who walked out to the middle of the floor, calmly took possession, sat down, curled his tail carefully around him, and mewed loudly. He had only one ear and looked like a hard case. Diana gave him a stern look.

"Where have you been? Do you think this is any time to come home?"

The cat mewed again.

"Oh, so you'll be fed now? So this is just the place where they keep the fish?"

The cat walked over, jumped on the couch, and commenced bumping his head against Diana's side while buzzing loudly.

"All right. All right. Come along. Show me where it is." He jumped down and trotted quickly over toward Demeter, tail straight as a smoke column on a calm day, then sat and looked up expectantly. He mewed again.

"Don't be impatient." Diana held a dish of sardines in the air. "Show me where to put it." The cat trotted over in front of the fire. "All right. Now are you satisfied?" The cat did not answer, being already busy with the fish.

Diana returned to the couch and reached for a cigarette. "That's Captain Kidd. He's an old pirate with no manners and no morals. He owns this place."

"So I gathered. How did he get in?"

"He let himself in. He has a little door of his own that opens up when he mews."

"For Heaven's sakes! Is that standard equipment for cats these days?"

"Oh no. It's just a toy. He can't let himself in my door. It opens only to my voice. But I made a record of the mew he used to let me know he wanted to come in the house and sent it to be analyzed and a lock set to it. Now that lock opens his own little door. I suppose that doors that open to a voice are somewhat marvelous to you, Perry?"

"Well, yes and no. We had such things but they weren't commercially in use. I've seen them work. In fact I believe that I could design one if I had to."

Her eyebrows lifted in surprise. "Really? I had no idea that technical advance was so marked in your day."

"We had a fairly involved technical culture, but unfortunately most of it wasn't used. People couldn't afford to pay for the things that the engineers could build, especially luxuries like automatic doors and television and such."

"Television isn't a luxury. It's a necessity. How else could one keep in touch? Why I would be helpless without it."

"Yes, no doubt you feel that way about it. People were beginning to say that about the telephone in my day. But the fact remains while we knew how to accomplish pretty fair television we didn't because there was no market. People couldn't afford it."

"I don't see why not."

"I don't know how to tell you. Perhaps I don't see either, except in some way I can't explain. But we did have a lot of unused or only partially used mechanical and technical knowledge. The application of any advance in invention or art was limited by whether or not there were people willing and able to pay for it. I served for a couple of years in one of the big aircraft carriers. There were boys in her—enlisted men—who used the most amazing technical devices—mechanical brains that could solve the most involved ballistic problems, problems in calculus using a round dozen variables, problems that would have taken an experienced mathematician days to solve. The machine solved them in a split second and applied the solutions, yet more than half of those boys came from homes that didn't have bathtubs or central heating."

"How awful! How in the world could they stay clean and healthy in such houses?"

"They couldn't. I don't suppose that I can make you realize just what the conditions were in which a lot of people lived. A classmate of mine at the Naval Academy joined the navy because he got tired of walking behind a mule and plowing. So he walked fifteen miles to town barefooted and slept on the doorstep of the post office. When the postmaster arrived in the morning he enlisted. He was selected for the Naval Academy and became one of the most brilliant young officers in the fleet and expert in the use and design of equipment that makes your automatic door seem simple. But his father and mother and brothers and sisters were still living in a one room dirt-floored cabin, dirty and sick from hookworm, anemia, and malnutrition."

"Why in the world would the government spend all that effort on machinery for an aircraft carrier when its citizens were living in such abominable squalor?"

"Well, I guess we had something like your private and public spheres of actions, Dian'. The lives of these people were in the private sphere of action, but national defense is public."

"But it's obviously the same thing. Any government official would know that it is dangerous to everybody to let people be hungry and sick. Why, from the most selfish standpoint possible, if people are sick, they can be the center of epidemic, and anybody knows that a hungry man is not responsible for his actions and may do something dangerous."

"I don't know how to answer you, Diana. We knew it in the navy of course, and we kept them clean and healthy and well fed, but to say that any government official would naturally know that—well, either men have grown very much wiser in a hundred and fifty years or something has happened to change the point of view."

"I don't believe that we are any smarter than people were in your day. I don't think such a thing is possible in four or five generations. But I don't see how anyone could be so short-sighted."

"Even if an official did have your viewpoint and wanted to do something, he would be bound to ask 'where is the money to come from?'. And no one could answer him. Cost of government was already too high."

"Where is the money to come from, Perry? Why, I never heard such silly talk. Where does any money come from? When the government sees a need for exchange, it creates it, of course. Why you had that in your day, Perry. It says right there in the original constitution, 'Congress shall have the sole right to coin money and regulate the value thereof.'"

"Yes, I remember that phrase. But that isn't the way it worked out in my day. Money was created by the banks, most of it at least—the important part anyhow. If the government needed money and couldn't raise it via taxes in time, it borrowed from the banks."

"But I don't understand—the banks are a part of the government."

"Not in my day. They were private institutions. It might be proper to say that the banks were the government. In some ways they were stronger than the government."

"But that would be sheer blind anarchy!"

"It was—pretty much."

"But see here, Perry. All this doesn't check. You came from 1939 when Franklin Roosevelt was president. I don't know a whole lot about history, but I do know that he is regarded as the first man in the new economic era. Why, there is a statue of him in Washington, showing him feeding the hungry."

"Yes, Mr. Roosevelt knew that all right. But he got very little cooperation, even from those he was trying to help. But it's my turn to ask questions: Tell me, is there no longer anyone hungry?"

"Of course not. Not in the United States at least."

"I meant the United States. Are there any sick?"

"Oh yes. Not many of course."

"What happens to them?"

"They are treated and taken care of to make them well. What else could you do?"

"Never mind. Is anyone out of work?"

"Out of work? Do you mean not working for money? Of course. At any one time I don't suppose you will find more than half the population working to make money."

"Don't those that work object to working while the others are idle?"

"Why should they? Everybody can't work all the time or nobody would have time to use what he has produced—no time to spend his credit. Everybody works whenever he feels the need of replenishing his credit—or if he has an occupation that he likes whether he needs more credit or not."

"Does everybody work part time?"

"No. Most professional people work regularly because they like to. Take a surgeon for example. He will work forty weeks every year. If he is famous and loves his work, his vacation will be as busy as his credit work. Take me for example, I work every week now and have for quite a long time, a broadcast like tonight every week, not to mention recordings for stories and songs."

"Is that one broadcast all the work you do?"

"I have to rehearse a lot and I'm expected to invent a new dance each week."

"How about people that aren't professional people, the various kinds of skilled or semi-skilled labor, and tradesmen and so forth."

"Some work full time and some part time. Quite a number of people work for several years and then quit. Some people don't work at all—not for money at least. They have simple tastes and are content to live on their heritage, philosophers and mathematicians and poets and such. There aren't many like that however. Most people work at least part of the time."

"Diana, is the United States a socialism now?"

"Why no, not if by socialism you mean government owner-ship of the factories and stores and farms and such. New Zealand has that kind of a government and I believe it works pretty well, but I don't believe it would be suited to the American temperament. But see here, Perry, I'm no economist. I've got a pal at the University of California who is. I'll get him to run up here in a day or two after you've studied up on history a little and he will be able to answer all of your questions. Which reminds me. If you are to have those recordings tomorrow, I had better order them." She stepped to the communicator. Perry heard her calling the University of California at Berkeley.

"Will you be able to order at this time of night?" he enquired.

"Probably not, not without paying an excessively high bonus. I'll simply set for recorded message and they will get the order first thing in the morning."

"How do you do that?"

"Either one of two ways. I can have my voice recorded, or write with the telautograph. Want to see the telautograph work, Perry?"

He stepped over to her side. "They haven't changed much."

"Do you mean to say that you could telewrite in 1939?"

"Uh huh. They weren't used much, but I remember seeing one in the Union Station in Kansas City. It was used for train orders."

"Hm—, maybe our mechanical marvels aren't going to sur-prise you as much as I had thought."

"I'm sure I'll find plenty to amaze me. But remember, Dian'. I was an engineer albeit in 1939. I take it you are an artist pri-marily. I may not be impressed at the things that you *expect* will impress me."

"That's probably true." She wrote slowly with the telautograph, stopping several times to think. Finally she signed it and closed the machine. "That will do for now. I've ordered a general catalog too so that you can pick out any records you may be interested in."

"Do you buy these records?"

"No, not unless you want to. There is a small charge for using them. If you find you want to keep a record permanently, you can pay for it and keep it."

"Do you have any here?"

"Oh yes, but not very many except for my professional library. I have quite a number of those, recordings of my own dances of course and a lot more of every sort of dancing. Most of the others are story records, just for amusement. Want to see some of them?

"Sure."

"I'll show you how to use the receiver as a reproducer at the same time. Now watch. This is the adapter switch. Turn it to 'rep'. Then you put the record in like so and fasten the end of the film with this catch. Then press the power button. No, don't do it yet. You control the volume of sound with this dial. Now push the power button." The machine whirred softly and the large screen came to life. A fool in motley appeared and laughed sardonically in their faces.

"Hi, brother fool," he shouted, "You want another of Touchstone's tales? Then gather round and attend me well. Touchstone Tells the Tale! Many, many years ago in ancient Greece there lived a wench of monstrous humor." A large hook appeared from the side of the screen and settled about the jester's middle. His grin changed to dismay and broke into a thousand pieces, reformed and spelled *Lysistrata: A Comedy of Manners*. Diana noticed Perry's reflex of recognition.

"You know it then?"

"Yes. Oh yes."

"Shall I turn it off?"

"No. Please don't." For the next hour they laughed and chuckled over the ageless farce of marriage and war. Perry was particularly delighted to recognize Diana among the Grecian wenches, and pointed out his discovery with a glee. Diana looked pleased, but protested when Perry insisted in whispers that Diana should have had the leading role.

Presently the play came to its rollicking finish, and the machine clicked to a stop. Perry found Diana smothering a yawn. She made a face at him. "Sorry, but I was up earlier than you were."

"I'm sleepy myself."

"Ready for bed?"

"I think so. Where do I sleep?"

"Anywhere you like. Where you were last night is as good as any."

Perry accepted the suggestion and made himself comfortable on that part of the couch. Diana lay down across the room, called out a languid goodnight, and with as little ceremony as a cat, curled up and appeared to fall at once to sleep. Perry lay on his back, eyes closed but head seething with confused impressions and idea sequences, each demanding immediate attention. Sleep seemed impossible but nevertheless in a very few minutes he sank into the soft warm glow that precedes it. Soon he was breathing slowly.

A scream of terror cut through the room. Diana sat up and switched on the light. Perry was sitting up also, his eyes staring, horrified. She ran to his side. "Perry, Perry, my dear. What happened?" He clung to her hand.

"I was falling. It seemed like I landed here in the dark. I'm all right now. It was just a bad dream."

"There. There. It's all right." She soothed and comforted him. "Just wait a minute. I'll leave the light on." She left him and returned quickly with a cup of the same steamy, spicy mixture that he had drunk the night before. "Now drink this slowly."

He touched her hand. "Dian', I know I'm being a baby, but will you stay with me for a little?"

"Of course, Perry."

When he finished his drink, she lay down beside him, put her arms around him, and rested his head on her breast. "Now just relax and be quiet. You're safe and I won't leave you." In a very few minutes he was sleeping peacefully. Diana held him a little while longer then gently uncurled herself and sat up. She massaged the pins and needles out of her arm and watched Perry's face. After a long time she bent over and kissed him quickly and softly on the lips. He smiled without wakening. Then she returned to her place on the couch. Now it was her turn to have trouble wooing sleep. Why had she kissed him? It was a silly thing to do. She wasn't in love with him. Of course not. She didn't know him and didn't feel any strong physical attraction for him. One didn't fall in love with savages anyhow. And that was just what he was, essentially. He hadn't acted like a savage though. Nevertheless, anyone brought up in the first part of the twentieth century couldn't possibly be a fit companion for a girl nowdays. He would be sure to be emotionally unstable. He *was* unstable; that crying out in the night proved it. He hadn't anything to fear. *But suppose I had just fallen to my death*, she thought. He wasn't dead. No, but he thought he was. No, he didn't either. It was very confusing. He had looked so hurt and lonesome. Then when he went to sleep he looked so young it had made her melt. That was why, just sympathy, just the way she had kissed the top of Captain Kidd's furry cap after she cut a thorn out of his paw. Just sympathy. But why had she urged him to stay until he got oriented? There were institutions for that, quite capable and better equipped than she was. Oh damn, why hadn't she turned Captain Kidd in when he first came mewing at the door and demanding attention? *Diana, you're a fool and any animal or child or man or woman that wants to can move you right out of your own home.* Hadn't she built this house for privacy? Hadn't she come here so she could take out her soul and examine it in private? And now how could she? What interesting eyes he had. Yet he didn't look at her, except to meet her gaze. Didn't he think she was pretty? Could she be getting *old*? Were the women in 1939 more beautiful than they were today? Or would he think so? But then what if he did? Certainly *she* was not interested.

Diana got up and fixed herself a cup of the sedative, drank it, sought a new place on the couch, arranged herself in a ball and fell asleep.*

*Diana grew up in a transport car. Both of her parents were interested in her and liked her and she, fortunately or perhaps in consequence, felt a warm affection and respect for them. Both her father and mother preferred the more casual hit-or-miss training that a child receives from interested parents to the presumably more scientific, certainly more systematic, training a modern child receives in our development centers. Her father had spent most of his active life in food technique. He was a man of considerable imagination and great talent in organization. Several of our present home comforts can be attributed in whole or in part to his effort. He invented the autotherm food container and induced others to develop it to the point that we now have it, cheap enough to use and throw away. Nearly forty years ago as an assistant engineer for the Cuisine Company (a forerunner of Universal Foods) he started the first agitation for natural texture in synthetic proteins. He left this company and founded Ambrosia, Ltd., while still a very young man, in order to permit two synthetic chemists to use all the credit they liked in their laboratory. The results we meet every day at dinner—sausages that have never seen a pig and soup stock that grew in a test tube.

His energies were not confined to food. His bitter controversy with Polenski over the merits of dry point etching and the current acid thermal process is remembered by all devotees of that esoteric art. His assertion that the modern man is better fitted physically, mentally, and emotionally to cope with the wilderness barehanded than his savage ancestors caused a storm of argument which reached a dramatic climax in his year of practical experiment on an uninhabited South Pacific island. He took Diana with him on this adventure, a slim girl-child of ten. His triumphant return, a modern Crusoe, hale, hearty, and filled with boasts is known to every romantic boy and was the basis for a flood of story records, written, directed and acted by lesser men.

Diana's mother was less spectacular but equally important in the development of the girl's character. She was a surgeon, of a line of surgeons and healers. Calm and cool, with large slender bony hands, more expressive than her placid face, she seemed detached from her surroundings and fully alive only when those delicate sensitive fingers were cutting the line between life and death. Although it was the father who encouraged the child to dance, it was the mother who insisted that she persevere in her studies until she produced a worthwhile result, a technique of her own.

Diana grew up with first one, then the other, of these assorted progenitors and occasionally with both when their several occupations permitted family life. Her mother selected the instructional records for the child's formal primary education and cultural orientation. Her father supplemented this with little excursions to cultural and industrial centers to make concrete what she learned from the recordings. On her mother's insistence Diana lived for two years in a development center during her adolescence in order that she might experience the practical realities of social self government and understand the background of a large portion of the population.

Ideal or not, Diana flourished in this environment and grew up, not only strong and healthy, but with a mind agile and uninhibited, a temperament sunny and free from boredom, a memory packed with a wide variety of information and skills arranged in reasonably efficient integration. The possible flaw in her character, if flaw it were, lay in her quick emotional sympathy, the ease with which she felt the pain and sorrows of others. It prevented her from following in her mother's career as a surgeon, as she could not manage the detached viewpoint necessary to protect the surgeon from the emotional impact of the suffering she treated. This joint in her armor led her too easily into emotional relationships, especially with the opposite sex. In her late teens she suffered a severe hurt through a love affair with a young poet, who was ill with a cycloid neurosis probably psychotic in character. He became obsessed with her dancing and took his own life while watching the climax of one of her emotional numbers. It is easy of course to say that he should not have been at large, but the reader knows as well as the writer that our preventive diagnoses are not infallible and that we cannot afford to take the risk of violating the customs on which our liberty is based.

In any case the results were very nearly disastrous to Diana. The physical effects were naturally pronounced in a character such as hers, hysterical gastritis, disordered metabolism of course; but the mental disturbance was intense. An immediate introversion, excessive timidity, and a terror of dancing were the gross symptoms. Her father dropped what he was doing and hurried to her, where he argued with the healers over her treatment, created a bedlam, and finally snatched her away to subject her to an uproarious picaresque six months that left her no time to think. Toward the end of the time, an unimaginative handsome young animal coaxed her back into a normal sex life. She quickly tired of him, and he of her, and she awoke one morning to find herself completely cured, and anxious, not only to dance, but to enjoy the world and the people in it.

Her illness may not have improved her dancing, but it widened her horizon. Although still strongly interested in dance, and firmly believing it to be the most living and personal of all the arts, she now found herself not only cured, but grown up, with an alert interest in all life, all knowledge, the whole cultural pattern. But her reputation as a dancer grew even as it became to her more and more a means whereby she had the opportunity to enjoy more fully the myriad other aspects of living.

The Author

IV

Diana awoke the next morning with a feeling that it was going to be a nice day. She stretched and yawned contentedly. As she sat up her eyes fell on Perry, tousle-headed and still sleeping. She sat still and then a smile stole over her face. Of course, that was it. She was no longer obsessed by the doubts and forebodings of the previous night. It seemed right and proper and very much fun to be helping a lost boy to find himself. Humming quietly she entered her refreshing room and prepared for the day. Perhaps she took a little longer with her hair-do than usual. In any case it was several minutes and a few more before she emerged pink and glowing into the living room. She glanced at Perry, and assured herself that he still slept, then quietly commenced preparations for breakfast. She was interrupted shortly by a voice behind her.

"Good morning."

"Oh, you startled me. Good morning, Perry. Did you have a good night's sleep?"

"Yes, but say—you look gorgeous!"

Diana blushed and dropped her eyes. "Don't try to flatter me."

"But you do."

"Is it the custom of your time to make such direct personal compliments?"

"Why, yes. Isn't it nowdays?"

"Well—, yes, if you wish and it's deserved."

"I think you are the most beautiful thing I've ever seen."

"But—Oh, bother. Hurry up and refresh yourself. Breakfast will be ready before you are."

Perry laughed, and ducked into the guest's refreshment chamber. Diana went determinedly ahead with her work. She mistakenly put a quantity of flour instead of tea in the steeper, turned boiling water over it, then stamped her foot and said 'bother' again, before washing out the pasty mess. Perry stuck his head into the room.

"Dian'!"

"Yes, Perry?"

"Is there some way I can shave around here? My face is a sight."

"There is a capillotomer in my 'fresher. You can plug it in in yours."

"What's a catillopomer?"

"Not a catillopomer, a capillotomer, a hair cutter."

"Will it shave?"

"Smooth as a baby. Here, I'll get it for you." She fetched it and showed him how to use it.

"Why, it's the old dryshaver, streamlined and with a college education."

"It's old fashioned all right, but I don't care much for depilatories. Quit playing with it and shave. I'm about to serve."

"In a jiffy."

"All right, as long a jiffy isn't over five minutes."

Breakfast was a dream of Hedonism. Clear winter sunshine crowned the snow on the far mountains. A light breeze made lacy patterns of the falls. Inside the glass screen two hungry healthy young people looked at each other over cups of steaming black tea and found the other in every way pleasant to look upon. In the background an orchestra in Honolulu played softly and substituted for conversation. Presently the toast was gone and with it the poached eggs and fruit cup.

Diana got up and put out her cigarette. "Your education begins today, my lad. Are you ready?"

"I've polished an apple for teacher."

"That sounds nice. Now for works. Let's pick out a few books. Here—yes, and this will do. And I mustn't forget the *Customs*. I wonder where I put it. Oh, here it is. And you might be interested in this—it's mostly engineering. Now let's see if the records have arrived." She stepped over and opened the receptacle. "Yes. Let's see what Santa Claus brought: 'Historical Panorama of the United States, sections 11–20, XXth Century, sections 21–28, XXIst Century', plus supplements to date and a continuous narrative summary. Integrated world history in four sections. You won't need the first two sections but you might run them anyway. 'Illustrative Customs for Children, infancy to puberty', in six sections. Same for adolescents, and the integrating series for full citizenship. 'Taboo: a History of Social Conventions'. That will keep you busy for quite a while and you can pick out anything you are interested in from the general catalog. There is a list of special catalogs in the front of the big catalog. If you want to go after any particular subject, you can get its catalog. By the way did I show you how to stop the reproducer and make it repeat a portion?"

"No, I don't think you did."

"I'll show you. It's useful in study, especially for a slow poke like me. You'll find that this particular historical series makes several references to this book of United States history. You can stop the machine if you like and read the reference and then pick up where you left off. I'm glad they sent this series. They were directed by the same master who wrote the book."

"Where had I better start?"

"I would forget the books for a while and charge right through the historical recordings. Then I would view all the customs records. Then tomorrow you can start to run them piecemeal with the books, if you like. But be sure to read the *Code of Customs* all the way through. Lots of the customs aren't illustrated in these records."

"OK, where's that first record? See if I put it on properly. All right—let'er roll." The cool calm voice of the announcer stated the title of the record and the period covered, then 'Washington, 1900'. Perry, staring into the stereoscopic picture, found himself floating over Pennsylvania Avenue facing west. It was winter and cold and grey. He moved along over a fairly dense traffic of carriages and hansoms, clop-clopping over muddy pavement and splashing through slush in car tracks. A street car clanged its bell and started. He floated over the tops of the vehicles and found himself approaching the White House. He entered the front door, proceeded to the West Wing and found President McKinley at his desk. Seated at ease near the President, but with his great frame exuding energy even in repose was the one and only Teddy, Teddy Roosevelt, the people's darling. "I tell you, Mr. President, the only way to handle it is to speak softly but to carry a big stick." The scene faded and others appeared with the voice of the commentator frequently in the background. Sometimes the voice carried the story and was merely illustrated by the living shadows. Again the picture presented the story and dialogue provided sufficient explanation, but constantly the scene shifted. At Kitty Hawk the Wright brothers lifted their 'crazy contraption' off the ground. The Panama Canal was dug and yellow fever conquered. 'Too proud to fight.' The *Lusitania*. War in the air. High Cost of Living. Automobiles poured over the continent. Chain stores melted into Tea Pot Dome and a market crash. 'My friends—' came out of a radio by a fireside and Boulder Dam climbed high. Then Perry leaned forward in tense anticipation as 1939 passed by. He kept very quiet for the better part of two hours except at first for a few ejaculations of surprise. After that, surprise left him. He stopped once to ask Diana for some cigarettes and again to get a drink of water. This time he discovered that Diana had gone out. A long time later he felt a touch on his shoulder.

"Don't you think that is about enough at one dose?"

"Oh!—Sorry, you surprised me. You're probably right, but it gets to be a vice." He snapped off the power. "It's as hard to put down as a detective story."

"What's a detective story?"

"A story about the solution of a crime. These were all the rage in 1939. Half the stories published were murder mysteries."

"Good Lord! Was murder that common?"

"No, but the stories were primarily puzzles—like a chess game."

"Oh—. But look, Perry, I called you to see if you would like a swim before lunch. Do you swim?"

"Sure, but where do we swim? Isn't it too cold?"

"No. You'll see. Come along." A door in the end of the room opposite the canyon opened directly outdoors, but instead of a January winter in the High Sierras, it was summer, summer in a tropical garden. The sun shone brightly on masses of flowers and on a patch of green lawn which bordered a little rock pool with clear water over white sand. The pool was just long enough for four or five strokes. Beyond the garden Perry saw winter and snow-capped peaks. Yet the garden and pool were apparently unprotected in any way from the rigors of the mountain climate.

Perry turned back to Diana. "Listen, Dian', I've believed everything else, but this is a dream. Put me out of my misery. How, how is it done?"

Diana smiled in delight. "It is nice, isn't it? I'll show you how it's done. Walk along the path by the pool. When you get close to the edge of the garden put out your hands."

Perry did as directed. As he reached the edge he stopped suddenly and gave a grunt of surprise. Then he cautiously ran his hand up and down what appeared from his actions to be a wall of thin air.

"Why, it's glass!"

"Yes, of course."

"It must have an amazingly low refractive index."

"I suppose so."

"Look, Dian', I can't see the stuff. Tell me where it is, so I won't bump into it."

"You won't. The garden is laid out to keep you a half meter or so from it and it's quite high enough overhead. The base of it runs all around here"—she indicated most of a semicircle— "From there it arches up to the house. If you look closely you can see the joint of the seal, and there it runs down the rock wall and back to the ground again. It is shaped like a giant bubble."

Perry mused. "Hm—I see. And that's why it doesn't need supports. But how did it get there in the first place?"

"It was blown in place, just like a bubble. It is a bubble. Look, did children blow bubbles when you were young?"

"Yes."

"Did you ever wet a dish or a box or a table top and blow a bubble on it and make it follow a shape you wanted?"

"Yes, yes, I begin to see."

"Well, first they painted the wall and a sheeting on the ground with sticky stuff—bubble mixture, right up to where the bubble is to stop. Then they put their bubble pipe gadget in the middle and commenced to blow. When the bubble just reached the proper size, they stopped."

"It sounds easy the way you tell it."

"It's not very. I watched them do this one and they broke four bubbles before one held up. Then it takes several hours to dry tough, and any little touch can ruin it until it does."

"I don't see yet how you can get glass to behave so."

"It isn't glass—not silicate glass anyhow, but a synthetic plastic glass. One of the technicians said it had molecules like very long chains."

"That's reasonable."

"I wouldn't know, but it's a sticky stuff when they decant it, like a white molasses, but it dries very hard and stiff like glass only it's tough, instead of brittle. It won't shatter and it's very hard to cut or tear."

"Well, it's a grand notion in any case. You know we had patios and outdoor living rooms and pools in gardens in my day, but it was generally too hot or too cold or too windy to enjoy them. And there were always insects; flies, or mosquitoes, or both. In my aunt's patio it was honey bees. It's very disconcerting when you're trying to sunbathe to have bees crawling over you and buzzing around your head."

"Are you sensitive to bee stings, Perry?"

"No. I can handle bees. They don't sting me, but they used to drive my aunt nearly frantic. The poor woman never did get any real pleasure out of her garden. They would sting her and she would swell up like a poisoned pup, and get sick to her stomach. Sad really, she did love her garden so and got so little fun out of it."

"Then why did she keep bees?"

"She didn't. One of her neighbors did."

"But that's not custom—Never mind. I asked you about bee stings because bees don't sting anymore."

Perry clapped his hand to his brow and gave a look of mock

agony. "Enough, woman enough! Tell me no more! No. Stop. One more thing. Answer me this question and I die happy. Do watermelons have seeds?"

"Did they used to have?"

Perry stepped to the edge of the pool, assumed a declamatory pose and orated: "Farewell, sad world. Papa goes to his reward! *Sic semper* seeds," nipped his nose between thumb and forefinger, shut his eyes tight and jumped feet first into the pool. He came up blowing to find Diana wiping water out of her eyes and laughing hysterically.

"Perry! You're a clown! Stop it!"

He didn't answer but asked solemnly, "Tell me, bird of mournful numbers, do blackberries still have seeds?"

Diana controlled her giggles. "Blackberries have seeds, you idiot."

"That's all I wanted to know." Perry's head disappeared and he gave a creditable imitation of a drowning man, accompanied by glugging sounds. Diana dived in, joined him on the bottom, and tickled him vigorously. Both heads reappeared. Perry coughed and blew.

"Wench, you made me strangle."

"Sorry." But she giggled again.

Some minutes later Perry lay on his side drying off and watching Diana, who was still in the pool. She floated with just her face and the curve of her breast appearing above the water. Her hair formed a halo about her head. The warm sun soaked into their bones and rendered them sluggish and contented. Perry chucked a pebble into the pool. It hit the water with a little chunking sound and splashed a drop on Diana's face. She turned on her side, took two effortless strokes to the side of the pool, and rested her hands on the edge.

Diana cut in. "Are you hungry, fella?"

"Now that you mention it, there does seem to be something missing."

"Then let's eat. No, don't get up. We'll eat out here. It's all ready."

She returned laden with a tray as big as she was. "Perry, you move over into the shade. You haven't the tan I have and I don't want you blistered."

Three-quarters of an hour later, Diana stirred out of a digestive calm. "Before you get back to your studies, I want to have you measured for some clothes."

Perry looked surprised. "Clothes—why, I had gathered the impression that they weren't necessary."

Diana looked puzzled. "You can't stay in the house forever, Perry. It's cold outside. I've planned a little picnic for tomorrow, but we'll have to get you some warm clothes first. And while we're about it, you might as well order some other things that you will need."

"Lead on, McDuff."

Diana selected a combination on the televue. A Semitic gentleman appeared on screen. He rubbed his hands together and smiled. "Ah, Madame, can I do you a service?"

"Thank you; my friend needs some costumes. A heavy and medium snow suit, first, and then some other things."

"Ah, that is fine. We have some new models, very dashing and sooooo practical too. And now will you have him take position?"

Diana nudged Perry into a spot near the televue, then turned the screen so that it faced him. The Semitic gentleman seemed ecstatic. "Ah, yes. A beautiful figure. It is a pleasure to make clothes for a man who can wear them. Wait. Let me think. I have it! I shall create a new model for him. With that proportion of the shoulders and that length of leg—"

Diana cut in. "Not today, thank you. Another time perhaps."

"But Madame, I am an artist, not a businessman."

Diana's lips barely moved. "Don't let him fool you, Perry. He's one part artist and three parts businessman." Then to the televue. "No, we need these clothes today. Please use a stock pattern."

"Service, Madame." He wheeled up a camera-like device somewhat larger than the one used to take Perry's palm print. "Is your friend exactly four meters from the screen?"

"Exactly." He fiddled with the camera.

"Is your screen corrected for angular aberration?"

"Yes." He made an adjustment.

"Now—front view. Very well, right side. Back view, please. Left side. Will you bend over, please? Extend both arms. That's fine. Now raise your knees in succession. That's all." The camera disappeared. "Will you examine materials?"

"No, make them all wool with cellutate lining. How about colors, Perry? Would dark blue suit you?"

"Fine."

"With white piping, perhaps?" The vendor's anxious voice joined them.

"Very well."

Diana also okayed the purchase of a pocket belt with a detachable kilt for travel and general public wear, some sport sandals, and a pair of light slippers for city wear. She firmly vetoed any discussion of ornaments, jewelry, knickknacks, and accessories, and refused to be drawn into considering any feminine frills for herself. The 'artist' finally gave up and the screen went blank. Perry returned to his studies. Record followed record and the afternoon wore away unbeknownst to Perry. Once, Diana came in and changed the position of the screen and propped Perry up on pillows. Later she brought him a cup of tea and a sandwich. Perry hardly noticed the interruptions. He was held by the endless, ultimate drama. Late in the afternoon the last supplement whirred to a stop. Perry got up and stretched cramped limbs. Diana was not in sight. He looked around, sighed, sat down and lit a cigarette. Presently Diana appeared in the garden door. "How far did you get, Perry?"

"I've been through them once right up to date."

"How about it?"

"Well, I feel for the first time as if I actually were in 2086. It's a lot to swallow at one dose though."

"I've invited an old friend of mine here this evening, Perry. He can help you a lot. He's a Master of History who used to be one of my teachers."

"Say, that's fine. When does he get here?"

"He should be here for dinner. He has to fly over from Berkeley."

Less than an hour later the visitor appeared. He was a thick set man, with broad powerful shoulders. His cranium was large, his eyes deep, his face homely and rugged. He gathered Diana in a bear hug that lifted her off her feet, kissed her on both cheeks, sat her down and started to peel off his flying kit. Perry judged him a well preserved fifty-five or sixty, and noted with interest that he appeared to shave his entire body with the exception of his bushy grey eyebrows. Diana introduced them.

"May I do you a service, my boy." It was more a statement than a question. "Diana has told me something of your case. We should have lots to talk about." His name, it appeared, was Master Cathcart.

Diana insisted on refraining from historical discussion until after dinner. Once it was over however, and Master Cathcart had persuaded a big bowled pipe to burn, he came right to business. "I am to assume, I take it, that you are for all practical purposes an inhabitant of 1939 A.D., well educated in your period, transported by some witchcraft to this period. Very well. You have been studying some records today? Which ones?" Perry ran through the list. "Good enough. Now suppose you summarize briefly what you have learned today and I will explain and amplify and answer questions as best I can."

"Well," replied Perry, "that's a large order but I'll give it a try. At the time of my accident, July 1939, President Franklin D. Roosevelt was in his second term. Congress had adjourned after wrecking most of the President's program. The war in Spain had been won by the fascists. Japan was fighting China and was apparently about to fight Russia. Unemployment and an unbalanced budget were still the main troubles in the United States. 1940 was a presidential year. President Roosevelt was forced to run for a third term through lack of an electable successor to carry on his policies. His nomination by the Democratic convention resulted in the defection of the conservative wing of the party to Republican Party. In the meantime the National Progressives had organized on a nationwide scale and put young Bob LaFollette in the field. The Republicans nominated Senator Vandenburgh. Vandenburgh was elected but polled considerably less than half of the popular vote and failed to get a majority in either house. His administration was doomed from the start. Very little was done for four years except for a half-hearted attempt to balance the budget by eliminating relief, but riots and hunger marches soon scared Congress into providing more and more for the dole. In the spring of 1944 the death in a plane crash of Mr. Roosevelt demoralized the remnants of the Democratic Party and most of them joined the Republicans or the Progressives. The Democrats adjourned their convention without naming a candidate. The Progressives named LaGuardia, the fiery little Mayor of New York, while the Republicans after many ballots picked Senator Malone. President Vandenburgh was as thoroughly discredited by circumstances he did not understand and could not control as President Hoover before him. Senator Malone was a midwestern politician, a typical demagogue of my period, if I'm any judge. The recordings show him red-faced and raucous, a man of the people. Malone ran on a platform of blaming everything on Europe and the radicals. He demanded instant payment of the war debts, which were pretty silly since the second European war was already on. He called for the outlawing of the Communist Party, protection of the American home, and a return to rationalism in education which he defined as readin', 'ritin', and 'rithmetic and a particularly offensive jingoistic patriotism. He advocated deportation of all aliens, laws to prevent women from holding men's jobs, and protection of the morals of the young. He promised to restore prosperity and promised everyone the 'American' standard of living. And he won, by a narrow vote in the electoral college. LaGuardia said afterwards that since Malone had promised them the moon, all he could offer was the moon with whipped cream, which didn't seem practical to LaGuardia.

"Once in office Malone ran things with a high hand. Congress was willing in the first session to pass almost any law he desired. One of the most important was the Public Safety bill which was in effect a gag for the press and other means of public information. Inasmuch as it was first used to suppress news of labor troubles which resulted from the discontinuance of the dole, the capital controlled press submitted to it without really knowing what they were in for. Then a law was passed which greatly increased the scope of the G-men or Federal enforcement agents and making them directly responsible to the chief executive. Malone staffed these expanded and greatly changed corps from his home state political machine. In the meantime, in spite of his controlled press, the people were getting restless. Even those who were still economically fairly comfortable had had swarms of the hungry, dispossessed, and unemployed turned loose on them. Malone was apparently afraid to chance another election, even a mid-term. Perhaps he never intended to. In any case he declared a state of emergency, using the mobs of unemployed as an excuse, and took over the internal civil government as an absolute dictator. He used the army and navy to quell any local difficulties. With his new secret service and control over the means of communication and propaganda this was feasible. By the way, the record states that he was able to use the army and navy to destroy the democratic form of government. I find that hard to believe, Master Cathcart. You see I was in the navy myself and I don't believe that the American Services were fascist minded. How do you account for it?"

"I'm glad you brought up that point, Perry. It seems likely that Malone had planned this from the very first. At least he anticipated having to use the military against the people. His technique was simple and almost foolproof. His information service inquired into the political sympathies and economic status of every officer in the fleet and in the army. Whenever an officer was definitely determined to be liberal and democratic, he was not removed or even framed in a court martial. Malone was subtle. Each such officer was transferred as soon as located to a noncombatant assignment; recruiting officer, Reserve Officer's Training Corps instructor, inspector of supplies, War College, Naval and Military Academies, and so forth. Whenever an officer was determined to be definitely militaristic, jingoistic, a potential sadist, he was placed in a key position over forces actually ready to exert armed force. To a lesser extent the enlisted men were weeded out. When he was ready to strike he had behind him a military machine he could bend to his purpose."

"But how about the National Guard?"

"Oh, that was more difficult at first glance. But the federal government owned and controlled the arms used by the Guard. Under the guise of replacement practically all of the ammunition in the hands of the guards was called in during the week before his coup. Of course had it been realized that all the ammunition in all units of the Guard was being called in at once, it would have caused trouble, but control of the nation's communication services plus the fact that each separate order was classed as a confidential military order enabled him to get away with it."

"That clears up my difficulty," said Perry, "I thought there was something fishy about it. If I remember, this dictatorship or inter-regnum, as the record referred to it, lasted only about three years. Malone was assassinated by one of his own henchmen in 1950. The commentator seemed to think that the regime was essentially unstable and would have broken down anyway very shortly. In any case Malone's assassination was the signal for an uprising all over the country. Inside of three weeks Malone's bullies had been killed or driven into hiding. The man who had been governor of Michigan at the beginning of the inter-regnum called all of the governors together. They selected one of the number as President Pro Tem and set a date for a general election. LaGuardia was elected. He served two terms."

"Very clear," put in Cathcart, "now let's talk about the rest of the world for a while. It was during Vandenburgh's administration that the second European war ran its course. With the collapse of the loyalists in Spain, the fascist states were ready to take on the democracies. France was torn with internal dissension and strikes. The Conservative Party was in power in England and apparently committed to a do-nothing policy. The Fascist powers struck, but the first world war was repeated. The democracies failed to fold up although they lost battle after battle. The end came, not through the intervention of the United States—Vandenburgh had no stomach for that—but through the economic collapse of Germany. She had entered this war in a physical condition much poorer than that of 1914 and she couldn't stand a long war."

"What happened to the dictators?"

."Adolf Hitler committed suicide by shooting himself in the roof of the mouth. Mussolini got out much more gracefully. He submitted his resignation to the king he had kept around during his entire tenure and the king appointed a new prime minister, a social democrat. But to my mind the most interesting thing about the peace was the peculiar terms of the peace treaty."

"Some sort of a league of nations, all over again wasn't it?"

"Yes, and no. A very brilliant young Frenchman, a descendant of LaFayette, argued that a continental government or federation was necessary if a lasting peace was to come, and argued further that a constitutional monarchy was the most stable form under which free men could live. And so the United Europe was created. But the romantic part is the man who was chosen to head this polyglot creation. The Hapsburgs and the Hohenzollerns were out for obvious reasons of bad blood and bad records. The English king was suggested but he aroused no enthusiasm, being rather negative in character and further handicapped by his shyness and speech impediments. None of the pretenders in exile had any real following. But one prince was available, who had long before captured the world's imagination. Edward, Duke of Windsor, who had abdicated the British throne in 1936 rather than accept the complete domination of his prime minister, became the choice."

"Well, I'll be damned!" muttered Perry. "I don't believe that was in the record."

"You only saw the summary records," explained Diana.

"Edward had returned home at the start of the war and demanded to be assigned to military duty. He displayed surprising talent, particularly as a creator of morale. It was largely due to him that the repeated losses of battles did not result in capitulation to the fascist governments. When his name was proposed, he was nominated by acclamation. He was reluctant to accept but finally agreed to do so provided his wife was given equal formal rank with him. This was agreed to over the protests of the British delegation and they were crowned in a ceremony that marked the end of the Bordeaux conference on 1944 June 12. He assumed the title of Edward, King of States and Emperor of Europe. Wallis was of course Queen and Empress. They say that the English queen never got over it."

"Swell!" Perry chortled.

"Edward made an able ruler. He had helped to draw the constitution of the new super-state and had insisted on several things, free trade among the sister states, a common currency, a joint army and navy, and a small one at that. All international disputes to be settled by the Imperial Tribune. The system worked well enough for a quarter of a century, in spite of creakings and adjustments."

"What put an end to it?"

"His death. He died in 1970, and left no heirs. Even while the Tribune was declaring Wallis regent, pending the selection of a successor, a company of local guards crossed a bridge in eastern Europe and seized a little town of less than a thousand inhabitants. There was some vague historical claim based on a battle nearly five hundred years before. They were resisted by the local constabulary who were joined by the veterans' organizations. In two days that whole border was in a state of guerrilla warfare and within a fortnight there was fighting all over the continent. It was hastened at least by Great Britain's refusal to recognize the regency of Wallis in spite of the Tribune's authority, and calling home her ships and troops."

"And that was the start of the Forty Years War?"

"Approximately. Some of the States stayed out at first and various ones dropped out from time to time. But for all practical purposes Europe was at war for the next forty years."

"How did it end?"

"It didn't end, not formally. It burnt out like a fire that has consumed all of its fuel. In 1970 Europe contained over four hundred million people, exclusive of the Soviet Union, Sweden, and Norway, none of which were heavily involved in the war. The Soviet Union of course had not been a part of United Europe anyhow. In 2010 which marks the approximate end of the war Europe is believed to have had a population of less than twenty-five million."

Diana blanched. Perry spoke up. "Do you mean to say that over a third of a billion people were killed in thirty years?"

"Not all by shot or poison. More people starved than were killed in battle. It was the breakdown of the economic organization that killed the masses rather than deadly weapons. People hardly ever realize the completeness of our economic interdependence. Communications were destroyed by the fighting. Distribution was upset. The credit system expanded and then collapsed, leaving people to depend on barter. Barter was about as adequate to take care of the involved economic structure as oars would have been for one of their battleships. Governments resorted to the exercise of angary and expropriation to provide for troops, but it amounted to foraging and the people regarded it as such. This dog-eat-dog system ran its natural course. The farmers hoarded and the city dwellers starved. From time to time the city dweller killed the farmer and took what he had. When that was gone the city dweller died for he had never learned the arts of husbandry. And the armies ran over them all. Of course this breakdown didn't occur all at once. For the first few years the industrial civilization ran faster than ever, but in the high fever of war, living on its own substance. But when enough crops had been destroyed, or not planted, enough granaries emptied, enough water works bombed that the pangs of hunger became general, then dissolution set in. A modern city is an almost incredibly helpless and delicate organism. It has lost its power to produce the actual essentials of life. In spite of its transportation systems, it cannot move as they found out in the evacuation of London. It is like an overgrown idiot baby in an incubator. It is completely helpless without the aid of the many servants that succor it. It cannot even think except in a slow ponderous collective fashion and it cannot think at all in an emergency. Its individuals can think, but a city is an organism in itself and must have a directing brain and nervous system. Destroy its waterworks. It dies. Stop its food supply. It dies. Remove its directing intelligence, it commits suicide. The cities went to pieces first.

"And the birth rate fell to lowest ebb in history. Part of this was due to contagious abortion, one of the many epidemics that swept the continent. Some of the sociologists find evidence that a large number of women refused to bear children. And lots of the men were sterilized, even when they weren't killed, by exposure to the rays that a beneficent science had handed to the field marshals. And so Europe died."

"How in the world did we stay out of it?"

"Partly luck, but mostly the genius and strength of character of one man. Franklin Roosevelt had proposed and partially developed laws that were intended to keep the United States out of war. These were strengthened by LaGuardia until the President had the power to completely withdraw the United States from a danger zone. In 1970 the United States had enjoyed many years of useful economic relations with Europe. But at the time of the death of Edward, there was in the chair at Washington,

President John Winthrop, elected by the Conservative Party and a man who might have been expected to repeat the mistakes of 1914. But at the first outbreak of trouble he suspended all shipping. When it became evident that a general war was likely he used the naval and air forces to evacuate our nationals and promulgated the Non-Intercourse Proclamation. Our diplomatic and fiscal agents were all withdrawn. Our commerce with Europe stopped in every respect. With minor exceptions, for twenty years no American citizen made a legal visit to Europe. Naturally it produced terrific economic dislocations in the United States. But he stood firm. At the time of the proclamation Congress was not in session and no regular was scheduled for five months. He refused to call Congress and his legal authority to do what he did was upheld by the Supreme Court. It seems likely that he would have defied the court if necessary. He was hanged in effigy, but by the time Congress met his action appeared justified to many. He was impeached but acquitted in his trial by a narrow vote, and the United States was saved in spite of itself. However before we talk too much about Winthrop we should go back a little in United States history."

"Just a second before we leave Europe entirely. What happened after the war?"

"We don't know, Perry. Not in any great detail. The Non-Intercourse rule has never been fully lifted and we have never resumed commercial or diplomatic relations. The population is increasing slowly. It is largely agrarian and the economy is mostly of the village and countryside character. Most of the population is illiterate and technical skill is almost lost. Our knowledge is incomplete although we maintain missions in several places for ethnological and sociological study. But now can you tell me what happened after the assassination of Malone?"

"Well, LaGuardia took office in 1951 and served two terms.

The chap that directed the recording seemed to think that his biggest achievement was a change in the banking system. He called it the Battle of the Banks."

"Yes, and it is important for it was a change that made possible our present economic system."

"Wait a second, please. What *is* the present economic system? Diana says it isn't socialism. Is it capitalism?"

"You can call it that if you like. I would suggest that you think of it as privately owned industrialism for the time being. LaGuardia destroyed capitalism as you knew it. He started out to found a publicly owned bank, the Bank of the United States."

"Wasn't the Federal Reserve Bank still in existence?"

"Yes, but the Federal Reserve was not, despite its title, a publicly owned bank. Nor was it a bank in the common use of the term. A private citizen couldn't borrow money from it nor place money in it. Only bankers could use it and they owned it. LaGuardia wanted to set up a real bank that would be owned by and used by the people. But the bankers fought him in every way. They controlled most of the newspapers, owned a good piece of the wealth in the country, and held mortgages of one sort or another on the rest. Their position was very strong in machine politics, too. So they set out to defeat him. And that got him angry. It appears from what we can find out that it was never safe to get the 'Little Flower' angry. He jammed his banking bill through by a combination of personality and intimidation and announced to the whole country that he was ready to lend money to all and sundry who might be refused credit at the private banks. You see the banks had created a panic and a wave of fear by calling loans and refusing to loan more money. LaGuardia restored confidence even before he was able to set up the machinery for handling a banking business. And by now LaGuardia was not willing to let things drop just by setting up his new bank. He had intended it primarily as a fiscal agent of the government to aid in the manifold financial dealings of the government with the citizens, started by Franklin Roosevelt. LaGuardia became determined to break the private bankers. He called in several students of finance and studied the theory of credit himself. He became convinced that ordinary commercial financing could be done for a service charge plus an insurance fee amounting to much less than the current rates of interest charged by banks, whose rates were based on supply and demand, treating money as a commodity rather than as a sovereign state's means of exchange. He proceeded to lend money on this theory. His cost accountants figured pretty accurately the service charge necessary and estimates were made to cover insurance. As the system developed the insurance feature was simply the pro-rate of the losses of the preceding fiscal period. The types of loans the government would make and the quality of paper it would discount kept the losses low and within a year the federal government would loan money to its citizens at an average interest of three-quarters of one per cent per annum.

"Then he dealt his final blow. His new banking law permitted the government to regulate the percentage of fractional reserves that private banks were required to keep on hand to meet withdrawals by depositors. As you may know if you have studied the banking laws of your period, the so-called fractional reserve was a dodge whereby a banker could loan money he didn't have and never had. It actually permitted him to create new money, based not on gold, nor on his own credit, but on the credit of his customers. LaGuardia proceeded to regulate with a vengeance. He ordered fractional reserves increased in a program that called for one hundred per cent reserves at the end of three years. The disgruntled bankers made a test case and took it to the Supreme Court. The Solicitor-General argued that the law and the order made under its authority were not only constitutional but that fractional reserves as hitherto used were clearly in violation of the constitutional provision giving Congress the sole right to coin money and regulate the value thereof. The Court upheld the administration on all counts in a famous decision written by Mr. Justice Frankfurter, and the manipulation of the money power was destroyed in the United States."

"Then private banks were destroyed?"

"Not entirely. They remained a useful institution for some people as depositories for they soon offered services to their customers that the Bank of the United States did not give. If you like to have your deposits received by messenger at your home or want to cash a check in the middle of the night, the private bankers will gladly oblige. And there was still plenty of room for speculative credit pools for people who wished to risk their capital in expectation of high return. The banks continue to lend money at high rates where the risk is great and not easily figured, but they have to lend real money now, not stuff that they draw out of the ink well. The fractional reserves decision put an end to that. You will find what an important part the speculative bankers played in the penetration of South America. They still play an important role. They supply an element of private initiative and enterprise in industry that government cannot hope to provide."

"What about the South American penetration? The records were rather vague or perhaps I had gotten out of my depth."

"Some historians call it rape rather than penetration. Up until 1970 the United States had been steadily losing ground in South America. During the reign of Edward Europe grew steadily more industrialized and found her greatest market in South America. The Asiatic market had been worthless since the 1930's and South America with its raw materials was in a position to reciprocate. On the other hand the United States was an agricultural export nation, and this annoyed several South American states, especially Argentina. But the Forty Years War changed all this. The United States had undergone an economic improvement as a result of the Banking Act which had decreased the spread between production and consumption by lowering the percentage of the cost charges, in a commercial article, unavailable for purchasing power."

"I don't follow you."

"I suggest that you note it down and wait until you study the current economic system. You were probably educated in the conventional economic theories of your period which were magnificent and most ingenious, but—if you will pardon me saying so—all wrong. But to return to our muttons; the improved economic condition produced the usual political reaction and a conservative administration was elected after LaGuardia. There still remained however considerable spread between production and consumption. It had always been the conventional point of view, especially in the economic beliefs of the Conservative Party, that a prosperous nation required a favorable trade balance or gold balance as it was formerly called. In simple language that means that a country is best off when it exports more than it imports. Phrased in that way it sounds silly, for it is surely evident that a country that ships out more than it takes in gets poorer every year in terms of real wealth. Nevertheless there was an element of truth in it, a very practical truth at that time. The economic life was organized in such a comical fashion that each year the country produced goods of greater value than the people of the country were able to buy back and use up. This was known as over-production and many were the esoteric nonsensical things said about it. But the situation was that simple. The system of necessity produced more than it consumed. Of necessity. You can go into the mathematics of it later. Being an engineer you are bound to see the truth of it, and will probably be vastly amused by it."

"Do you mean to say that that was all there was wrong with business in the United States in my day?"

"That was all. And all of your labor troubles, and poverty, and physical suffering were as unnecessary as they were tragic."

"That seems preposterous. If it was as simple as that it could have been fixed. I could work out some scheme to fix it myself, half a dozen schemes. Why in the navy we wouldn't have put up with any such damn nonsense. Why didn't somebody see it?"

"Some people did, C.H. Douglas, Goulds Gainesborough, Bronson Cutting and a few others, but it was almost as difficult to convince people of the fact as it had been to convince an earlier generation that the world was round. In each case the fact was true and the fact was simple but the sturdy common sense of the man who had been brought up to believe in a flat earth or a 'favorable trade balance', rejected the truth. The socialists understood this truth of course, but they insisted that there was only one solution. There were many good solutions for so simple a problem. We believe nowadays that we have a solution more suited to the United States than socialism. But come, we are getting a long way off from South America.

"From 1970 to the turn of the century a partial solution was found. Our excess wealth was poured into our sister continent and it was developed as a new frontier. Gold mined from the Chilean Andes helped for a while to preserve the fiction of a favorable trade balance. After that and in addition to it, almost any sort of wildcat financing was acceptable that would keep up the flow of goods to the south. The private bankers turned to this rich field of exploitation and convinced the public that the new El Dorado lay under the Southern Cross. The whole shaky business piled up until practically the entire continent was mortgaged to the skies in return for goods that we couldn't use ourselves and would have poisoned us if we had kept them. But the Latin temperament had a simple solution. I sometimes wonder whether it was planned or was the inevitable result of the the circumstances. But when the due day came each government folded up and a new government calmly repudiated the commitments of its predecessor.

"The first incident of the A.-B.-C. War occurred in 2002 April. The Argentine government had refused to recognize its debts to us both public and private, and several stiff notes had been exchanged. Our South American squadron was ordered to Buenos Aires. Chile and Brazil each informed the United States that any display of force in Argentina would be regarded as an unfriendly act.

"Nevertheless the squadron was not recalled. It steamed into the harbor and had no more than anchored, two old aircraft carriers and an odd dozen of minor craft, when it was attacked from the air and sunk to the last man, before a plane could rise. We don't know yet who did it, but we do know that both the Chilean and Brazilian navies and air fleets had made a rendezvous some two hundred kilometers off Buenos Aires."

"How did the war work out? I found the record account a bit sketchy for my professional taste."

"Why, Perry, you aren't really interested in *killing*, are you?" Diana was perturbed and incredulous.

He patted her hand. "No Dian', not at all. But the matters of the strategy and the tactics involved and the weapons used are of intellectual interest to me, just as you might be interested in the ceremonial dances that accompanied the Aztecs' Blood sacrifices.

The wrinkles smoothed out from her brow. "Yes, I suppose so. But it does seem barbaric."

"I imagine the weapons would have been largely familiar to

you, Perry. The United States had not been at war for many
years and it is a matter of history that few weapons are developed
in peacetime. The military mind clings tenaciously to its accustomed ways—if you will pardon me. The strategic principle of
exterior lines determined the war. Neither side was equipped to
deal any telling blow on the other. They were too far apart and
there was too much terrain involved. There was no commerce to
raid as practically all the shipping had been between the United
States and South America. Each side was able to raid the cities
of the other, but armies of occupation would have necessitated
extended lines of communication to protect at a serious strategic disadvantage. The most startling single incident in the war
was the raid on Manhattan."

"Tell me about that."

"One would think that Manhattan would have been evacuated
early in the war, but it was extremely inconvenient to do so and
the public had been assured that no enemy force could possibly
get that far north. As a matter of fact, practically all the fighting
had been below the equator. Except for two raids in the Gulf and
one on Palm Beach, none of which did much damage, the United
States was untouched. But in 2003 December two aircraft carriers, the *Santa Maria* and the *Reina Borealis* raided Manhattan.
They had proceeded to New York by a route that took them far
east in the Atlantic and by luck and partly by foresight they
reached the North Atlantic without discovery. They were aided
by the weather for the last thousand kilometers had to be made in
a thick fog. They attacked at noon, dropping out of a cloudy sky
with a ceiling of less than two hundred meters and in some places
lower. The attack must have been worked out with great preci-
sion, for each ship seemed to know exactly where to go. The
bridges were destroyed first, and the landing platforms. It must
have been a terrifying sight to see those great helicopters settling

out of the clouds and proceeding leisurely to destroy their objectives while the more agile fighting planes that escorted them buzzed around like hornets. The tubes under the rivers were bombed also. A helicopter would settle at the last station, its crew would gas the bystanders while a working party commandeered a train and loaded aboard the explosives. Then with controls and time bomb on board the train would make its last run."

"How much damage was done?"

"The damage was practically complete. The water works were destroyed along with the power stations. The skyscrapers were almost completely wrecked. Incendiary fires were started throughout the city. It was remarkably efficient, for warfare, as explosives were not thrown around at random but carefully placed to do maximum damage. It is believed that the helicopters made two or three trips. The weather made the whole thing possible, of course, particularly the gas attack that completed the job."

"How was that?"

"After the attackers had apparently exhausted their supplies of high explosives, they systematically patrolled the island, remaining always in the clouds and dropped gas containers. They must have returned to their floating bases time and again for they kept this up for thirty-six hours."

"You speak as if they had no opposition."

"There was opposition, surely, but consider—You are a pilot. How would you attack an enemy ship in a cloud bank."

"I couldn't."

"That's the answer. They destroyed Manhattan and nearly eighty per cent of its population. Although it wasn't conclusive, hardly more than an exhibition of frightfulness, it lead indirectly to the end of the war."

"Why was that?"

"Five out of six of the heads of the leading international banks were killed in the raid on Manhattan, not to mention the destruction of a large part of the records of the financial dealings that had started the trouble. And of course hundreds of the small fry in the banking racket. With the ring leaders gone Congress listened to the people of the country who had never wanted a war in the first place. An armistice was declared in 2004 February. The terms of the peace included moratoria on international obligations which was a polite word for cancellation, and established a Pan-American export-import bank to provide for resumption of trade on what amounted to a cash and carry basis."

"Anything else?"

"That was about all. The destruction of Manhattan was checked off against the raids on Rio and Buenos Aires. But the most important result was the twenty-seventh amendment."

"That's the war referendum amendment, isn't it?"

"Yes. Did the records tell you how it works?"

"Well, I gathered that it was an arrangement whereby the people had to vote on it before war could be declared."

"That is true as far it goes. In effect the amendment states that, except in case of invasion of the United States, Congress shall not have the power to declare war without submitting the matter to a referendum. The article sketches out briefly the machinery for holding the referendum and sets a time limit in which to accomplish it. But the most amusing feature is the provision saying who shall vote in the matter."

"Doesn't everybody?"

"No, only those persons vote who are eligible for military duty."

"Aren't women permitted to vote?"

"Yes and no. If the current laws make women eligible for combat duty, they vote. If not, they don't vote."

Perry whistled. "I'll bet that caused an uproar."

Cathcart grinned as if savoring the joke. "It certainly did. Militant feminists screamed and frothed at the mouth. Then it was pointed out to them that the proposed amendment made no mention of sex and that they could, if they chose, make women eligible by including them for military service in the implementing bill."

"But that isn't practical."

"On the contrary. As a matter of fact the law did include women for a number of years. Women can be used in the place of men in practically all military positions. Not as effectively in many of them, but they have been used many times. Your military history should have told you that."

"I guess you're right. Yes, I'd forgotten the Battalion of Death. And they make very good pilots of course."

"At the present time a limited class of women are eligible for service and would consequently vote on a war question."

"But see here. It seems to me that it is unfair to leave it in the hands of those who are eligible to go into the service. If there is any one thing I've learned from history I've studied today it is that war affects everybody in the country, that it can kill off an entire population. Why we knew that even in my day."

"What you say is true. But the non-combatants don't expect to be killed—not seriously. In the A.-B.-C. war if those bankers who were killed in the raid on Manhattan had expected to be bombed and gassed, there wouldn't have been any war. But they didn't. They thought the war would be fought far away by the professionals. No, the great mass of civilians never see war as anything personal to themselves, unless it is brought home to each one that he, John, will have to fight in person. That is why nations used to declare war so easily and then be forced to use conscription to fight the war. The country wants to go to war. Oh surely. 'John Brown's Body.' 'Make the World Safe for Democracy.' 'Britons never will be slaves.' But if the war is more than a skirmish you have to draft men to fight it. With all due respect to you, Diana, women were worse than men about it. It's always possible to get women stirred up to a war fever. Half of the men who do volunteer in a war instead of waiting to be conscripted, do so because some woman who thinks it's glorious and romantic is urging them or shaming them into it. In peace time women are emotional pacifists, but when the bands start to play, they are much more easily stampeded than men. What's on your mind, son? You look thoughtful."

"I was thinking of an organization that used to give me the cold shivers, the Gold Star Mothers. They were formed after the World War and a woman had to have had a son killed in the war to be eligible. They had meetings and officers and conventions and national presidents and so forth, just like a lodge. It made my flesh crawl."

Diana interposed. "But, Perry, I should think such an organization could be a powerful force for good."

"It could have been, but it wasn't. If they had devoted themselves to making another war impossible, it would have been fine. But it was just another lodge, just another woman's club. But let's get back to the subject. I'd rather forget it."

Cathcart resumed his discourse. "I haven't told you about the neatest feature of the amendment. As we have said, only those who could fight could vote. Those who voted to declare war automatically enlisted for the duration of the war. The ballot even told them where to report the next morning. Those who didn't vote were the next draft, and those who voted no the last draft."

Perry looked puzzled and slightly annoyed, "But that puts a premium on cowardice, doesn't it? If war is declared, they should all have to take the same chances. If I had my way, I would just reverse the scheme."

"Don't be hasty, Perry. Stop and think. Is it a premium on cowardice? Perhaps it is. But isn't it just as likely to be a premium on common judgment? Perhaps the war isn't worth fighting. I've studied history all my life and I can remember but two or three wars that seemed to me to be worth fighting, and I have my doubts about those. In any case, if a man takes the responsibility of voting to plunge a country into a situation that may destroy it and is bound to kill and maim a lot of its citizens, shouldn't he have to accept the consequences of his decision by being in the first line of fighting? There is a stern justice about it. Under this rule no man could cast a vote that would send a fellow human being out to face poisonous gas and shots and burning rays without being ready to stand alongside him and suffer the same fate."

"But see here, in a democratic country, we are all in the same boat. Why shouldn't everybody have to defend the country alike?"

"Your reasoning is sound, Perry, but it doesn't apply to the case. You have forgotten that if the United States is invaded, no referendum is necessary. To be exact if any part of the North American continent is invaded, or if a fleet approaches our home waters with evident hostile intent, Congress can act without consulting the people. The referendum applies to situations such as the First World War, or the Spanish-American War or the War of 1812 or the A.-B.-C War. As a matter of fact the President has ample power to act, even without consent of Congress, to repel invasion or to succor our nationals abroad. No, the purpose of this amendment is to permit the people to decide for themselves whether or not an incident or series of incidents constitutes sufficient reason for them to want to go outside our own country and fight someone else. Of course the munitions makers didn't like it nor a lot of the financiers and industrialists, but it was democratic and reasonable and the people voted it in anyhow, once they understood it. But the munitions makers fought it tooth and toenail and eventually cooked their own goose in the process."

"How?"

"At the next session of Congress there was the usual bill introduced to take over the entire arms industry and make it a government monopoly. But this time the munitions men were in bad repute and Congress passed it."

Perry laughed. "Served 'em jolly well right, didn't it? But seriously, while this scheme seems to fit modern conditions, I don't believe it would have worked in my day."

Cathcart's shaggy brows lifted. "Why not?"

"Too cumbersome. It would take weeks to get ready for the election and weeks more to be sure of the count. By that time the whole strategic situation could have changed and lost us the war, if we went into it."

"I think you overrate the difficulties, Perry. I believe that I know your period as well as an historian can for I have made a special study of it. If Congress was debating a war resolution, wouldn't everybody in the country know about it? The President habitually spoke to the country by radiotelephony, correct? So if he were to address the country announcing the outcome of the congressional vote and calling a war referendum, everybody would be listening, would they not?"

"Ninety-nine per cent or better."

"Very well then. Calling the election is easy. How soon could it be held? No need to wait for the people to inform themselves and consider the merits; if the situation is actually grave, they will have been following it for weeks and probably have made up their minds long before Congress acts. The next question is how long would it take to do the physical acts necessary to conduct a balloting? Everybody in the country of voting age knew or could find out very quickly the location off his usual precinct election polls. And each of those polling places had officials designated at the last regular election. Printing the ballots would be fairly simple, there being but one point to vote on, or they could be kept printed at all times, and let the name of the enemy be written in or assumed. Counting the ballots in each precinct would be a simple matter as well, twenty minutes at the most. The only new technique would be in collecting the returns. Tell me, there were telegram dispatching bureaus all over the country, were there not?"

"Oh yes, probably one within ten minutes of every polling place. I begin to see your point."

"Then let telegraph clerk in the country be considered a special election official. With a reasonably efficient system of intermediate clearing and tabulating, the final figures should be in the President's hands within an hour after the closing of the polls."

Perry nodded his head. "Yes, that is feasible, entirely feasible. You make me feel rather stupid that I couldn't see it."

"You needn't feel so. I have simply described with a few minor changes some of the provisions of the original implementing act. You had adequate organization and sufficiently rapid communication in your day. All that was needed was the decision to use them. As a matter of fact the method has worked practically perfectly since it was adopted."

"It has been used, then?"

"Three times since it was adopted. Each time the people rejected war and each time, in my opinion, history has justified them. And so the United States has *not* committed suicide. Yet in each case you may take it for granted that Congress would have plunged us into war. The simple fact that it called the referenda indicates that. You made another point, however, the point about the strategic necessity for a quick decision. This arrangement not only lost no time, valuable in strategy, but actually gained time."

"How do you figure that?"

"Because the first draft is mobilized the day after war is declared. That saves at least six weeks over all previous methods of conscripting an army. Furthermore adequate preparations could be made in peace time to provide fully for such an army, and any amount of training or arming that prudence indicated could be undertaken without fear that arming itself would lead us into war. It was a means whereby a peaceful, non-imperialistic, civilian-minded people could be fully prepared for any possible war."

Perry nodded his head vigorously. "It certainly sounds like a foolproof scheme. I admire the professional features about it quite as much as the political. I'm glad you pointed them out. There were a lot of peace plans afoot in my day, but I didn't have much use for any I ever heard about. Most of them seemed to be based on the notion that the United States being unarmed and untrained would keep us out of war. I've read some history, and I was convinced that it was the one sure way to get into a war."

"I believe you are right, Perry. Of course there is one objection to the referendum plan that was made by a number of people."

"To wit?"

"It appeared in many different forms, but it always boiled down to the same thing. A contention that the people didn't know what was good for them and were too stupid to be trusted with so much power. It amounts to a total disbelief in the democratic form of government. Strangely enough it came from the very groups who are loudest in their protests of affection for the American form of government, and 'Americanism' whatever that is, if it is not democracy. The people who made this objection were schoolteachers, preachers, officers of veterans and patriotic organizations, professional demagogues et cetera. Interestingly enough the army and navy did not oppose the scheme, even though they were denied the right to vote in the referendum."

"I'm pleased to hear that but not surprised. The professional military man is the last to believe any romantic nonsense about war, even though he may be calloused to it."

Diana took advantage of a momentary lull to put in a word. "I don't want to interrupt this conversation but I'm getting sleepy. Master, do you have to go back tonight?"

"No, but I want to get away first thing in the morning. Will you put me up over night?"

"Of course. Happy to have you any time. You men can stay up as long as you like and fight all the battles you wish. I've fixed a pot of coffee and you'll find a tray of sandwiches by it. Nighty-night." She patted Perry's cheek, blew a kiss to Cathcart and glided off into the shadows at the far end of the room. Perry followed her with his eyes. Cathcart noted his gaze and spoke:

"That's a fine girl there."

"Hunh?—Oh! Yes, yes."

"I suggest we emulate her example shortly. However as I must go back in the morning, let's trot over the past eighty years as quickly as we can and bring you up to date. Give me a quick sketch of the salient features of the history of the country from the turn of the century."

"Well, the war was over in 2004. We have just been talking about the results. Hard times commenced to settle on the country about 2006, but it took several years for it to develop into a full sized depression, partially because the Bank of the United States didn't fold up and partially because of the premature retirement of war bonds and payment of a war bonus. But unemployment mounted steadily each year. In 2010 Wendell Holmes was elected president. Between 2011 and 2015 he instituted the economic reforms that are now the current practice. Business picked up and things ran along pretty smoothly until the late twenties, when a movement started that was known as the New Crusade, or Neo-Puritanism. It seems to have been some sort of a religious revival that eventually caused a lot of trouble. It reached its height in the middle thirties and then for about a year there were riots all over the country. President Michèle straightened out that mess and some constitutional reforms grew out of it. From then until the present time I don't recall any outstanding event. Lots of little ones of course and a lot of new inventions but nothing that appeared to change the course of history."

"Yes, that is true. The past half century has been a period of steady development with no spectacular changes but rather a slow growth and steady social progress. We appear to have reached a period of dynamic equilibrium in which mankind can develop his arts and perfect his sciences in reasonable comfort and safety. It might surprise you to see all the change since the end of the New Crusade, but it would be impossible for me to put my finger on any one thing and say 'Here the change occurred'. However, it is not necessary. You will gradually see for yourself now that you have the general framework. Do you have any questions about this period?"

"Yes, two things are bothering me. I don't understand the economic reforms under Holmes, and I don't see what this New Crusade was all about. It sounds screwy."

Cathcart grinned. "It's a good thing my professional research gives me some knowledge of the idiom of your period. It *was* screwy. But let's take 'em in order. We discussed before the cause of economic depressions and I asked you to take on faith the idea that the only thing that caused depressions was a financial system that automatically caused a spread between goods to be bought and money to buy them, or 'over-production' as it was euphemistically called. I'm not going into the mathematical theory even now. You can take it up later with an economist or in several books I can recommend. But President Holmes was one of the few men to occupy the White House who had sufficient insight and mathematical ability to see the trouble, the reasons behind it, and to devise a cure. He had a powerful weapon to work with, the Bank of the United States, and he had the free intellect necessary to do what needed to be done without clouding the issue with a lot of moralistic tape. In fact he helped to formulate a realistic social ethic that justified his new departure. To begin with he saw the 'over-production' or, as he looked at it, under-consumption or shortage of purchasing power. He directed a staff of actuaries to supply him with approximate figures showing the percentage of under-consumption and its dollar value for the past year. Then he undertook to make up the missing purchasing power by literally giving away through the Bank of the United States the necessary amount of money. He was aware that to do so without some control over prices would result in inflated prices and a new spread between production and consumption. So he held back about half of the newly created purchasing power and used it to control prices in the following manner: All of the retailers of consumption goods in the country were invited to join in the New Economic Cycle. If a dealer joined he agreed not to raise his prices over what they were when the new regime started. On the contrary he was to sell all his goods at a ten per cent discount, and the Bank of the United States would hand him the difference on presentation of his sales records. Then Holmes proceeded to give away through the Bank twenty-five dollars per month to anybody who would take it. Naturally business boomed. Prices didn't go up because all of the business went to the merchants who had joined the agreement.

Presently all the other merchants joined, too, in order to get in on the rush of business. Factories re-opened, labor was needed and unemployment disappeared like snow in July. The country hummed. And that is a thumbnail sketch of the present situation, Perry. No unemployment, plenty of well paid work for anybody that wants a job, and enough credit issued every month to anybody that wants it to keep body and soul together in decency."

Perry looked bewildered. "Wait a minute. It looks fine at first glance, but where did he get the money? Not from taxes, surely, with the country already broke. And not from the private bankers. They were ruined in the war."*

*For the benefit of the reader who is arithmetically inclined:

(A) Value (Price) of consumption goods produced
    in 2010 $540,000,000,000.00

Average income per person $2,413.33

(B) Total of personal income (Wages, dividends,
    insurance, pensions, etc.) $434,400,000,000.00

(C) Difference or under-consumption $105,600,000,000.00

Practical check:

(D) Value of estimated excess in inventories
    (under-consumption) $110,400,000,000.00

Error $4,800,000,000 or ±4.45%

(E) Empirical control figure $\frac{(C+D)}{2}$ $108,000,000,000.00

Divide by population of 180,000,000 to obtain
    under-consumption per person per year of 2010 $600.00

Divide by 12 to obtain under-consumption per person per month $50.00

Issue one-half of this directly $25 per month per person

Ratio to (A) all consumption goods produced of (E) unconsumed consumption goods is one to five or 20%. Discount is to handle one-half of this. Therefore discount is 20%.

Q.E.D.

I have taken the liberty of using round numbers. The exact figures from the Washington Archives show $27.813 per month and discount of 11.87%.

                                            The Author

Cathcart grinned. "He got the cash money the same way we have gotten all cash money since Roosevelt put the gold back in the ground—right off the printing presses. But he didn't have to print much of it. The checks were issued at the Bank and the merchant and a great many others had accounts at the Bank and very little cash money changed hands. The bulk of it was mere bookkeeping entries, made by the bank clerks. Holmes had implemented what the bankers had known for centuries but were barred by LaGuardia from doing—taking money out of an inkwell. What's the matter, son? Still not satisfied?"

"Well, I don't know. Everything you have said seems okay, but how about this? If you keep pouring money into a country indefinitely, you are bound to get inflation, fixed prices or no fixed prices."

"You don't pour it in. You add just enough to keep it running. Each fiscal period the additional amount is the closest possible approximation of the amount necessary to prevent a spread between consumption and production, based on the value of the nation's inventories."

"But why do you have to keep *adding* money all the time?"

"I said I would stay away from theory but I'll give you this hint to chew over: the amount necessary to add each period is theoretically equal to the amount of savings invested as capital in the preceding period. And one more hint: Doesn't it take more money to run the country's industry now than it did when George Washington was President? But now let's pass on to the New Crusade. It's getting late."

"OK."

"It is difficult to assay the causes of any religious movement. There appear to be mass movements of the human spirit that we do not fully understand. Karl Marx attempted to interpret all history in terms of a rigid materialistic causation, but how does that account for the Children's Crusade? Carlysle would have us believe that history is no more than the acts of certain great men, heroes. I find that equally hard to believe. Would George Washington have been more than a gentleman planter if England's rule of the colonies had been more liberal? It is my belief that history is a story of the action of individuals, acting according to their characters in the environments in which they find themselves. A change either in character or in environment would change the resulting action. In the interplay of lives there are strong characters—Carlysle's Heroes—who exert powerful influences of personality and intellect on their fellow men, and thereby shape the environment in which less dominant creatures act. If these strong characters are born in a period and are able to reach an environment in which their peculiar talents find maximum expression, they will write their names large on the pages of history. 'There is a tide in the affairs of men, which, taken at the flood, leads on to fortune.'

"Such a dominant character was Nehemiah Scudder, founder of the New Crusade and leader of the Neo-Puritans. He found the opportunity to use his exceptional talents in the Middle West in the third decade of this century. He was first heard of about 2030 as an itinerant evangelist of an obscure fundamentalist sect. He preached over most of the Mississippi valley, and although not prominent enough to make a splash in the news of the day, he had a reputation in his denomination for the forcefulness of his preaching, and the virulence with which he called the vengeance of the Lord upon the erring brother. But his fortunes took no great change until the death in 2023 of a Mrs. Rachel Biggs, the septuagenarian relict of a wealthy shoe manufacturer. Mrs. Biggs left four million dollars outright and that much more in trust to establish and maintain a tabernacle and television station to be used by the Reverend Scudder. We have had our radio priests and our political preachers many times before, but while most divines are tuned out at once, Brother Nehemiah was able to project his magnetic personality through the broadcaster and those who heard him once were thereafter his followers, if they were temperamentally ready for his brand of fire and brimstone. He was able, also, to choose and inspire other preachers to help him in the organization of his rapidly growing spiritual following. About 2024 he interpreted certain passages in the *Apocalypse* to mean that the new Jerusalem was here and now, that Armageddon was at hand, that his followers were called on to take up the fight. He organized the Knights of the New Crusade to implement him for Armageddon. This organization was modeled in nearly every respect after the Ku Klux Klan of the previous century, even to many details of ritual, uniform and constitution, which Brother Nehemiah had not bothered to change.

"In order to understand what happened subsequently and to appreciate the great power which Scudder wielded, it is necessary to understand the man and the people among whom he worked. He was a man of tremendous physical vitality and nervous energy, of middle height but powerfully built. His manner and speech suggested his backwoods origin. Deep set eyes under bony brows burned and gleamed and glared. His voice was normally low and mellow, but could scream and shout praise if need be. His mouth was large, his lips full and loose. In rest they were sensuous but in speaking they expressed a sadistic delight in his work. As to his private life, not much is known. He was married and his wife accompanied him and served him, but from time to time other female acolytes were added to his staff. The obvious conclusion is possibly not true, as there is a persistent story that the man, in spite of his great strength, was actually sexually impotent.

"A large portion of the population was ripe for such a leader. In the New World, since it was first settled, there have been two strongly dissident elements in the social body. One was anarchistic, and tolerant; the other sternly authoritarian and fanatically moralistic. It is a mistake to believe that our forefathers came to this continent in search of religious freedom. On the contrary they sought a place in which to exercise their own brand of religious totalitarianism. It is probable that the religious persecutions and moralistic intolerances practiced on dissenters by the colonists of New England were more severe than any from which they had fled. It is surprising that the Constitution contained an apparent guarantee of religious freedom. This seeming oversight may be attributed to two things, the mutual suspicion with which each colony viewed the other, and the staunch feeling for liberty felt by Thomas Jefferson who wrote the provision. It is very significant to note that the religious freedom clause was an injunction to the federal government. It did not limit the states. At one time the State of Virginia had an established church, and religious intolerance had been practiced, under the law, in every state in the Union. In addition to the puritanical factor in the American culture, there was the Roman Catholic strain, strong in some parts of the country, which supported many of the same intolerances as the Protestant churches.

"All forms of organized religion are alike in certain social respects. Each claims to be the sole custodian of the essential truth. Each claims to speak with final authority on all ethical questions. And every church has requested, demanded, or ordered the state to enforce its particular system of taboos. No church ever withdraws its claims to control absolutely by divine right the moral life of the citizens. If the church is weak, it attempts by devious means to turn its creed and discipline into law. If it is strong, it uses

the rack and the thumbscrew. To a surprising degree, churches in
the United States were able, under a governmental form which
formally acknowledged no religion, to have placed on the statutes
the individual church's code of moral taboos, and to wrest from the
state privileges and special concessions amounting to subsidy.
Especially was this true of the evangelical churches in the middle
west and south, but it was equally true of the Roman Church on
its strongholds. It would have been equally true of any church;
Holy Roller, Mohammedan, Judaism, or headhunters. It is a
characteristic of all organized religion, not of a particular sect."

Perry interrupted. "All this may have been true in 2020 but I
saw no particular evidence of it in my day. There were churches
of course and I went to Sunday School when I was a kid and
chapel when I was a midshipman, but Lord, I didn't notice
them after I grew up. They didn't bother me and I didn't bother
them."

Cathcart smiled wryly. "What one has never had one doesn't
miss. It might be instructive if I were to name over a number of
the laws, and customs having the effect of law, prevalent in your
period whose origins may be traced directly to some powerful
organized church or churches."

"Please do."

Cathcart ticked them off on his fingers. "Sunday closing laws;
tax exemption for church property; practically all laws relating to
marriage and the relations between the sexes—including laws
forbidding divorce, country-wide rule permitting only monogamous marriages, laws against fornication and other taboo sexual
relationships, and laws forbidding birth control; laws prohibiting
the teaching of certain scientific doctrines, especially man's kin-
ship to other animals; all laws of censorship, for moral reasons, of
the press, stage, radio, or speech; certain taboos of word and
speech forms; laws prohibiting certain parts of the body being

exposed to view; laws prohibiting the drinking of alcohol per se; laws against smoking cigarettes; any law which takes a paternalistic attitude toward the citizen with the purpose of ensuring his moral perfection rather than the purpose of regulating his conduct to prevent him from damaging other persons and, vice versa, prevent others from damaging him."

"But surely most of the laws that you mention arise from common sense rather than from religion?"

"You believe so because you were reared in the environment that the churches created. You were conditioned to regard them as the natural order of things. But it is a matter of historical record that in cultures where the organized religion held different views on morals, the exact opposite of every law I have referred to has had its day. But again we are getting away from the Reverend Scudder and his band of holy fanatics. In spite of what I have said the American churches fought a rear guard action for four hundred years. It is a far cry from the blue laws of early day Massachusetts to the tolerance and easy morals of the period under discussion. The libertarian spirit had great hold especially in the cities. With the perfection of technique for controlling conception and the elimination of contagious diseases associated with sexual intercourse, the sexual customs of the people were undergoing a rapid metamorphosis. The New Economic Regime produced more changes in moral relationships and made divorce easier. It produced another effect, too, in destroying the moralistic nature of work for work's sake. All of these things were offensive to a person of an old fashioned point of view, and none found them more distasteful than the Reverend Nehemiah Scudder. He preached against them, predicting Hell's fire and brimstone for the ungodly people of the United States! He denounced the pleasures of the flesh, all frivolities, the scandalous clothing, the demon rum, dancing, gambling, worldly music, light minded literature, and vanities of every sort. He called on his followers to stamp it out, fight the battle of Armageddon, and be led at once into the New Jerusalem, where the godly would never die, but live forever, singing hymns and praising God. Furthermore he advised his flock as to just how they might accomplish this happy end. He had a genius for organization and used it to weld together the most effective minority group ever seen in American politics. In the first place he claimed to represent the whole population and claimed a majority of the population as his personal following.

"Such was the effect of his organized agitation that he convinced the easy-going unorganized mass that his adherents were in the majority. In particular he convinced the politicians that he controlled enough votes to turn an election. In response to this belief, which may or may not have been justified, he began to accomplish through political means many of the changes in law which he desired, and what he could not get legally was obtained by his night riders, the terrorist Knights of the New Crusade or Angels of the Lord as they were variously known. There is a latent streak of sadism in the best of us. The Reverend Scudder turned it loose.

"During the period from 2025 to 2030 no man was safe in his home. The night riders might come knocking at his door and spirit him away to be flogged and perhaps tarred and feathered for such crimes as neglecting to attend church or a disrespectful attitude toward the movement or any fancied slip from the stern moral code of the brethren which might occur to the fanatical intolerant mind of a Crusader. Or his daughter might be torn from her parents, stripped naked and branded with a hot iron as punishment for some innocent frivolity regarded by the brethren as mortal sin. Or a merchant might find his store windows broken and his stock vandalized for the crime of employing an ungodly man. By 2028 Scudder had an iron grip on the Mississippi Valley and was a strong force throughout the country. Blue laws controlled the whole life of the valley. Not a vehicle moved on Sunday. Churchgoing was obligatory in many places, and it was safer to do so in any case. Women wore somber clothing which completely hid their bodies. Dancing, singing other than hymns, games and other vanities were verboten. Higher education was discouraged. Idleness was dubbed vagrancy and treated as a crime. Scudder was looking forward to two national changes, the abolition of the distribution of the credit checks without work in return, and the open establishment of the church.

"However terror breeds terror and persecution brings its own reaction. The Libertarian element in the population, normally unorganized, were forced into protective coloration, but were not defeated. Under the pressure of necessity they organized, secretly and underground. They placed candidates in the field for their next congressional election and prepared to win at any cost. An underground terrorist group was formed by the more headstrong which undertook to hand the Knights some of their own medicine. The more conservative turned their attention to the coming election and flooded the country with pamphlets which denied that the Scudderites were more than a small part of the population and urged the people to vote their convictions. Election day was a shambles and the counting of the ballots resolved itself into a multitude of little battles between the Knights and the embattled individualists. When the smoke had cleared away it became evident that Scudder had lost the election. He had been heavily defeated on both coasts and clearly lost the majority of the seats in the larger cities of the valley. Even if he were conceded all the disputed contests in his rural strongholds, he nevertheless had lost every state but Tennessee and Alabama.

"The members of the new congress who had been elected on an anti-Scudder ticket were pledged to constitutional reforms to prevent a recurrence of loss of individual liberty from any cause. In consequence several hundred amendments were proposed in the first few days of the term. The parliamentary impasses resulted in a clever piece of law making. At a caucus of the Libertarians it was proposed and agreed to that a small representative committee draft and submit to the caucus an amendment in the form of a new constitution which, if adopted and ratified, would supersede the old constitution in toto. The committee consisted of five men and one woman, great minds all of them; Cyrus Fielding, Rosa Weinstein, John Delano Roosevelt, Ludvig Dixon, Joseph Berzowski, and Colin MacDonald. Fielding presided and apportioned the work. I wish we had time to go into the details of their discussions. They labored night and day for nearly four months. Fortunately we have a record of their entire proceedings which you can study at your leisure, and there are several excellent abridgments available. Their report was submitted to the caucus on 2028 April 20 and was debated in caucus for three weeks, but the members of the committee had done their work so well and in particular had been so skillful in retaining most of the wording of the original document, the new amendment was approved by the caucus without change and submitted as a single bill signed by every member of the caucus. Its adoption of course was a forgone conclusion. It was ratified by the thirty-seventh state on 2028 November 12.

"I won't go into the minutiae of the document but several changes are worthy of note tonight. The most important was the addition of a new restriction on the power of government. Henceforth no law was constitutional that deprived any citizen of any liberty of action which did not interfere with the equal freedom of action of another citizen. Pardon me, I have stated that badly. These are the words of the new constitution: 'Every citizen is free to perform any act which does not hamper the equal freedom of another. No law shall forbid the performance of any act, which does not damage the physical or economic welfare of any other person. No act shall constitute a violation of a law valid under this provision unless there is such damage, or immediate present danger of such damage resulting from that act.'

"Do you see the significance of that last provision? Up to that time, a crime had two elements; act of commission and intent. Now it had a third; harmful effect which must be proved in each case, as well as the act and the intent. The consequences of this change can hardly be exaggerated. It established American individualism forever by requiring the state to justify in each case its interference with an individual's acts. Furthermore the justification must be based on a tangible damage or potential damage to a person or persons. The person damaged might be a school-girl injured or endangered by a reckless driver or it might be every person in the state endangered by the betrayal of military secrets or injured by manipulation of commodity prices, but it must not be some soulless super-person, the state incarnate, or the majesty of the law. It reduced the state to its proper size, an instrument to serve individuals, instead of a god to be worshipped and glorified. Most especially it ended the possibility of the majority oppressing any minority with that hackneyed hoary lie that 'the majority is always right.'

"In another place in the constitution, corporate persons were defined and declared to have no rights of any sort except wherein they represented rights of real persons. Corporate persons could not be damaged. An act committed against a corporate person must be shown to have damaged a real person in order to constitute an offense. This was intended to clip the wings of the corporate trusts which threatened to crowd out the man of flesh and blood.

"Another new civil liberty was defined, the right of privacy. You will understand that better as you study the code of customs. Several other reforms were instituted, most of them obvious, such as the direct election of the president, and a re-definition of the 'general welfare' clause in order to give greater freedom in changing the details of government in a changing world. There were two important changes in the method of legislation. The House of Representatives was given the right to pass legislation over the veto of the Senate. There had been under consideration the abolition of the Senate, or at least to make it proportionately representative, but an obscure clause in the original document prevented this without the unanimous consent of all the states. Perhaps the most striking change was the power vested in the chief executive to initiate legislation and force its consideration. Under this provision the President with the aid of his advisers could draft bills which automatically became law at the expiration of ninety days unless Congress rejected it. The ninety days had to be while Congress was sitting of course."

"Suppose Congress wasn't in session?"

"The President could call it if he saw fit."

"Suppose the matter was too urgent to wait ninety days."

"Congress could accept it at once if there was need. Sometimes the President asks them to do so."

"Did Congress lose its power to initiate legislation?"

"Oh no, not at all. They could pass any laws they wanted and reject any laws they chose to. But if there was great disharmony, either branch of the government might force an immediate general election. The President could do so by dissolving Congress; the Congress, by a vote of no confidence. The latter vote was in the House alone, the Senate wasn't empowered. That is the least but one of the major changes. The new constitution called for a re-codification of law every ten years and laid a strong injunction on all law makers to use simple language and to avoid abstractions. A way was opened here to invalidate laws on constitutional grounds simply because they were not in clear English."

"I like that," commented Perry. "I always have thought that lawyers had deliberately clouded the issue by the cock-eyed way they talk. I had a course in school once in order writing. Although it was classed as English composition, the criterion was not style, nor literary merit, but whether or not the meaning was unmistakable. I think it would have done most lawyers a lot of good to have taken it."

"I'm sure of it. Well, that about clears us up, Perry. The past sixty years have been largely development and growth which you can best appreciate by seeing it. If you will excuse me, I'm going to bed."

"A sound idea. But I want to thank you first for the trouble you have taken for me. You have been very patient."

"Not at all, son. I enjoyed it. Someday soon I want to question you at length about your recollections of your period. If you actually have authentic and detailed personal memories of your time you will be doing me a great service."

"It will be a privilege and a pleasure."

"Well, goodnight, son."

"Goodnight, sir, and thanks again."

V

"Going to sleep all day, sleepy head?"

Perry stretched and yawned, then grinned up at Diana.

"What time is it?"

"Late enough. Daylight's wasting. Master Cathcart is gone long since. If you want breakfast with me you'd better hurry." Perry jumped up and ducked into the refresher. When he returned ten minutes later, tingling from his shower, Diana was setting near the window a tray from which rose appetizing smells.

"What have we here? Buckwheat cakes. Sausage. Fresh pineapple. Diana, you are a jewel. Will you adopt me and feed me like this every morning?"

"Sit down, silly, and eat." She made a face at him, but her eyes were shining. "Hurry up. We're going places today."

"Where?" The coffee cup poised in the air.

"Round and about. Most any place you want to. The great wide world. What would you like to see?"

"I don't know—yet."

"Well, that's where we'll go."

After breakfast Diana lit a cigarette, then popped the dishes into the fire. She turned to Perry. "Better put these on. Your other things are already in the car." 'These' were a pair of sandals with zipper fasteners and ornamental straps. He slipped them on and hurried after Diana who had opened the outer door. Perry found himself not outdoors, but in a small reception hall. On his left Diana's shapely legs were disappearing up a flight of steps. He hastened and caught up with her. They emerged in a moderately large hangar, containing at the moment what was obviously an aircraft but reminded Perry of an illustration from some lurid Sunday supplement. It was egg-shaped, about eighteen feet long and twelve feet high. It was supported by three retractable wheels, two at the blunt or forward end, and one at the stern. Mounted at the small end of the egg was a screw propeller with three five-foot blades. At the topmost point of the egg shaped body was a small cylindrical projection from which streamed aft a sheaf of flat blades about fifteen feet long and perhaps eighteen inches wide at the widest point. Perry guessed that this unfolded into a rotor for helicopter flight. He attempted to count the blades in the gloom and decided that there were either five or six. No wings were in evidence but Perry noticed that there were slots about four feet long on each side near the top amidships. Diana confirmed his guess that these housed wings that spread when needed. But search as he might he saw no sign of a control surface; rudder, stabilizer, nor fins.

The body was a dull copper color, except for the front end and the sides back to midships, which were plastic glass. The door was just abaft his enormous view-port on the starboard side. Diana swung it open and they stepped inside. The interior was very roomy, there being nearly five feet of clear floor space thwartships and almost that much abaft the twin pilots' chairs. A lazy bench ran around the outer wall except for the space forward of the chairs, where it was replaced by a belt of instruments with clear glass above and below. Perry saw that the level inner floor plate and the corresponding curved outer hull were largely of glass.

Diana seated herself in the right hand pilot's chair. "Come sit beside me, Perry." He did so and examined the dual controls in front of him. Diana touched a lever control and the car rolled out on the platform. She grasped the joystick and pulled it toward her, thumb pressing a button on the end. Perry heard a soft hum and a slight haze appeared over the car. The rotor had unfolded. The hum grew to a high-pitched whine, then died away. The car trembled and he noticed a slight feeling of heaviness. He glanced down between his feet and watched the mountain with its crags and pine trees drop away. A few minutes later Diana moved the stick forward to the vertical. Perry felt as if he were riding in an express elevator which had just stopped at the top floor. The car hovered about two thousand feet over 'Diana's mountain'. She turned to him. "Now where shall we go?"

"I don't want to go any place until I learn to fly this thing."

"I'm not exactly a flying instructor, but I'll try. You saw me take off. First I started the main motor with this switch turned to 'helicopter.' I pull back the stick to rise straight up. With the stick vertical the car hovers. The stick won't move unless you press the button on the end. Push the stick forward—so—and the car lowers. Then return it to vertical when you are at the altitude you wish. In landing you settle it down slowly with a slight pressure forward."

"Suppose the main motor stops while you're in the helicopter?"

"It settles down on the rotor. The wheels snap out into place. They are held retracted magnetically by a field off the main motor. You settle down pretty hard—It's about like falling ten meters at sea level, a little harder in this thin air. But the carriage takes most of the shock and this pneumatic upholstery soaks up the rest. It is pretty much of a jolt however. Anyone standing in the cabin should lie down quickly on the couch."

"Suppose it fell over water."

"The car will float. If you can start the rotor again, you can even take off again. I've done it with this one from Lake Tahoe. If you can't take off, you can just sit there and wait to be rescued."

"Now tell me how to maneuver this baby."

"Turn the main control switch from 'helix' to 'plane'. The wings come out,"—Sure enough, Perry saw them spread on each side—"and the screw starts. As it gathers speed, it drags more and more current, and the rotor slows down and stops and folds up. If you stop the screw by throwing the switch back, or if something happens to it, the rotor starts. The wings don't retract until the rotor is maintaining lift. See, there goes the rotor." The great vanes passed by, turning more slowly each revolution, finally stopped, folded back on each other like a Japanese fan, and disappeared. "We are flying now. If I pull back on the stick now the speed increases. When the air speed meter shows the speed I want I return the stick to vertical. If I pushed the stick forward the speed slows. If I slow to stalling speed before I reach it the rotor will start."

"How do you change direction?"

"If you push the stick sideways, the car turns in the same direction. When you are on your new course you return the stick to vertical."

"Does that both bank and handle the rudder? Say, I didn't see a rudder nor any other control surfaces. Why should it turn?"

"There aren't any control surfaces. The car is gyro stabilized. We rotate the car around the rigid reference frame of the gyros and let the screw push away in our new direction."

Perry nodded slowly. "That seems all right, except that she must side slip like the very devil on a turn."

"That's right, Perry, but ordinarily it doesn't matter. If you need to prevent it, you can turn past your new course and hold it there until the side slip is killed."

Perry's face cleared. "Yes, I suppose so, but I would hate to try to fly a tight military formation in her."

"You couldn't. This is a family model, for quiet people like me. It isn't very fast and it's as nearly foolproof and automatic as they can make it. They claim that if you can use a knife and fork you can fly a 'Cloud House'."

"What speed does she make?"

"I cruise her at about five hundred kilometers. I could make five hundred and fifty but there's a nasty vibration at that speed. I may need a new propellor." Perry whistled. "If that is a moderate speed for a family car, what's the record these days?"

"About three thousand. That is with rockets of course. But I don't like a rocket ship. They make me nervous and they are devilish to handle. Give me my old-fashioned electric runabout. I'm in no hurry."

"Which reminds me. I gather this baby must be electric drive, but how?"

"The rotor and the prop are driven by induction motors. The power comes from storage batteries. The gyros each have their own induction windings. They run all the time."

"Storage batteries—I should think they would be too heavy."

"These aren't heavy for the power they store. They call 'em chlorophyll batteries because the principle involved is supposed to be similar to the photosynthesis of plants. But don't ask me why. I'm a dancer, not a physicist. However there are some new models on the market that make their own electricity from coal."

"Directly?"

"I don't know. It doesn't burn if that's what you mean."

Perry slapped his thigh. "Edison was working on that when he died."

"Too bad he didn't perfect it. We've had it only about ten years. See here, Perry, want to try the controls?"

"Yes indeed. Wait a minute though. How do I change altitude when I'm in 'plane' combination."

"You can get as much as ten degrees dive or climb by changing this setting. It rotates the car about the horizontal gyro axis. You can use that when hovering with the rotor to keep from drifting in the wind, provided the wind isn't more than seventy-five kilometers."

"In that case you could maneuver by rotor if you wanted to, couldn't you."

"Yes, but it's slow of course. Do you know what all your instruments mean?"

"You keep an eye on the instruments. I'll fly by ear for a while." Perry took the car up a couple of thousand feet and cautiously put her through her paces. Presently when he had the feel of the controls he undertook to see what it would do. He soared and dropped, flew straight away and slewed her into sudden turns. He discovered that he could jamb her about one hundred and eighty degrees and stop her dead with the propeller. After this stunt Diana touched his arm:

"Perry, if you knock off the propeller, we'll have to go home on the rotor." He looked crestfallen.

"Oh, I'm sorry. I thought anything she could do, she could handle."

"That is very nearly true. But my prop may be out of balance, you know. In any case the screw itself is a gyro and you were processing it on a rigid frame."

He set the controls at neutral and turned to her. "Diana, if you are a dancer and no physicist, how do you know so much about mechanics?"

She looked surprised. "Any schoolgirl knows that much."

"I can see education has improved." He returned to the controls and tried new stunts; stalling, changing combinations, maneuvering on the rotor. The flight brought them back near the canyon—'Diana's canyon' as Perry regarded it—and the waterfall caught Perry's eye. He lowered away cautiously and eased the craft slowly over toward the veil of water until they hovered halfway down and a hundred feet from the falls. They both sat in silent contemplation for several minutes until a shift in the wind forced Perry to return to the controls. He rose out of the canyon and settled down in level flight. Then he spoke. His voice was low and fervent. "Boy, but that fall is something!" He turned to Diana. "It's nearly as beautiful as you are, Dian'." She looked up and met his eyes for a moment, then dropped her lids, without replying. They were flying west. Presently Diana spoke.

"Where are we going, Perry?"

"I hadn't thought about it. Where would you suggest?"

"Would you like to see San Francisco?"

"Fine!"

"Then let me set the course."

"I can do it. I know this country." He located the South Fork of the American River and followed it by eye until it joined the Sacramento River. Presently Diana got up and went to the rear of the car. When they were approaching Sacramento she announced lunch. "Can't do," answered Perry. "I'm coming into traffic." She peered over his shoulder.

"I'll set the robot to circle Sacramento and pick up the San Francisco beam. You mustn't fly in traffic until you have qualified in the rules. Now come to lunch."

Hot soup. Stuffed eggs and celery. Oatmeal cookies and grapes. Cold milk. When it was inside Perry felt no desire to move. He lay on his stomach with his head over the edge of the lazy bench and watched the ground slip by the deck port. Diana regarded him lazily. Presently the ground changed to water.

FOR US, THE LIVING

"Coming into San Francisco!" he cried, jumped to his feet and seated himself in the bow.

"Don't touch the controls, Perry," Diana cautioned. "They are on full automatic." Perry didn't answer for they were slicing across the bay bridge.

"Dian', is that the same bridge?"

"I believe so."

Perry looked proud. "They had engineers in my day, too."

"Indeed they did."

"Why, there is the Ferry Building. Don't tell me that has stood all these years."

"No, that is a replica. It's a museum of California history."

"There's Nob Hill! And the Fairmont Hotel."

"You're right, but I don't see how you recognized it. It's only been there ten years."

"I can see how it's not the same building. But it's in the right place." The car changed course and commenced leisurely to circle the city in a clockwise direction. Several other aircraft were in the same circle at the same speed.

"The streets are decked over, aren't they? What's that moving under the glass decks?"

"Those are the streets, with people traveling on them."

"But how? I don't see any automobiles or other vehicles, yet they are going pretty fast."

"The streets move in strips. The strip nearest the buildings goes five kilometers an hour, then next ten and so on to the middle. Those have seats on them and travel forty kilometers."

"How about the end of the line?"

"The end of the line? Oh, they travel in loops. If you stay on one you come back to where you started. The cross traffic is on a lower level, naturally. Shall we land, Perry?"

His brow furrowed. "What do you think? I probably don't

know how to behave. Besides I can't go into a city like this, can I?" He indicated his bare condition.

"No real reason why you shouldn't, except to avoid being conspicuous. But the public kit you bought yesterday is by you in the locker under the bench you are sitting on." Diana dug it out, and gave it to him. Perry donned it. It consisted of a kilt of bright blue silk hung on a broad leather belt with pockets and hooks in it. A strap over one shoulder helped to support the belt. Slashes in the kilt were lined with bright silver stuff which glittered as he moved. The belt and strap were black with chromium fittings which matched his sandals. Diana surveyed him.

"There. All set? Then I'll land us." Diana put the car down carefully through a maze of traffic onto a platform on Nob Hill. Before leaving the car she picked up a garment of her own and slipped it on. It was a Grecian tunic of black velvet, caught at the right shoulder with a jeweled silver clip. The right side hung open. The left shoulder and breast were bare. Perry whistled.

"Dian', you look perfectly gorgeous in that outfit, but in my home town they would toss us in jail and throw away the key."

"What for?"

"Indecent exposure."

"How silly. Let's go."

Diana received a check from the parking attendant, and they started for the stairs. It was cold on the platform. Perry felt goose flesh form on his chest and a sharp wind fluttered his kilt. Diana appeared not to mind. But it was warm in the stairway. As they rode to the street level Perry glanced at the other passengers. Apparently he and Diana were sufficiently clad. Most of the women wore as much as Diana, but several of them wore more provocative clothes. Passing the seventh level he noticed leaning in a doorway marked CORECTIV MASAJ a big Scandinavian girl clad only in a bored look. No one seemed to take special note of her. The men's costumes were varied. Many of them wore coveralls of heavy cloth. These Perry judged to be mechanics from the platform. A goodly number were dressed much as Perry was. He noticed one old gentleman in a Roman toga, who read a newspaper as he rode. But in a moment they debarked at the street level and Perry was too busy to worry much about clothes. They were caught in a swirl of foot traffic at the landing which separated him from Diana. He felt a wave of panic as he looked for her and failed to find her. Then a little warm hand slipped into his and he heard her voice. "Let me hold your hand. I nearly got carried away." He looked down at her face and knew that she was being diplomatic, but he didn't care. He held her hand tightly.

"What do you want to see, Perry?"

"Gosh, I don't know. Suppose you show me around a bit. If I think of anything, I'll tell you."

"All right." They proceeded along a wide corridor toward the street. The corridor was lined with brightly lighted little studio shops. Perry glanced at the displays as they walked. Most of the items seemed to be handcraft of various sorts, curios and beautiful things, some familiar in conception and use, some unintelligible. The Chinese, Japanese, and Indian shops seemed most familiar. In a few cases prices were marked. These seemed surprisingly high to him. He asked Diana about this.

"Why, naturally they cost a lot, Perry. These things are handmade. They are worth whatever the artist asks for them, if you want them enough to pay his price. A lot of them are queer ducks though. If you appreciate something they have made and you can't afford to buy it, they may just give it to you."

"But how can these hand workers compete with factory production?"

"They don't compete. Their work is for people who appreciate individual creation. The value of the things they make has nothing to do with the cost of the materials or the usefulness of the article. They are aesthetic values, that can't be standardized."

"Suppose people won't pay for an artist's work?"

"In that case he can do as he likes—either go on creating and keep the results or give them away—or stop and do something else."

"I didn't make myself clear. How can he go on creating if people won't buy?"

"He lives on his heritage checks, or he works for pay part of the time and works at his art part of the time."

Perry fell silent. They passed a row of public visiphone booths and came out on Mason Street. Perry had his first view of traffic on the moving ways and was made a little giddy by the sight. The crowds of people in front of him all appeared to be pedestrians but they moved at various speeds, those furthest away moving the fastest. It reminded him of times when, on a dance floor, he had whirled with a light-footed partner and then stopped suddenly. He glanced back at the adjacent building to steady himself. Then he looked back at the street. The movements gradually ordered themselves in his mind. He saw that each moving strip was about eight feet wide. He counted six strips to the middle of the street. The last strip carried a continuous bench on its far side and facing him. People were seated on this bench, reading, talking, and watching the life around them. Between their heads Perry saw flashing past in the opposite direction the heads of the passengers on the other side of the street. Overhead the glass canopy stretched from side to side from the window level of the second story, perhaps twenty feet in the air. On his left a pedestrians foot bridge arched daintily over the ways. From beneath the moving ways came a whisper and purr of machinery. Diana squeezed his hand. "Want to go for a ride?"

"Sure! Baby ride merry-go-round." He started to step on the outer strip.

"No, no, Perry! Face against the motion of the strip. And step on with the foot nearest the strip." Perry safely negotiated the first strip. "Come on, Perry, off the edge of the strip. Get inside the red stripes at once. Otherwise you might interfere with someone changing speeds."

Perry looked down and saw that the center three feet of the strip was bounded by red stripes. Several people within earshot glanced toward them curiously at Diana's words, but turned quickly away, except for one small urchin about six years old who surveyed Perry with a slow dispassionate stare. The next four strips were traversed without trouble and they settled down on the cushions of the bench. Diana smiled at him. "All right?"

"Easy once you get the hang of it. Just Eliza crossing the ice." Diana gurgled. He watched with interest the passengers around him. The urchin who had favored Perry with his attention was now staring at the opposite bound traffic with his nose pressed against the glass backboard which rose above the back cushion of the bench. His mother steadied him with one hand while she talked with another woman. The traffic was fairly heavy and Perry watched them come and go with interest. His eye was caught by a plumpish middle-aged woman in a striking purple and white robe. She carried in her arms a bright-eyed shaggy terrier who wiggled and attempted to get down. The woman was looking back over her shoulder and talking to a companion. She collided with a man moving off the fifth strip, lost her balance and sat down very suddenly on her broad posterior just at the joint between the fourth and fifth strips where she lay, shrieking, while she turned slowly round and around. The terrier bounded away and attained the sixth strip, where he ran up and down barking at the passengers on the bench. As his mistress passed slowly out of sight, several other passengers helped her to her feet and brushed her off. Perry whistled to the dog, who acknowledged the overture by jumping to the bench beside him and applying a warm wet tongue to Perry's chin and neck, "Down, boy, down! That's enough." Perry grabbed his collar. "Now what do we do? We've been joined." He grinned. Diana rubbed the dog's head. Then she got up from the bench.

"Come along and bring your friend." She moved quickly to the fifth strip, Perry close behind, then to the fourth and to the third. She stopped on the second. "We should see her soon." Presently the purple and white robe showed up on the fourth strip. Diana, Perry, and the dog moved to the third and boarded the fourth as the woman came abreast. She swooped down on the dog.

"Chou-chou! Did mama's darling get lost? Was um fwightened?" She kissed its nose and hugged it. The dog wore an air of patient forbearance. "Thank the kind people, Chou-chou. They rescued you." She turned to Perry and Diana. Diana gave him a sidewise glance and tugged his belt. They skipped onto the fifth strip and quickly over to the sixth. Diana sat down and sighed deeply.

"Safe at last." They sat for a while and watched the passing buildings. A few minutes later she pushed an elbow in his ribs. "Look over to your left." She whispered. The purple and white robe was some yards away moving along the strip towards them. "I think she's looking for us. Come along. Here's where we get off." They threaded quickly through the crowd toward the outer strip and were shortly on the stationary walk. "That was close."

"Why was she looking for us?"

"Maybe she wasn't, but I took no chances. I can't stand to be slobbered over."

"What do we do now?" They were standing by the entrance of a large squat building of synthetic marble. Over the entrance Perry read UNITED STATS POST OFIS, Tub Stashon A. Diana followed his glance.

"Want to see how the tubes work?"

"Sure." They went inside, across a broad foyer and mounted a flight of stairs to a mezzanine. Diana led to the far side of the balcony. They leaned over a rail and looked down into a broad deep room whose floor level Perry judged to be below the street. Diana pointed down, and to the right.

"See them coming in there. Then they go on the belt and are sorted." Canisters of various lengths but of a uniform thickness, about eighteen inches, streamed out of a round hole and were deposited one after the other on a conveyor belt. Every few feet a mechanism leaned over the belt. Occasionally relays would click and a broad hook would roll a canister off the belt and pull it onto another belt running crosswise underneath the first. The crosswise belts then carried the canisters off to the right and left.

"Who operates the selectors?"

"They are automatic. An electric eye scans the destination tag. If the appropriate symbol corresponds, the grabber swings out and hooks off the can. See that first selector that is so busy? The one with three arms? That takes all the San Francisco traffic. Its belts unload in another room about as big as this where they are sorted for the local stations."

"I suppose the tubes run on compressed air."

"Only on short jumps. On the trunk lines they shoot along in a partial vacuum floating in a magnetic field that pulls them along. They make tremendous speeds on the long jumps."

"Suppose I wanted to mail a letter to New York. Would it ride in one of those cans all by itself?"

"Yes, but there isn't much sense in writing a letter when you can call up on the visiphone, or write on the telautograph."

"No, I suppose not. Say, I'd like to take one of those selectors to pieces."

"Perhaps you can if you care to apply for permission. But there is nothing fancy about them. Seen enough?"

"I guess so. What now?"

Diana glanced at a chronometer on the wall. "It's ten minutes past thirteen. We could run out to the rocket port if you like."

"Say, that's fine. Let's go!" They went back to street level and rode the first strip to an intersection where they dropped down one flight to the crosstown shuttle. This they took to a station marked TUB EKSPRES TU ROKET PORT. An attendant sealed them in a cylinder containing heavily cushioned chairs. Diana sat down and laid her head back against a head rest and told Perry to do likewise. A light glowed above them for a few seconds, then cut off. Perry suddenly felt very heavy and was pressed into the cushions. Then he was suddenly normal weight again.

"Brace your feet, Perry." The sudden increase in weight pressed him forward this time. Then normal weight returned and the door opened.

"Where are we?"

"At the port, about fifteen kilometers south of town."

"San Mateo?"

"No, west of there near Pillar Point." They climbed out and proceeded up a ramp to a waiting room, where swarms of people moved about and clustered at the far end. Diana glanced at an illuminated notice board and then at the chronometer beside it. "Hurry, Perry. We are just in time."

"For what?"

"The Antipodes Express. It arrives from New Zealand in

four minutes. Hurry." He followed her up a ramp into a gallery with windows facing the field. Several sightseers were already there. Diana turned to one of them, a boy about twelve. "Is she in sight yet?"

"Uh huh, she's circling. See?" He pointed for them. Diana and Perry squinted at the sky.

"I'm afraid I can't make her out."

"She's there all right. There go the field lights. The screens'll be up any minute now."

"What kind of screens?" Perry inquired. The boy looked at him curiously.

"Say, you haven't been around much, have you? These kind of screens." Dark amber glass shutters were settling over the view windows. "You look at a rocket blast with your naked eyes and you'll wish you hadn't."

"Thanks, son. I don't know much about rockets."

"I do. I'm going to be a rocket pilot when I grow up. There she comes. She's the good old *Southern Cross*. See how pretty she rides? That's old Marko himself. He don't bounce 'em." The ship, a faint silvery sliver, circled toward the earth. She rode with her bow lifted perhaps twenty degrees, and her tail jets streaming behind her.

"Looks as if she were climbing."

"No, no." Superior Knowledge was faintly scornful. "He's riding her in on her tail. Old Marko don't pull out the plug till he's ready." The ship circled again lower down and on a narrower course. The tail jets snuffed out, then a brilliant light flared from her keel. "There goes her belly blast. Oh boy!" The youngster's eyes shone. The blast reached down toward the earth. Soon it splashed around the field. Steadily the ship lowered until the blast was almost point blank and the splash filled the halfmole landing circle and concealed the ship. Then the blast ceased and the ship lay before them. The boy chortled. "Did you see that? Just as steady as a rock on her good old gyros. And he just slid her down like sliding down a rope. Not even a side jet. Not once! What he aims at, he hits. Marko's going to drive one to the Moon someday; you wait and see. And I bet I'll go along, too."

A little cart was rolling out toward the ship and unfurling a long matting as it went. Perry asked the lad about it.

"That's the asbestos rug. You wouldn't want to walk on that field in those sandals after the belly blast hits it. You'd fry. The cart's just the baggage cart." They watched the passengers debark, then strolled about the station for a few minutes.

"Any place else you want to go, Perry?" Diana presently inquired.

"Have you any suggestion?"

"I'm getting a little weary of the crowds. Let's get back." Fifteen minutes later they were on the platform where they had left the Cloud Horse. Diana surrendered her receipt and her car was run out onto the take-off flat. Inside, she shucked off her tunic and tossed it on the bench and had the car in the air before Perry was out of his belt and comfortably settled. Once seated he lit a cigarette and handed it to her. "Where are we going?"

"Would you like to go swimming?"

"Swell. Where?"

"I know a little cove down near Monterey that is sheltered from the wind. The water may be a bit chilly."

"Let's try it."

Diana switched to 'plane' combination and gave it the gun. In fifteen minutes they were over Monterey Bay. Diana continued past Point Pinos for a few miles, circled, changed to helico, and settled down in a little cove which faced southwest. The waves broke gently on a narrow ribbon of beach. On each side shoulders of granite jutted out onto the sea. They opened the door and stepped out. The air was almost still and the afternoon sun beat down on them. The sand was warm underfoot. The sea smell, ripe and tangy, stirred in their nostrils. They walked toward the water but soon the joy of being alive lifted them up and they felt compelled to run. They splashed into the water, yelling and laughing. Perry charged along and dived head first onto the face of a breaker. He came up and dog-paddled in the back wash. Diana's head broke beside him.

"This is swell." He gasped.

"A little bit chilly. Look out! Duck!" He turned around just in time to catch a wall of green water in the face. He came up blowing, and swam over to where Diana stood laughing at him. His hand struck bottom, he dropped his feet and stood beside her.

"This is grand, Dian'. I wish we could have done this in my day."

"My goodness! Didn't you?"

"Swim raw I mean. We swam but we wore swimming suits."

She looked incredulous. "I've read about it, of course. But it seems so ridiculous—so unsanitary." She shivered a little. "I'm going to dry off, Perry. I'm cold."

"One more dive and I'm with you." She moved off up the beach. When Perry returned he found her by the door of the car, rubbing herself briskly with a big fluffy towel. He picked up a second towel which was lying in the door. "Turn around and I'll rub your back." She turned obediently. When he had finished, she scrubbed away at his back, then stepped away and snapped him with her towel. "Ouch!" He rubbed the spot ruefully. "Was that nice?"

She grinned impishly. "No, but it was fun."

"You ought to be paddled for that."

"You'll have to catch me first." She was off down the beach, hair flying, legs flashing. He took off after her and ran her down. He grabbed her from behind, she struggled, and they fell down together, a laughing disorderly heap. He tussled with her and tried to turn her over into a favorable position for a smacking, but she was lithe as an otter and nearly as slippery. Their contortions brought their faces close to each other. He bent his head down and kissed her on her lips. She became instantly quiet, not relaxed but tense. In sudden alarm he searched her face. Her expression was serious but she did not seem angry. Slowly he bent his head again. She made no move, but did not draw away. His mouth touched hers gently. Her body relaxed and melted into his and her lips parted slightly as her right arm went about his neck. They held still for a long time.

There are kisses and kisses. Some are given in sport and some in passion. There are formal kisses of greeting and departure, and there are perfunctory pecks of accustomed affection. Once in a great while lips meet and two spirits merge for a time and the universe is right and complete and the planets wheel in their proper places. Once in a while the lonely, broken spirit of man is healed and made whole. For a while his quest is over and his questions are answered.

She lay quiet in his arms. "Oh, Perry."

"Dian', Dian'."

Presently she stirred. "Let's go back to the car." They arose and were surprised to find muscles stiff and cold. The warm glow of the interior of the car was welcome. "Shall we go home?" He nodded and she drew back the stick. The shadows on the beach were lengthening and the car's shadow flew out ahead of them to the east. She leveled off and shifted combinations. Presently her hands left the controls. "I've set the robot on Reno. Let's move back." They seated themselves side by side on the cushions.

"Cigarette?"

"Thanks." He lit it for her and one for himself. A long silence. Presently he spoke.

"Dian'."

"Yes, Perry?"

"I didn't say so, but I suppose you know that I love you."

"Yes, I know."

"Well?"

"I love you too, Perry."

Neither spoke for a long time. The quiet whir of the screw and the clicking of the robot marked the growth of time. He kissed her. When their lips parted she left her head on his shoulder. The room filled with their thoughts. In course of time a bell tinkled and a little light flashed on the instrument board. Diana arose hastily. "We're abreast of home. I must take over." Quickly she slid into her pilot's chair and changed course to the right. Five minutes later she spoke. "Look down and see if you can pick out our field."

"I see a light below."

"Work this switch and see if it blinks."

He did so. "It's ours all right."

"Will you land us, Perry?"

"Why, yes, if you wish."

"I want you to."

He set them gently down. A few moments later Captain Kidd was telling them in blasphemous terms what he thought of people who stayed away all day. There seemed to be some mention of inconsiderate, something about no sense of responsibility and a distinct intention of writing to the *Times*. Diana hastily procured a saucer of milk and one of sardines. He accepted her apology—tentatively.

When Perry came out of the refresher, he found Diana at the

food preparer, her hands fairly flying about the place. He called
to her.

"Dian'."

"Yes?"

"You've still got your sandals on."

She glanced down and smiled. "So I have. Your supper will be
ready the sooner." She placed a few more items on the tray.
"Here, set it up." She dived into her refresher and returned in less
than five minutes, sandal-less, her hair fluffed out and her body
glowing from a quick shower. She slid into her seat. "All ready?
Get set. Go!" They ate like starved children for a few minutes.
Then their eyes met and they both laughed without knowing
why. They finished more slowly and Perry chucked the dishes in
the fire. He returned and sat down beside her. The evening
passed without much talk. They sat and watched the fire and listened to the music Diana had selected. She read some poetry to
him. After that he asked her if she had anything by Rudyard
Kipling and she produced a thin volume of his verses. He found
what he sought and read aloud *The Mary Gloster*. Then he kissed
a cheek wet with tears and made it damper with his own. A long
time later she smothered a yawn. He smiled and spoke. "I'm
sleepy, too, but I don't want to go away and leave you."

She looked at him, round eyed and serious.

"You needn't leave me, unless you wish."

"But—See here, darling, I want to marry you, but I don't
want to rush you into anything you might regret."

"Regret? I don't understand you. But as far as I am concerned we are married now, if you wish it so."

"I suppose we could run out tomorrow and have the ceremony performed."

"There is no need. These things are in the private sphere.
Oh, don't make it complicated." She began to cry.

He hesitated for a moment, then picked her up in his arms and laid her on the widest part of the couch. Then he lay down beside her. A coal in the fire cracked and firelight flickered about the room.

VI

Perry *pressed back on the control stick and his plane shot higher and higher. He had to fly high because the Princess, his passenger, lived back of the Moon. He struck a bank of keys and plumes of fire shot from the tail of his plane and the plane climbed and climbed. He felt a swelling in joy within him at his own skill and the power of his plane and the warm beautiful knowledge that the Princess loved him and rode beside him. The Princess smiled and reached out a graceful little hand and caressed his face. Her face grew closer to his. The plane and the Moon faded away but the face of the Princess was still close beside him.*

"Awake, darling?" Her head was on the thick of his arm and her hand rested softly on his cheek. He blinked. His eyes blurred and crossed. He blinked again and she came back into focus.

"Awake? Oh, I guess so. Almost, anyhow. Good morning, beautiful. I love you."

"And I love you."

When their lips parted, he spoke again. "Why?"

"Why what?"

"Why do you love me? How did I find you? Why was I singled out for this end? Who am I to claim your love? Why are you so wonderful and beautiful and why do you love me?"

She laughed and hugged him. "I can't answer any but the last. I'm not wonderful. I'm a very ordinary human woman with a lot of failings. I'm vain and I'm lazy and sometimes I'm bad tempered and cross. I'm beautiful because you think I am. And I want you to tell me that I'm wonderful and beautiful every morning of my life."

"And every night and every day." He kissed her again.

Later she stretched and yawned and made little contented sounds. "Hungry?"

"I guess I am. Yes, I am. If I could make magic in that witch's den of yours I'd bring you your breakfast in bed."

"It won't take but a moment. But thanks. Will you have yours in bed?"

"No, I'll come joggle your elbow and get in your way." He followed her to the kitchen nook.

"Tell me, Diana, when were all these fresh fruits delivered?"

"Last summer, mostly. I unfreeze them as I need them. Father picked out my supplies. He's in foods."

"Your father? Is your father alive?"

"Surely. Why not?"

"And your mother?"

"Yes. She's a surgeon. Why? Did you think they were dead?"

"I didn't think so consciously. I just hadn't thought about it. You were you. I didn't fill in your background. Say, does your father keep a shotgun around the house?"

"Whatever for?"

"It just seemed possible that he might think I'd wronged our Nell."

"Wronged our Nell? What does that mean?"

"It's just an expression. What I mean is this: If he knew about us, wouldn't he disapprove pretty violently? After all we may be married to each other but the world doesn't know it."

"But why should the world know it, or Father, unless we choose to tell him? And even if he didn't like you—and I'm sure he will—how would that affect us? He would never dream of mentioning it. Listen, Perry, you must realize that marriage, as an institution, has changed enormously. We talked about this once before. Marriage isn't a public contract anymore. It's strictly in the private sphere. You and I love each other and want to live together. We are doing so. Therefore we are married."

"Then there isn't any ceremony, nor any contract?"

"You can have all the ceremony you want if you care to apply to any of the churches. But I hope you won't ask me to do it. It would embarrass me terribly, and make me feel—well—dirtied."

His brow wrinkled. "I don't understand some of your customs darling, but the way that suits you suits me."

"We could draw up a domestic economy contract if you want one. Personally I'd rather not bother. We both have comfortable credit accounts and it would just mean a lot of unnecessary records. Let's just be casual about it. Even if you didn't make any money, we probably couldn't manage to spend my income."

"I don't want to be a gigolo."

"What's a gigolo?"

"A man who lets a woman support him in exchange for love making."

Her lip trembled and tears welled up in her eyes.

"Perry, you shouldn't have said that to me."

"Sweetheart! Please—Oh, Lord, I'm sorry, I truly am. I didn't mean to hurt your feelings, but good heavens, I don't know the customs of this topsy-turvy world."

The tears stopped. "OK, darling. I should have made allowances. But let's say no more about credits and contracts. We don't need to."

•   •   •

After breakfast Perry re-opened the subject. "Dian' darling, there is just one thing that worries me about this casual modern way of getting married. What about children?"

She looked at him levelly and soberly. "Do you want to give me a child, Perry?"

"Why, no. Well, no, I don't mean no. I'd want to, I suppose, if you wanted to. I wasn't thinking about us personally; I was thinking about children in general. Say, have I already? I mean do you think it likely?"

"No, not until we decide to and want to."

"That's good. I mean of course it would be an honor and a privilege, but there is your career—and as for me—Look, Dian', how can I be a father?"

"Why not, Perry?"

"You know. This isn't my body."

"I think it is, Perry. Perhaps we can find out."

"Suppose you wake up some morning and I'm not in this body anymore—Suppose Gordon comes back?"

She put her arms around him. "I don't think that will happen, Perry. Don't ask me why for I don't know. But I feel sure of it just the same.

"But you ask about children. Children aren't a financial burden as they were in your day. A child's own credit account is enough to support it. A child can live with its parents if it wants to and they want it, or if it chooses, it can grow up in a development center. If parents separate, the child can go with which ever it chooses."

"It sounds awfully cold-blooded."

"It's not, really. In most cases children spend most of their childhood with one or both parents. Usually parents will insist on a child spending at least a year or two in a development center to be sure that the child is adjusted to social living. Take my case for example. I lived with one or the other of my parents practically all the time until I was eighteen, except for two years in a development center between fourteen and sixteen."

"You say one or the other of your parents. Aren't they married anymore?"

"Oh yes. But they are not very domestic, and their work keeps them apart a lot of the time. But take the case of my half brother Pharion. He's the son of a very talented actress who fell madly in love with Dad for a while and wanted a child by him. But they never married. He grew up in a development center almost entirely because he didn't like his parents. He was a sober minded boy and they were both too frivolous for him. Then there is my half sister Susan; she's mother's child by another great surgeon. I don't believe they were in love at all the way you mean it, but I am sure that they both hoped that their child would be a genius in surgery. Sue has lived with mother all her life."

"That sounds polygamous to me."

"No—I really don't think you could call it that. There is no custom against polygamy or polyandry, if anyone wants to. I have two friends, girls, who live together. They have a friend, a man, who lives with them most of the time. Of course I don't know but I think they are both married to him."

Perry shook his head. "I don't understand it. It seems unnatural."

"Don't worry about it, darling. You will understand in time."

Perry was much too busy for the next several days to trouble his mind with misgivings and doubts. He was happy, happier he thought than he had ever been in his life—or lives?—he could not be sure which was the proper term. Life was a picnic, a honeymoon, a delightful and interesting school, a Cook's tour, and the land of the Lotus Eaters, all rolled into one. He listened for hours to records of events that fascinated him, studied new techniques and advances in science in a medium that made his early day studies seem left handed and awkward, trudged through the mountain snows with Diana, watched her rehearse her dances, listened with her to gorgeous music and stirring drama, flew about the country-side in their car, and spent the nights in his darling's arms. Their intimacy ripened and grew. She encouraged him to talk of his early life, his childhood in Kansas, the adolescent triumph of winning an appointment as a midshipman, his school days, his life in the service, the things that he had seen and experienced, and the evaluations that he placed on all these things.

Meanwhile, as he observed the life of the modern world, listened to the records and studied the code of customs, he found in talking with Diana that his opinions had changed from the world that he had left, and that he was beginning to assess that past life from the point of view of a citizen of the modern world. That which had appeared to be the natural order of things, now seemed grotesque. Values lumped together as "sportsmanship" now appeared to be the stupid exhibitionism of savages. Things that were known as "sport" now appeared to range from harmless but pointless play to callous sadism. Nice points of "honor" between "gentlemen" struck him now as the posturing of peacocks. But most of all he came to despise the almost universal deceit, half lies and downright falsehood that had vitiated the life of 1939. He realized that it had been a land of hokum and cheat. The political speeches, the advertising slogans, the spit-licking, prostituted preachers, the billboards, the ballyhoo, the kept press, the pussy-footing professors, the incredible papier-maché idol of "society", the yawping Neanderthal 100% Americanism, paving contracts, special concessions and other grafts, the purchased Senators and hired attorneys, the corrupt judges and cynical politicians, and over and through it all the poor desiccated spirit of the American peasant, the "wise guy" whose motto was "Cheat first, lest ye be cheated" and "Never give a sucker a break." The poor betrayed overgrown lunk who had played too young with the big boys and learned a lot of nasty habits, who had deluded himself with his own collective lies, whose father had deluded him from the best of intentions and who would in turn delude his own son from the same good intentions. The pillar of the community who taught his son that a man has to "go with a woman" but the women you marry are somehow different from the women you "go with." The mother who encourages her daughter to "make a good match" but wants to "run out of town" her sister from across the tracks who strikes a more generous bargain. The whole tribe, lying, lied to and lied about, who had been taught to admire success, even in a scoundrel, and despise failure, even in a hero.

Perry came to despise and be nauseated by all of these things, but he did not hate the people from which he came, nor loathe himself for being one of them, for he knew these people, and he knew that they were good people, warm-hearted and generous, yes, and brave and courageous. He knew that any one of the posturing morons among those 100%ers would dive under the wheels of a locomotive to rescue a child, that the crooked real-estate promoter would buy a meal for any hungry man, and the vicariously ambitious mother would go without food to buy her daughter a party dress. He knew that kindliness and generosity were as universal as deception and cut-throat competition. Perry realized that not one in a thousand men had ever had a chance to act the decent, honest creature that he potentially was. He knew that the ordinary man from 1939 was too weak-willed and too naïve to stand up against the system in which he found himself.

The thing for which Perry most admired the Americans of his period was that in them, potentially, lay 2086. In a short century and a half these callous, kind hearted, gullible, deceitful bumpkins had stumbled and zig-zagged into a culture they could be proud of. Somehow or other (Cathcart's explanations seemed too simple now) the universal longing of the older generations that things might be different for their children had borne fruit. Perhaps that alone had accounted for it. Perhaps to have the desire for better things for our children, and our children's children, than we had for ourselves is to *be* immortal and to *become* divine.

Perry had ample opportunity as the days marched by to see this culture as well as to hear about it and view it in shadow show. He visited the socialistic state of Wisconsin which had grown up in its own direction within the framework of the federation. Diana and he spent several days in the Gulf States where there still remained the large group of blacks not yet assimilated by the white majority. Here he found a culture as free as the rest of the country—perhaps less highly mechanized, but undoubtedly richer in arts, and social graces, and zest for living.

Gradually Diana introduced Perry to her friends and helped him over the rough spots in adjusting himself to new social customs. After a few weeks of the casual, easy, good-humored atmosphere of her circle of acquaintances, he felt, and she agreed, that he was ready to get by in any company without betraying the peculiar circumstances of his life. He had acquired some of the modern liking for privacy and decided not to expand the number of those who knew.

• • •

One morning about six weeks after his advent Diana announced that she expected a visitor. Perry looked up with interest. "Who is it? Anyone I know?"

"No. It's a young fellow named Bernard. I used to be very close to him. He's a dancer, too. We used to be partners."

"What do you mean, 'used to be very close to him'?"

"Why, I was very fond of him. We lived together about a year."

"What!"

"Why, Perry, what's the matter?"

"What do you mean? Do you mean you lived with him in the sense that we are living together now?"

Her face grew dark. "You've no right to ask that sort of a question. However, I will answer. We lived together, as man and woman, as you and I are doing."

He strode up and down, a black look on his face. Finally he turned and faced her. "Diana, is this your way of telling me that you are through with me?"

She reached out and placed a hand impulsively on his arm. "Why, no, darling. No, No."

He shrugged off her grasp. "Then why do you invite this old flame of yours here? Are you trying to humiliate me?"

Her face was white and tense. "Perry, Perry darling! Nothing of the sort. You mustn't think such things. He is coming because he has occasion to. He and I are billed to appear in a series of dances together. He's coming here to work out the choreography and rehearse."

"Why hadn't I heard about it?"

"There was no reason to discuss it, Perry. We signed the contract last fall and we don't open until the first of May. But now we must rehearse."

He looked up and his face had cleared a little. "You used to love him, Diana?"

"A little. Not as I love you, Perry."

"He means nothing to you, nothing at all?"

"I wouldn't say that. I'm still very fond of him and he was very good to me. We just got bored with each other and split up, but I still count him as a staunch friend."

He looked sulky. "Staunch friend, my foot. I'll bet he's still nuts about you."

Diana looked hurt and bewildered and seemed about to cry. "Perry, Perry, darling. I don't understand you. What is this all about? What have I done to harm you? We were so happy, so very happy, and now all this. It seems so silly. Why? Why?" Tears welled up and spilled over. Perry wore the harassed indignant look of the eternal male confronted with the incomprehensible irrational feminine viewpoint.

"Good Lord! What do you expect? I guess I'm as tolerant and broadminded as the next one, and I've never thought it was my business to go poking my nose into your past, but can't you see that this is a bit thick? When a guy shows up whom you admit is an old lover of yours, and you want me to receive him into the house as a friend of the family, it's too much. Anybody'd be jealous. Don't you think I have my pride?" His face settled into sullen, stubborn lines and the corners of his mouth twitched. "The free and easy business may be all right for casual lovemaking, but apparently you didn't realize that I was serious. *I* thought we were married. *I* thought you felt the same way about me. I didn't know what all this casual immorality you showed me amounted to." He passed his hand over his face. "OK. I've been a sap. But don't you worry. I'll pack up and be out of here in no time. Thanks for everything you've done for me of course. I'll figure up what I owe you and pay you back right away."

Diana stood rigid, her hands clenched and her face screwed up like that of a child whose world has crumbled about her. Scalding tears pressed out of her tight shut eyes and splashed on her breast. He turned to go. She moved quickly and clung to him. "Perry! Perry! No! Don't! What have I done? I don't understand. Please, darling, please. Anything, but don't just leave me alone." She sobbed brokenly. Perry patted her awkwardly. Her sobbing continued. He turned her face up and wiped at her tears.

"Don't cry kid. I can't stand it. And let me go. It's better that way. Stop it, kid, please. Oh Lord, what can I do?" The sobs abated, and died away. She sniffled and gulped.

"Perry, it's some awful mistake. But tell me that you love me and you're not going away."

He looked troubled. "Well, I don't want to go away. Listen, Dian', I love you and I want to stay. Look. Will you call up this mug and tell him to stay away?"

She looked unhappy. "I can't Perry. He'll be here any minute."

"What can we do then?"

"I don't know."

"Christ!" He strode over to the view windows and stared out, his fists jammed against his hips. Diana waited. Then he turned. "Look, Dian'. I guess I'll have to be polite to this guy for today. After he's gone we can figure out what to do about your contract and so forth." She started to speak, then fell silent. "Well?"

"All right, Perry." He smiled and took her in his arms and kissed her. He felt the warm glow of one who has done a magnanimous thing. He could not know that she was still deeply troubled.

As they were finishing lunch they heard the thump of a careless landing overhead. Shortly the door light glowed and there was admitted their guest. He was a young man, tall, well muscled and beautifully made. Perry noted with dissatisfaction his obvious good looks. He greeted Diana with "Hello, beautiful!," swung her off her feet, kissed her, and set her down with a flourish. Diana turned uneasily to Perry.

"Bernard, this is Perry."

The visitor seemed momentarily startled, recovered himself, made the ghost of a formal bow and muttered, "Do you a service?" Perry acknowledged as briefly.

Bernard turned to Diana. "Dancer?" Diana shook her head. Bernard continued, "OK. Let's get going. I've got a lot of brand new stuff and, baby, it's hot. Look at this." He pulled a roll out of his belt, then shrugged off the belt and threw it on the couch. "This one now. It's historical, see? I'm an army aviator and you're a war nurse. We do the first half in costume with lots of action, then in the finale we duck the costumes and it's all symbolical. The score is Radetzky's *War Birds* with my own arrangement." They fell into a discussion of technical terms which Perry failed to understand. He went over to the reproducer, selected a record and cut in the earphones. Grimly he kept up the pretense of studying for the better part of two hours. Finally he realized that he had played a record on engineering materials and processes three times and remembered none of it. He snapped off the machine and turned and watched the rehearsal. There was no avoiding the fact that Bernard was graceful and handsome. His shoulders were broad and his hips narrow and he moved like a black panther. His body was the true golden bronze all over and his profile could have been the model for a Greek coin. Except for a slight petulance of his features in repose Perry could by no rationalization regard him as effeminate in spite of his occupation. At the moment they were rehearsing a phrase in which Diana leaped into the air and was caught by him as he turned. Bernard seemed dissatisfied.

"No, beautiful, no. You're not in time. It goes like this: Tata Tata, tata tata, thrrrrrump, bump bump." He illustrated in pantomime. "Now try it." The music started and Diana whirled and came out in a long flying leap. Bernard caught her from a turn, swung her about and set her down. "That's better. Now once more." He caressed her upper arm. Perry felt his jaw muscle tighten until hard lumps and an acrid smell came into his nostrils. Diana whirled again and leaped to be swept from the air like a netted butterfly. Bernard gave a shout. "Bravo! Bravo! That's it!" He retained her in his arms and planted an enthusiastic kiss on her mouth, then hugged her to him. Perry was on his feet and striding across the floor.

"Put her down!"

Bernard looked up with surprise and annoyance across his face. "What did you say?"

"Put her down!" Perry grasped his arm roughly. "Cut out that stuff. Put her down."

"Do you know that you are being offensive?"

Diana squirmed loose and stood between them. "Perry, please! Bernard, don't pay any attention. Perry, please go back and sit down."

"Just a moment, Diana." Bernard stepped toward Perry. "Your words require explanation. Why were you offensive?"

"Offensive! Pah!" Perry gave a short hard laugh.

"He obviously is not rational. Come, Diana." Bernard placed a hand on her shoulder.

Crack! Perry's left fist connected with Bernard's jaw and he went down in a heap. He struggled to his knees, fingered his jaw, and looked at Perry with an expression of utter amazement.

"Get up and defend yourself." The amazement increased.

Without moving Bernard spoke. "Diana, get behind me. He's dangerous." Instead she broke from her shocked immobility and flung herself on Perry.

"No more, Perry! No more! Oh God, look what you've done already."

"Diana, come away from him. We've got to get out of here." She turned, still clinging to Perry.

"No, he won't hurt me. You get out. Go. Go at once."

"I can't leave you alone with him."

"Yes, go. I'm perfectly safe. Get out." Perry finally spoke. "Do as she tells you. I won't hurt her, you fool. But get out or I'll cut you to ribbons."

Bernard backed toward the door, hastily grabbing his belt as he did so. As he opened the door, Diana stopped him. "Bernard!"

"Yes?"

"You won't do anything?"

"Do anything? I'll have to report it." He slid through the door and closed it. Diana burst into tears. Perry stared at her.

"What did he mean by that?"

Between sobs she explained. "He's going to report you for violating a major custom. And then they'll come and take you away, and you'll have to be examined to find out what they'll do with you." She burst into tears again. "Oh, Perry, why did you strike him? Oh dear, oh dear, we were so happy."

"What do we do now?"

"There's nothing to do."

"Do you think I'm going to sit here and let that young punk send the police after me on a measly assault and battery charge? Say, can I take the air car?"

She turned in sudden alarm. "Perry! You're not going away?"

"Why not? I can be miles away before they get here. Then when this quiets down I'll get in touch with you."

"Perry, don't think of it. You couldn't stay in hiding. You'd be picked up the minute you tried to use your credit account. It's impossible and it would just make things worse."

The visephone light glowed. Automatically Diana answered

it. The image of a kindly looking woman with a brisk official manner appeared in the screen. "Office of Public Safety at Truckee. Are you Diana 160–398–400–48A?" Diana nodded, too miserable to speak. "Is there a citizen there called Perry?" Another nod. "Let me speak with him, please." Defiantly Perry placed himself in range. "You are Perry?"

"Yes."

"We are informed by Bernard 593–045–823–56G that you experienced a major atavism today involving an antisocial violence. Do you recall anything of that nature?"

"Yes."

"How do you feel now? Any impulse to break custom?"

"I'm all right."

"That's good. The field investigators will be along shortly. Can you arrange to come along with them today?"

"I have to, don't I?"

"It would be better. A quick investigation is always more satisfactory."

"They'll find me here. I'll come."

She smiled. "That's sensible. You'll be well in time. Very well, then—Clearing." Her image faded.

For the next half hour a morose silence filled the room. Diana hesitated to speak and Perry was busy with his own unhappy thoughts. Finally came the door signal for which each had been uneasily but impatiently waiting. Diana opened the door and admitted two pleasant, clean cut young chaps. One of them spoke. "You're Diana? And you must be Perry. Truckee safety Office. I'm Bill; this is Leslie. Believe there's a service to do you?"

Perry made a wry face. "You could call it that." The second young man looked anxious and stepped forward.

"How do you feel, buddy? Need any immediate treatment?" He glanced at his partner, who answered.

"No trauma or gross lesions. Let's check your pulse. Hm—a little high, nothing startling."

Perry pulled his wrist away. "Cut it out. I'm all right."

"Okay. I don't like to give a sedative before the preliminary examination. That pulse won't hurt you. Got everything you need? Let's go." Diana donned a tunic. "You coming too, sister? Okay."

Shortly thereafter Perry found himself being ushered alone into an office in the Truckee Civic Hall. He was greeted by the occupant, a middle-aged, grey haired black man, who thumbed through a stack of papers and presented him with a sheet. "Here's a resumé of the report about you. Look it over." Perry glanced over the paper and handed it back. The official looked inquiringly at him.

"Any truth in it?"

"Do I have to answer questions? Don't I get to see counsel?"

"Why certainly, if you wish. But it saves unpleasant delay and mistakes if the state knows the facts at once."

"Oh well, I don't deny it. The report is correct as far as the general facts go."

"Very well then. We can skip the preliminary examination in that case. Consider yourself remanded for examination and disposition. Will tomorrow be satisfactory?"

"Good Lord, you seem in an awful hurry. When do I see my counsel?"

"You needn't be examined so soon, if you object. Who is your counsel? I'll have him sent in."

"I don't know any."

"Very well. I'll assign one." He touched a button and Perry was shown out. In the course of the next two hours he was assigned to a room (cheerful, clean, reasonably comfortable), given a card of special customs to read, weighed, measured, photographed, blood tests made, fluoroscoped, metabolic rate checked, and a dozen other items of clinical examination performed. When he was finally back in his room, tired and extremely confused, he sat down and tried to order his thoughts.

The door light glowed and an attendant entered, grinned and uttered the formal, "Service."

"Service," answered Perry. "What do you want?"

"Here's your menu. Check off what you want. You wanta eat here or in the refectory?"

"Here, I guess. Say, what is this joint; a hotel, a jail, or a hospital?"

"It's a detention center. Say, ain't everything been all right? You want anything?"

"No, thanks. Can I televue someplace? I need to get a message out."

"Sure, it's in that panel there by the window."

"Thanks." The attendant left and Perry tried to call Diana. There was no answer. He tried a second time and desisted to answer the door light. Diana stood in the door. Presently she disentangled her arms from about his neck and he saw that she was accompanied. Her companion was a spare intellectual man of about thirty-five who greeted Perry cordially. Diana introduced them.

"Perry, this is Master Joseph. He's here to help you. He's your counsel."

"Well, young fellow, if what Diana tells me can be considered as objectively correct, you have one of the strangest cases I've ever dealt with." In a few minutes Master Joseph had put Perry at ease and had drawn out of him the salient details of the event that had landed him where he now was. Then he inquired into the past few weeks of his life and the incredible story of his renascense. The talk turned to Perry's life in the twentieth century. Master Joseph seemed to have an inexhaustible curiosity concerning the social customs of that period, the beliefs men lived by, and Perry's opinions of the *mores* of both periods. While they talked, Perry's dinner arrived and he expressed embarrassment that he could not invite them to eat. Joseph answered that he could, if he wished, and signaled the attendant. After dinner the talk continued. Perry asked him what his chances were. Joseph considered this.

"Well, you are undoubtedly in violation of a basic custom. The Court will be sure to find affirmatively."

"What's the punishment?"

"Punishment?" Joseph's eyebrows raised. "There is no punishment. You have several serious psychological blockages and you will be requested to submit to treatment."

"What kind of treatment?"

"I don't know. Whatever your attending psychiatrists prescribe."

"Psychiatrists? What the hell? Do you think I'm crazy?"

"No, but I think you are badly in need of reorientation by psychiatry."

"What does a lawyer know of psychiatry?"

"I'm not a lawyer. I'm a psychiatrist."

"Then why were you sent to me as counsel?"

"Lawyers aren't private counsels. Those in court work are technical assistants to the court. I'll get one to see you if you wish, but he probably won't be much help. A lawyer is likely to regard any irregularity as most irregular—which it is of course." He grinned. "My advice is not to worry and get a good night's sleep. I'll order a sedative for you. No, Diana, you'd better not stay tonight. I want him to rest." He arose to go and studied the evening sky through the window while Perry and Diana said good night.

VII

Shortly after breakfast Perry was interviewed at length by a board of five psychiatrists. Joseph was present and facilitated the work. The talk seemed inconsequential. At one point one of them engaged him in an animated discussion of the effect of the invention of flying on the logistic problem in warfare. For some reason the others seemed to follow this discussion with interest. Another inquired into some details of customs or 'rates' observed by midshipmen, and as to what extent a midshipman's life differed socially from that of a civilian student. By lunch time they seemed satisfied and adjourned.

Perry's trial was set for fourteen o'clock. It turned out to be anticlimactic. On counsel's advice he stipulated the facts in the complaint and requested a trial without jury. The examining judge found affirmatively and read the findings of the psychiatric board. Then he spoke to Perry:

"Young man, according to the board you are for all practical purposes unacquainted with our customs in the field of social correction. In the terms you are familiar with you have been found guilty and I am about to pass sentence. In other terms familiar to you, you have been diagnosed and found to be sick and I am about to prescribe for your illness. You don't have to take your medicine unless you want to, but I hope you will. The findings of the board are encouraging if somewhat startling, and I think you will have a complete recovery."

"May it please the Court?"

"May it what? Oh yes, surely. Go ahead."

"What is the alternative to taking treatment?"

"The alternative is Coventry, by which I mean that you will be delivered to the gate of a reservation set aside for non-cooperative individuals, along with your credit turned into any chattels you choose. Or, if you prefer, you may emigrate to any country willing to receive you."

"What happens if I enter Coventry?"

"You must enter the gate. What happens thereafter is no concern of the state."

"How long must I stay in the reservation?"

The judge shrugged his shoulders and did not reply.

"I'll take treatment. I was simply curious about the other."

"Very good. I see from the report that certain typical moral reactions may be expected from you with a general classification of aristocratic. Do you recognize my authority?"

"Yes, Your Honor."

"I am going to ask you to make me a promise. You need not if you prefer not to. I want you to promise that you will refrain from doing any violence to any person whatsoever including yourself for any reason whatsoever until you are pronounced cured or until you come to me and tell me that you withdraw your word. Will you do it?"

"That's fair enough. I promise."

"Good. I want to parole you to someone not in need of treatment himself. Who is your next friend?"

Perry looked disconcerted. "Why, I don't believe I have any." As he spoke, Diana stepped forward. The judge smiled.

"Is she your next friend?" They both nodded. "Very well

then, you must understand that she is responsible to me that the instructions of this court are carried out." He turned to Diana. "Take him to the State Correction Hospital at Tahoe. The Chief Clerk will help you with the details. That's all. Goodbye and good luck."

In the air car Diana set the controls and turned to Perry with anxious concern in her eyes. "Well, darling, how do you feel?"

Perry considered this. "I don't know. I was braced for a pretty unpleasant outcome, but I've been treated very decently. On the other hand I have to go off someplace away from you and submit to treatment of indefinite duration and unknown sort. It's humiliating and I don't feel happy about it. I don't like to be regarded as crazy because I know that I am not."

Diana patted his hand. "Nobody thinks you are crazy, darling. They think that you are suffering from bad emotional reactions through faulty training. Now they will attempt to re-train you so that you can be happy."

He grasped her fiercely. "Do those fools think that they can train me out of loving you with a bunch of fancy phrases?"

She kissed him tenderly before she answered. "Not at all, darling. You'll love me just as much or more, but you'll be happier in it, because you won't be all cluttered up with a bunch of false reflexes and wrong identifications."

"You may be right but I can't see it. I don't see how you can change human nature."

"You'll understand that better in a few days. Relax and don't worry about it now. Come here and let me hold you." She took him in her arms, cradling his lean young shoulders like a baby. She smoothed the wrinkles from his brow and closed his eyes. Presently the little stubborn lines about his mouth ironed out and he breathed more slowly. Diana suspected that he was sleeping and was still. The miles slipped by underneath. Then she roused him gently. "Perry. Perry, dearest. It's time to land."

"I wasn't asleep."

"No, but it is time to land. See below—that flat over there to the left. Put her down as close to the buildings as you can find room."

"Right-O."

Inside the administration wing, Diana gave Perry his instructions. "Ask for Master Hedrick and tell them who you are. They'll tell you what to do." They were asked to wait for a few minutes. When Master Hedrick appeared, he turned out to be an unimpressive little man, rather thin, with scanty grey hair and a quick bird-like manner. He trotted up, hand outstretched.

"Ah, there you are. We've been expecting you. Welcome to Shangri La."

"Shangri La?"

"Just a poetical expression, an old man's fancy from a piece of classic literature I read when a boy. You've probably never heard of it."

"I've read it." Perry spoke abruptly.

"Oh, you have really? Then you'll appreciate the allusion. Not quite as Elysian as the original perhaps, but very beautiful, very beautiful." Master Hedrick beamed as if he personally had weeded the gardens. "And we try to make the place have the same effect, the same effect. Hope to, hope to." He cocked his head on one side and regarded them with chipper benignity. "But here, what are we waiting for? Visitors to Shangri La must be fed first. Have you lunched? Then perhaps some tea, or a liqueur? No? A cigarette?" Perry took one from the proffered pack. It was already lighted when he withdrew it. He regarded it with some surprise. Hedrick beamed anew. "Clever, isn't it? Designed for me by one of our guests. Very clever man, but a little too preoccupied with mechanical devices. Designed one intended to blow up the earth. Didn't work, but he doesn't want to anymore. Designs integrating fabricators instead. Very ingenious. Very ingenious. Never could understand them, but they work like a top, like a top. But come, you're not settled yet. Want to live in bachelor hall? No, of course not. We have some lovely apartments. Or how about a cottage?"

Perry didn't answer, but Diana diffidently suggested that they see the latter.

"Yes indeed. Come along." He led them at a quick trot downstairs and into a passage where a moving way delivered them to another stairway. They climbed the stair and found themselves in a pleasant comfortable living room complete in all necessary details except kitchen equipment. A fine view window faced out over Lake Tahoe. No other buildings were in sight. Hedrick indicated a path that lead to the right along the shore. "The main buildings are a couple hundred meters down there," said he. "You'll prefer to walk in fine weather. Now I'll leave you for a while. Just make yourselves at home. We won't really get busy until tomorrow." He trotted away.

Perry glanced after him. "Funny little guy. What is he, kind of a glorified janitor?"

"My heavens, no. He's the chief psychiatrist and director of the whole institution." Perry whistled, then he changed the subject.

"How soon do you have to go?"

"Why, I don't have to go. I don't have a broadcast until Tuesday."

"Do you mean they will let you stay here?"

"Surely. Why not? I'll have to be away a good deal because there is no place to rehearse here, nor to broadcast. They may want me to leave you a good bit of the time, but I'm certainly staying over night and most nights—if I'm asked." She lowered her lashes.

He placed a finger under her chin, turned it up and kissed her. "Of course you're asked."

The next morning Hedrick appeared and asked if he might come in and talk for a while. The men settled down to becoming acquainted, as Diana announced that she was going to run over and pick up Captain Kidd. The conversation rambled on for hour after hour. Perry found himself led into doing most of the talking and doing so with great freedom. The little man was curiously disarming. His bird-like twitter and mild ways broke down the younger man's reticence. Gradually he found himself talking about factual events alone. To it all Hedrick offered a sympathetic attention, his head cocked on one side, his eyes bright and alert. When he arose to leave, Perry inquired somewhat nervously as to when the treatment would commence. Hedrick beamed. "It has commenced. Didn't you know it?" Then he departed, having promised to arrange as soon as possible for a competent economist to come in for a chat, which Perry had requested.

The talks continued, both with and without others present. Hedrick turned over a part of Perry's case to Olga, a sturdy blond earthy person who seemed out of place on the staff of a psychiatric institution. She had the hips and breasts for childbearing and the calm eyes of the natural mother. But Diana assured him that Olga had more than once collaborated with Diana's mother in complicated brain surgery. Olga directed Perry in a more comprehensive study of the modern world than he had undertaken with Diana's help. In addition to technical and nonfiction works, Olga selected for him many fictional and dramatic works which she urged him to read or view. The two women got along together like old friends. Often Olga would appear with some book or record that she wished Perry to absorb, then the ladies would go for long walks in the surrounding hills. During Diana's numerous absences Olga would frequently eat and spend the evening with him.

Olga required Perry to do considerable writing, which he referred to facetiously as his 'homework' or his 'examinations'. There was an entire series in which he was asked to define terms. In the earlier papers the words to be defined were comparatively simple, such as 'walking', 'road', 'apple', 'cat'. Perry started in on these blithely determined to show that he positively was not chasing butterflies. But these papers came back to him with discrepancies and confusing terms pointed out and with a request for more nearly unmistakable definitions. He grew hot and sweaty and struggled with attempts to say in words just exactly what he meant. Then his second attempts came back with a congratulatory note on the care with which he had made his definitions, but with a comment on his definition of 'horse': 'Does this definition include clothes' horse, saw horse, horse play, horse dice? Please examine your other definitions with this comment in mind.' Grimly he sat down to modify the definitions which he had believed to be so beautifully exact. He hit upon the following dodge, a phrase which he added to each definition: '—and many other meanings, determined by the context, the speaker and listener, and the idiom of the period.' Finally he stated the proposition that a word is adequately defined when it is used in such a fashion that it means the same thing to the listener as it means to the speaker. He sent this in with the hope that it would settle the matter. He was soon undeceived for he was requested the next day to define 'human nature', 'patriotism', 'justice', 'love', 'honor', 'duty', 'space', 'matter', 'religion', 'god', 'life', 'time', 'society', 'right', and 'wrong'. After three days of fruitless struggle in an attempt to do something with these words, he sent back the following statement: 'Insofar as I am able to tell these words have no meaning whatsoever, for I am unable to devise any means of defining them so that they mean the same to the speaker as to the listener.' The answer that came back was cryptic: 'Let the problem lie, but do not abandon it. Could you design a turbine without a knowledge of calculus and of entropy?' He was then requested to formulate a mechanics of a pseudo-gravitation based on a law of attraction by inverse cubes instead of inverse squares. He became fascinated with the beautiful logical consequences of this problem and produced a monograph on the resulting ballistics. He was then asked if he could design sights for a gun to be fired under the postulated conditions. This request struck him as ridiculous and he demanded an explanation of Olga.

"Olga, what is all this rigamarole? What possible use is it for me to design a worthless gun?"

Olga smiled a long slow smile. "I would like to tell you the meaning but I can't. If you knew the meaning the rigamarole would not be necessary. But you must discover meaning for yourself. We are trying to help you discover the meaning of the words you didn't define."

"I'd like to lay hands on the guy who thought up this last little joke." She took his hand and placed it on her shoulder. "You did? Olga, I thought you were a pal of mine."

"I am, Perry, but it's part of my business to see that your treatment is approached through fields you understand and to watch its effect on you. However I think we can skip a step at this point. You obviously don't want to bother with designing this gun sight. But you could design it, could you not?"

"Certainly. Nothing to it. You see—" Perry launched into a flow of the technicalities used in ordnance and ballistics, and described with sweeps of his hands what would happen to a shell unlucky enough to be constrained by an inversed-cube type acceleration. "—and all this is in vacuo, of course. I wouldn't attempt to predict without empirical data the effect of a gaseous medium constrained by the same field."

"That's enough, Perry. I didn't understand a third of what you said, but I'm convinced that you could design the gunsight. Suppose we had such a gun and set it up here. Could you hit that sailboat over there across the lake?"

"Of course not."

"Why not?"

"Why, the mathematical formulas under which it was designed don't apply to the conditions under which the gun is fired. The more carefully you aimed the more certain you would be of missing."

"Does that suggest anything to you, Perry?"

"No, not off hand."

"You remember those words you didn't define—Weren't those words the names for things by which a man guides his life?—Honor, love, truth, justice, duty, and so forth?"

A look of dawning comprehension came into his face. "Yes, yes, I think so."

"Aren't these things just as powerful to move a man as the hunger of the belly or the stirring of the loins."

"Yes, yes indeed. More powerful."

"Then they *aren't* meaningless. But like that gunsight, unless the meaning you attribute to them bears a correct relationship to the world in which you act, you cannot possibly use them as guides to go where you wish to go. Yet without these guides, a man himself is as meaningless as a gun that can't be aimed."

"You make it sound very plausible, yet a man is not a shell in a gun and truth and honor are not gunsights."

"No, they aren't. Let us drop the analogy before it leads us into absurdities. Nevertheless I think you see that what I said is true, quite independently of the analogy. Men are moved to act by very complicated motivations tagged duty, love, sin, and so forth. You yourself are moved by them and yet you are unable to define what you mean by these terms. You have accepted these concepts more or less unconsciously yet you know so little about them that you cannot possibly know whether they lead where you want to go, or to disaster. If you attempted to pilot a plane with as little knowledge of the controls, you would be sure to wreck it. You are here because you did such faulty piloting of your own life, and smashed another person in the chin in the process."

"Granting that what you say is true—and I don't concede yet that I was wrong to hit that fellow—how do you discover proper meanings for these words that will enable me to conduct myself properly by them?"

"How did you discover how to design gunsights that would enable you to hit the mark?"

"Why the theory of gravitation makes it a mathematical necessity."

"Are you sure? I seem to remember that the theory of gravitation was turned upside down and inside out in your lifetime. Did that cause all the gunsights to be junked?"

He slapped his thigh. "By God, you're right. Exterior ballistics evolved by purely empirical means, trial and error. Whenever we got enough data to analyze we invented formulas to fit. We never tried to make the practice fit the theory. When the theory didn't fit, we junked it and made up a new one. But it worked. We built machines in that way that were marvels of accurate prediction," he said and thought, then his face clouded. "But how can you apply that technique to the problems of living?"

"Well, Perry, so far as I know there are just two ways of working out a practical theory of human relations that will enable us all to live happily together. One is the hard way of trying to work out empirical principles from what we know of the real world. The other is by divine revelation. I won't say that the second way is impossible, but we moderns have grown to distrust it. Our conclusions in 2086 from the first method are embodied in the current code of customs. He who complies with that code will live with reasonably little conflict in 2086 whether he believes that the code is a list of final truths or simply rough generalizations. The code embodies our 2086 meanings for these troublesome words that you could not define. You have other meanings, unspoken, and in my opinion your meanings are both inaccurate and dangerous, for I believe that if you were able to define your code in spoken objective words you would find that your code did not correspond to the real world around you."

"But that still doesn't tell me how you arrive at these customs, or empirical formulas for conduct, or whatever you care to call them."

"Much as you perfected the art of ballistics. By a willingness to junk theories that didn't fit the facts. For example, the churches, by and large, set their faces against divorce. Divorce was a 'sin'. No attempt was made to study marriage and divorce objectively, divorce was 'sin' by divine revelation and that settled it. It is almost inconceivable the amount of harm that was done by that one false generalization alone. By rejecting the dogmatic viewpoint and examining the problem in its environment we reached quite different conclusions. In the 2086 environment divorce is not a 'sin', although it is possible to conceive different social patterns in which divorce would be 'sin'. Consider again the subject of clothing as a taboo. Again a dogmatic generalization for social conduct decreed that it was 'wrong', 'dishonorable', 'immodest' to appear unclothed. Original sin was involved, complicated aesthetic ideas were given a false objective reality, and so forth. An amazing mass of philosophical nonsense was written on this one taboo alone by people who would never think of taking off their clothes in the presence of others in order to see what it felt like. Their faces were resolutely set against such irreverent experiment, even as the scholasticists of the Middle Ages refused to watch any experiment which threw doubt on the perfection of Aristotle's Mechanics, and yet the experiment was always available and easy to perform. In 2086 from purely experimental considerations, the clothes taboo is destroyed. It does not appear in our code of customs, and one may dress or not as convenience and personal aesthetic taste indicates.

"Again, take politics. For centuries philosophers attempted to formulate the perfect state, reasoning from their own unexamined prejudices, which they usually assumed to be divine revelation. In 2086 we consider that the 'perfect state' is a meaningless sound having no objective reality. Instead we set up a political system to achieve whatever we wish to accomplish in 2086. We have no notion that it would have suited 1000 A.D. nor that it would suit contemporary Europe nor that we will leave it unchanged in the future. But we do believe that we have evolved a technique by which we can make the state serve our purposes in any age."

She glanced at the chronometer. "I have other things that I must do now, and I believe that you should think over and develop for yourself any new ideas from this talk. Bye bye!"

VIII

These exercises in realistic thinking continued in various ways. Perry found himself unable to distinguish between activities which were a part of his treatment, events simply intended to entertain and thereby keep him happy in his environment, and activities which he had selected for his own edification or fulfillment. Early in his stay he had expressed a desire to continue with his study of modern mathematics. He was given every facility to do so, but in time lost interest in the face of other activities and, especially, his rapidly growing friendship with Olga. He was surprised to receive a call from Hedrick who urged him to pursue his mathematical studies to the limit and, if possible, to develop some new aspect of the art. Perry inquired if this were standard psychiatric procedure. Hedrick hastened to reassure him, "Not at all, not at all, but if a person under treatment has a mathematical pre-disposition the development of that bent may be used very handily to clear up his particular difficulty. Yours is a case in point. You think very admirably in the field of physics in which your terms are almost entirely mathematical. You are able to make useful predictions and are able to avoid fallacious identification of terms. You are able to appreciate and even invent little mathematical jokes based on a deliberate confusion of terms. You can 'prove' to me that one plus one equals one or air cars won't fly, for our mutual amusement. This does you no harm because you have deliberately confused certain terms and used them with different meanings in the same problem in order to achieve a willfully ludicrous result. When your thinking in social relationships reaches the same order of development, you will no longer be tortured by the emotional upsets that impelled you to consult us."

"Is that all that insanity amounts to, a confusion of terms?"

"Oh my, no. Even in your own case confusion in terms is not the only problem. You not only confuse the various meanings of some terms, but you also fail in certain respects to perceive the pattern of your structural relationship to your environment. This produces trouble which may be likened to that experienced by a thirsty traveler who believes that a heat mirage is a lake. Your trouble is not of that simple order of perception of physical phenomena, but in a much higher order of abstraction. Yet it is as difficult for me to explain to you the exact nature of your trouble as it would be for you to explain a mirage to an ignorant savage. Your only hope of getting the savage to understand a mirage in the fashion in which you understand it would lie in giving him a long course of basic instruction in modern science, having first—and this is very important—un-taught him a thousand superstitions and false identifications with which his mind is crowded. You are now in the process of unlearning your errors and superstitions. At the same time you are beginning to teach yourself a more satisfactory concept of the cosmos. But I haven't answered your question. You are not insane, any more than our savage. You are simply confused, as the savage was. In each case the confusion can be eliminated by proper training. Yours might well have taken place in a children's development center had you been of the proper age. Moreover, because of the maturity and exceptional ability of your mind we can enable you to re-train yourself in a fraction of the time necessary to train a child.

"With respect to other methods of treatment, naturally if a person is truly insane, suffering from physical lesions, whether congenital, traumatic, or pathological, we treat by physical means, surgery, chemical therapy, physical therapy, and so forth. Frequently there is little we can do other than care for them, keep them from harming themselves, or others, and prevent them from reproducing. But in any case in which the brain and nervous structure are not injured, we have not yet failed to achieve a satisfactory re-training into a state of full sanity. Yours is not even a difficult case, my boy. I feel sure that both of us will be satisfied with the result."

Perry stirred uneasily in his seat. "What you say may be true and I would hesitate to contradict you in your own field. Certainly I have acquired a lot of new ideas and new concepts and new ways of thinking about things in the past weeks. Nevertheless, I don't feel any different about the thing that landed me in this mess. I'm still in love with Diana, and I'm jealous as hell of her. I enjoyed taking a poke at that guy Bernard and would enjoy doing it again. I don't want any man to lay a finger on her. In spite of my inability to define human nature, I think you know what I mean by the term, and I think its in human nature that I should feel as I do, and I don't see how you can change human nature, mine or anybody else's."

Hedrick smiled and put the tips of his fingers together carefully, cocked his head on one side and replied, "You are right, my dear boy, entirely right, except about the immutability of human nature, in which you are partially wrong. I am quite prepared to believe that you are physically jealous of your woman in an acutely emotional manner. It is true that this emotion results from your own 'human nature' and that it is potentially present in all males and also in females, although it arises in females from a different source of more recent origin and less deep seated in character. The jealousy of the male for the female may be observed in animal life, in the battling of tom cats, the duels to death of stag deer, and the fighting cock bird. It is present in all animals, human and otherwise, and is both a necessary consequence and a determining cause of the survival of all bisexual life. It is very simple. The male who was unwilling to fight other males for the privilege of sexual intercourse did not reproduce; his line died out. Each generation, by and large, was descended from males who would fight for the females. Any factor in human nature which is necessary or helpful to the continuance and propagation of life may be termed a 'survival factor' and each generation will exhibit by necessity these factors; sexual urge, belly hunger, group loyalty, heliotropism, whatever they may be. You may term, if you wish, the resulting complicated manifold of instincts, desires, reflexes, emotions, and so forth, 'human nature', 'animal nature', or the 'nature of life'. But you must remember that these are complex terms, implying many factors, and arising from myriad environmental circumstances in the history of the race. And you must remember that environments change. Now, a factor in 'human nature' remains a survival factor only as long as the environment continues to make it so. For example on a dairy farm sexual jealousy is no longer a survival factor for bulls; on the contrary a bull is not allowed to fight; his major survival factor is his ability to breed daughters who are big milk producers. It is useless to argue that he is in an artificial environment; the distinction is a specious one. A man-made environment is as 'natural' as that of the jungle, unless you insist on a purely verbal distinction that divorces 'Man' from the rest of nature.

"Perry, you now find yourself in an environment in which the factor of physical sexual jealousy is no longer a survival factor. On the contrary it decreases your chances to survive. Yet the factor still exists in your 'nature'. You say 'that is that' and that nothing can be done about it, which would be true if you were a bull, but you are not a bull and there is an essential difference between modern man and other animals. Men are able consciously to examine their motives, emotions, and so forth, and by a conscious process to inhibit or divert a reaction, reflex, and so forth. He can control his emotions or modify them by conscious application, and thereby change 'human nature'. You think not? Let us consider the case of another survival factor, the fear of falling from a height. You ride in air cars. Are you afraid of the height? Does it cause you any nervousness? Does it upset your digestion, prevent you from sleeping nights, cause you to wake screaming from nightmares? Today the fear of heights is potentially present in that inherited matrix you call 'human nature'. It's nearly as old as the sex urge."

"Say," put in Perry, "you're right. I've had such dreams lately as a result of a fall. But I'm not bothered anymore—not in the least."

"Let's take another case, belly hunger. It is the oldest factor of all reaching back past the origin of bisexual life. If 'human nature' is not subject to change it should be the strongest of all and uncontrollable. Do you drool and slobber at a display of food? Do you fall on it like a wild animal? Do you snatch it from the plate of another? Do you sit up nights worrying about it? Yet it is there and basic. A change in environment would develop it to the point where men would fight for it, claw crusts of bread from dust bins, steal, rob, kill. You can supply many examples from experience and history. Do you begin to see that the active exercise of the factor of sex jealousy is today as stupid, as silly, as uncouth, and as unnecessary as the feeding habits of the jungle?"

Perry nodded soberly. "I begin to see, rationally at least. I'm afraid my emotions won't change quite so readily."

"Don't let that worry you. Proper emotional habits may be acquired like other habits—by conscious exercise over a period of time. If you control your acts along the pattern you desire, and exercise your will, your emotions will change. That may seem unlikely but I assure that it is a report of observed fact. Analogy in the cases of other primitive urges may make it credible to you.

"Before we go further, I would like to point out to you that the factor of sex jealousy as present in you and as exercised in the environment in which you matured was not always present in the same way in all times, places, and culture. Polygamy is, of course, well known to you, if not through experience, at least by report. It is a matter of reported fact that women in polygamous cultures were not made unhappy by the practice. The early Mormon culture is a case in point. Polyandry is less well known but was common in Tibet for a long period and worked very satisfactorily. In certain parts of Asia in recent times it was a common practice for a host to loan his wife or daughter to a guest for the night. It would have been bad form to refuse. Among certain of the Eskimo tribes it was the accepted practice in very recent times to exchange wives for considerable periods usually for reasons of domestic economy. To have disputed the practice or stirred up a fuss about it would have been thought barbaric, not to say immoral. Among certain of the Polynesian tribes promiscuity before marriage was the accepted rule. On the other hand among the Zulus as late as the twentieth century, a maid ready for marriage was examined by a committee of elder women. If they did not pronounce her a *virgo intacta*, she was beheaded. In contrast to this, among many people prostitution was a religious rite, reaching the extreme point in at least one highly developed culture wherein a woman could not marry until she had passed at least one night as a public prostitute. The illustrations from anthropology are endless. I have cited enough to show you that the manifestations of male sex jealousy occurring in the culture in which you were reared are not the result of an inflexible law.

"The case of female sex jealousy of the male differs greatly from that of the male. Female sex jealousy is primarily economic in origin, that of the male is primarily biological. The desire for sexual intercourse is not an important survival factor in the female. She may be impregnated without it, or even in the face of a strong contra-desire, as in rape. The dominant survival factor for the female is the need for protection and support during gestation and while caring for infant children. This will take the form of possessive sexual jealousy in any environment which requires her to capture the full attention of one man to achieve the end. It is not necessary that she be consciously aware of this. It is automatic. By and large, in such an environment, only the females who function in that pattern are able to reproduce. Many environments do not lay this requirement on the female. Yours did, to a marked degree, if the literature and records of your period are correct.

"From all I can gather the competition among women for the exclusive attention of one man must have been as fierce and ruthless as any jungle battle. It appears from history that the women of your period and before were able to freeze into law and creed that a man must take one woman and support her and her children to the exclusion of any other interest. A woman who connived with a man to break this stringent code of battle, as in adultery, was destroyed by her sisters as completely as they were able.

"Nevertheless, even in your day, the signs of environmental

change and consequent changes in your 'immutable' human nature were in evidence so far as women were concerned. They were gaining greater economic freedom and consequent greater sexual independence. They no longer needed to the same extent the economic support of husbands. It was even possible for a woman of foresight and ability to bear and rear children without the economic support of a male. With increased knowledge and use of practical convenient methods of controlling conception women were liberated somewhat from the pressing necessity for capturing a man and holding him. With the advent of the New Economic Regime women no longer required the services of a man to support herself or her offspring. For the first time in history women reached the dignity of social equality with men. Up to that time any equality with men granted to them was spurious, a mere verbalism, having no real foundation in fact.

"The social consequences were of enormous importance both to women and to men. For the first time in history men and women could mate as equals without fear of concealed motives. Life was enormously enriched thereby. Love between the sexes could develop aesthetically in a way never before possible. Freed of the twin vices of masqued rape and masqued prostitution, it developed a beauty, a variety, and a richness limited only by the imagination and sensitivity of the individuals concerned. Not only did it glorify the love between man and woman but it made possible a deeper, less antagonistic, relation between man and his brother, woman and her sister, for the primary causes of rivalry were gone. Gone for men as well as for women. Why?

"You recall that the primary cause of sex jealousy in men was the desire for intercourse. In former cultures other men might lure away a desired woman with economic bait or capture her bodily. Now that the woman is no longer subject to coercion but is a free agent, the competition between males for a woman's charms is necessarily by gentler means. Excesses of jealousy are likely to defeat their own ends and lose a woman completely. You are lucky that your chosen woman was sufficiently primitive in her emotion and loyal in her intellect that she decided to stick by you. Many women would have told you to go to the devil and taken up with a less selfish man."

Perry was startled to hear himself called selfish. He started to speak, then thought better of it and held his tongue, his face a study in mixed emotions. Hedrick continued.

"As a matter of practice a man usually finds that he has lost nothing at all by ceasing to respond to the emotion of jealousy. Strictly from a biological point of view there is much data to prove that potential capacity for sexual indulgence is much greater in most women than it is in most men, so much so, that an average woman could be the mistress of, let us say, two or three average men without loss to the men. On the spiritual side there is enough of the 'Mother of All Living' principle in the nature of any woman to permit her, if she chooses, to be the source of spiritual refreshment to many men. Any man who believes the contrary is a fool who judges the soul of woman by the paucity of his own. He need only look at the mother of any large brood to know that the capacity of a woman to replenish the soul with her love is limited only by the scope of her field.

"I speak now of the ordinary run of men and women. In some cases a man may be a sufficient companion in every way for more than one woman, in which case the situation is reversed but is otherwise similar."

"Do you mean to say that such combinations as you have described are the usual order today?"

"Not at all. Not at all. We Americans in 2086 remain, by and large, monogamous. If for no other reasons, the approximate fifty-fifty balance of the sexes, habit, and convenience would make it so. In addition to that, it takes time for a rich love to mature and one does not lightly throw away such a possession. You think that you are in love with Diana today, my boy, but if you are still with her ten years from now, you will wonder why you graced so thin and feeble an emotion with that name! No, we pair off and stay paired on the average, but that does not preclude the formation of other associations either more temporary, or less deep, or both. No one partner in life can supply all the possible richnesses of living to another. I speak now not only of physical sexual associations, but also of associations mental and spiritual, such as I observe that you are forming—You'll pardon me saying so—with our good friend Olga."

Perry blushed to his hair roots.

"No, no, son. No cause for embarrassment. I invaded your private sphere because I am your physician and have occasion to. Olga is a fine woman, finer than you now imagine. Your association with her is bound to do you good in every way. I am happy to see it." Master Hedrick yawned and glanced at the chronometer. "If I don't turn in fairly soon I shall need a stimulant in the morning to attend properly to my duties. I've just one more thing to say; I want you to make a list of the things you expected to protect or obtain by driving this other young buck away from Diana. Be as explicit as possible and mind how you use your terms. Take as long as necessary and let me see the result. By the way, when do you expect her back?"

"Tomorrow, probably. She just ran up to Chicago for a special broadcast."

"That's good. There's a rather interesting job over in surgery tomorrow that she would like to see. Diana's mother is coming here to perform a dexter cerebrectomy. You might drop in too, if such things interest you. Accident case. Very sad. Young rocket pilot."

"Thank you, sir. I think I will if Diana is back."

Hedrick arose and knocked out his pipe.

"Just a minute, sir. Doesn't anyone maintain a lifetime monogamy anymore?"

Hedrick desisted from tickling Captain Kidd's belly and considered this. "Very possibly. There are a lot of possibilities in a hundred and ninety million people. Seems unlikely though. You might try your hand at working out the equation of probability involved, if it amuses you. I think you'll find enough data on file over in the Archives to give it a try. Well, good night."

"Good night, sir."

IX

"I would have come to see you sooner, but the problem presented unusual features that required study." The speaker was a little stoop-shouldered man with a bulging bald head. He addressed Perry over a glass of sherry in the latter's cottage. "When Master Hedrick told me that he wanted me to explain the theory and practice of our present economic system to a man with the point of view of America 1939, I thought that he was in need of some of his own treatment. But when he elucidated I realized that I was confronted with the most startling problem in pedagogy I had ever undertaken. I wasn't able to undertake it without preparation. I had to search out and read much of the literature of your period and then spend several days in meditation in order to try to feel the period, understand the point of view, evaluations, and the fallacies of your time."

Perry shifted uneasily in his chair. "I didn't intend to cause you so much trouble, Master Davis."

"No trouble at all. You have done me a service. This is a most fascinating approach to the subject that has been my principle interest. By preparing to explain it to you, I understand it better myself. First tell me what you know of the present system."

"Well, in the first place it has retained private enterprise in industry. There I suppose it's a form of capitalism."

Davis nodded. "An inadequate word, but let it stand."

Perry continued, "However, although production, and so forth, is private enterprise, each citizen receives a check for money, or what amounts to the same thing, a credit to each account each month, from the government. He gets this free. The money so received is enough to provide the necessities of life for an adult, or to provide everything that a child needs for its care and development. Everybody gets these checks—man, woman, and child. Nevertheless, practically everyone works pretty regularly and most people have incomes from three or four times to a dozen or more times the income they receive from the government. There is no such thing as unemployment because there is always a demand for more production. Consequently wages are high. However prices are low, and to make the situation even more confusing, merchants regularly sell goods at less than cost, and the government pays them the difference. That is the general set up, if I understand what I have been told. It sounds impossible, an Alice-in-Wonderland business, filled with contra-dictions that deny common sense. It disturbs me. It challenges my reason. I'd be less annoyed at a perpetual motion machine."

Davis smiled. "I appreciate your difficulty. It is necessary first to clean your mind of a number of the errors, superstitions, and half truths that went by the name of 'economics' in your day. Consider for a moment the physical facts of the situation that you see around you. Disregard the money aspect for a moment and think in terms of goods, people, production and consump-tion. What then is the situation?"

"Well—I see that everyone has a pretty high standard of liv-ing, they live in good houses, and eat plenty of good food, and they have plenty of the comforts of life. That's the consumption side. On the production side I see factories and farms, and so forth, that produce at a high rate with lots of labor saving machinery. Nobody has to work very hard unless he really wants to. Anybody that does gets a big return for it in terms of goods and services."

"Do you see any difficulty in the picture now—still leaving money out of it?"

"Well, no. The physical wealth is there and the work done is enough to turn it into a high standard of living."

"Now describe 1939 in terms of physical economy—again leaving out money. Be careful not to use any term that implies money, such as wages, debt, price, and so forth."

Perry grinned. "You're preparing a trap for me. I can see it coming."

Davis was serious. "It's not a trap. It's a necessary expedient to lead your mind around its ingrown economic errors and enable it to think correctly. Go ahead and describe it."

"Okay. The country was just as rich in natural resources—richer as a matter of fact. We had plenty of factories to fabricate raw materials, but lots of them were shut down. Our farms produced liberally, plenty of good food, enough to feed everybody well. We had the technical knowledge, tools and materials to produce an abundance of luxuries and comforts, and in fact we did, for our retail stores were stocked to the ceilings with every sort of desirable article. That is the production side. On the consumption side about half of the population had less to eat than it needed and that of poor quality and wrong variety. In other respects they were worse off, living in houses that were fire traps, and disease breeders, frequently without running water and with primitive heating systems. Most of them had no medical or dental attention and were rotten with disease. My dentist once told me that four-fifths of the population never received dental care in their lives. The next third or so of the population just barely got by. They lived in fair comfort but in the fear of slipping back into squalor. A small group at the top had more than they needed of everything. While I'm speaking of consumption I suppose I should mention that we made a practice of destroying annually a large part of our production, especially food. Some people considered this wasteful, and we devised means to produce less rather than destroy part of what we had produced. But it came to the same thing."

"You speak of a small group that had too much. Do you know what the result would have been if everybody had consumed share and share alike?"

"As a matter of fact I do. I used to worry about that and worked it out on my slide rule in 1938 from some figures quoted in *Time* magazine. That was a news sheet published in those days. The average national income came to about one hundred and thirty dollars per month per family, which wouldn't have been a very high standard of living. But the same figures showed that only thirty per cent of the population had that much or more, seventy per cent had less. I have to mention money at this point, but I'll translate it into goods. A family at that standard of living would live in a cheap house, drive a second hand car, set a decent but not fancy table, have a radio, and go to the movies occasionally. But they would have no reserves, and sickness, accident, or the loss of a job would land them almost overnight in squalor."

"Then—still speaking in physical terms—was this average standard of living the best the country was capable of, by and large?"

"Oh no. Not nearly. The country was able to produce at least twice as much as was actually produced. Some authorities said three times or more. But anyone could see by looking around him that much more could have been produced. For one thing at least ten million people were out of work."

"Very well, then. You have described two different economic

systems in terms of the physical realities involved. Now which one of them denies common sense, which one challenges your reason?"

Perry smiled. "You've sprung your trap, just as I anticipated. The 1939 system is the ridiculous one, certainly—when you look at it that way. But that still doesn't explain your cock-eyed financial arrangements."

"The paradoxes you appeared to find arise from flaws in your training. They have no reality. I am about to state an axiom: Anything which is physically possible can be made financially possible, if the people of a state desire it."

"That sounds good, but is it true?"

"Yes, if the people of the state understand finance. Tell me, what is money?"

"Money—money is a lot of things. It is a medium of exchange, based on some precious metal, usually gold. It is also a commodity, bought and sold, and rented out for interest. And it's capital for industry."

"Which one of those things is it?"

"Well—when you come right down to it, I guess money is gold."

"That's what J.P. Morgan thought, at least he told a Senate committee that in 1912. I wonder whether he was lying or deluded. Try this definition: 'Money is anything which can always be swapped for goods, or services.' I believe that you will find that to be the only characteristic common to all money, and common to nothing else. How much money does a country need?"

"How can anybody answer that question?"

"Apparently nobody tried to before the present economic regime. Money was expanded and contracted in a most senseless fashion. The panic of 1907 for example was produced by a deliberate contraction of money. But the answer to the question is simple, and arises from the nature or purpose of money as we defined it. A country needs enough money to enable its citizens to perform all desired exchanges of goods and services. Your 1939 system did not accomplish this; our 2086 system does."

"But look—there was plenty of money in 1939. That doesn't make sense."

"Haven't you just told me that in 1939 there were millions of people who needed things they couldn't buy? And weren't there merchants who had all these things and wanted to sell them very badly, yet couldn't sell them? Wouldn't all this have been very different and vastly improved if the people in dire want had had that money in their pockets to buy from the merchants who had to sell or go bankrupt? Isn't that a shortage of money?"

"Yes, of course. But where are you leading me?"

"Patience. In 2086 the government gives money to the people to do that necessary buying."

"Yes, I know. Master Cathcart told me that the government got this money off the printing press or out of the inkwell—in other words fiat money. How can it be worth anything?"

"We decided that money was anything which *always* could be swapped for goods and services. That implies that the person who accepts it believes that he can do likewise. Therefore money is money as long as everybody believes it is money. There is a touchstone which will enable you to determine whether or not people will believe in money: Can you use it to pay taxes? Will the government give you something for it of value, postal service for example? If the people collectively as a state will accept it, then so will the individuals. Our 'fiat' money qualifies. The United States will accept it in exchange for things of value. That is no longer true of your gold. It can't be used for taxes. You may or may not be able to swap it off, it isn't money, and you may be stuck with it. As a matter of fact all United States currency has been 'fiat' currency ever since the United States suspended gold payments in 1933. Since that time the gold standard has been simply a fiction convenient in party politics. However I believe that your principle difficulty is in understanding why it is necessary for the government to create new money and give it away to the consuming public. In order to understand that, it is first necessary to understand the mathematics of the relationship between prices and purchasing power.

"Before we go into the mathematical theory, let me state the fact which we are to explain: In 1939, and before, the sum total of the purchasing power of the public was always less than the total price of the goods offered for sale. This is just another way of saying that 'overproduction', with its attendant unemployment, poverty, labor warfare, and so forth, was a chronic condition. As a matter of fact it is not necessary to understand the mathematics behind it as long as you observe the fact, just as it isn't necessary to know how a house caught fire in order to see that a house is on fire and to realize that something must be done about it. I stated that 'over-production' was chronic and that it is identically the same thing as saying that the public as a whole didn't have the money with which to buy the goods offered for sale. You will certainly agree that such was the condition from 1929 to 1939. It was generally recognized and the government even went so far as to partially make up the spread between prices and income by direct relief—giving money away—and wages for made work—giving money away with a moralistic sugar coating. This would have been sensible had the government created the money by fiat. Instead they borrowed it from the *banks* who created it by fiat. This was silly as it piled up a national debt to be reckoned with in the future and the money wasn't one whit sounder under the fiat of the banks than it would have been by government fiat. For please understand that the money lent the government by the banks to provide relief did not come into existence until it was borrowed. The bankers took it out of an empty vault—they fished it out of the inkwell. This may be hard to believe but it is the literal truth. Every time a bank loaned money in those days it created it. Of course President Holmes would successfully reclaim this practice for the government decades later, but at this time it was entirely imprudent.

"But to return to 'over-production'. Before 1929 in the period after the World War until the market crash, the spread between production and consumption was absorbed in several ways; an enormous increase in private credit or debt especially in the development of installment buying, exploitation of foreign fields particularly in Central and South America—which means to give away goods and get engraved paper in return, which later turns out to be worthless; and in losses suffered by practically all farmers and many businessmen. You see, a large percentage of businesses failed even in boom times in which case their inventories were sold below cost.

"The condition in the World War years is simple to understand. During war, production goes at maximum speed for the war machine and burns up the excess. Of course an enormous load of debt is created which must someday be cancelled in some fashion. Before the World War there were many years in which the pattern was similar either to the boom twenties or to the depression thirties. In either case production always ran ahead of consumption and was disposed of in the usual ways; by the creation of debt, by destruction of price values through bankruptcy, by sending more goods out of the country than were taken in, or by outright destruction of goods as in war, or, as was done in peace time, by crop destruction.

"The case in which more goods are shipped out each year than are imported deserves special mention. For many years this was regarded as the ideal economic condition although any child can see the absurdity of it, but it was called by all sorts of fancy names; 'Favorable Gold Balance', 'Favorable Trade Balance', 'The American Plan', 'Cornerstone of American Prosperity'. It was taught in the public schools as a natural law."

"Yes," mused Perry, "I remember being taught that in grammar school. My geography book devoted a whole section to telling how necessary it was."

"As a matter of fact it was as vicious as it was silly. Each nation tried to sell more than it bought, and this was the basic cause of every war in modern times. The stupidity of the idea should have been obvious, but the nature of the financing system made it inevitable. Since production *always* exceeded consumption by a wide margin throughout this period,* it was necessary for a nation to get rid of its excess as best it could or suffer severe economic upset at home. Many were the devices to promote this, for example, the 'protective' tariff and the subsidizing of the merchant marine.

"There was only one period in which this peculiar financial fallacy was suited to the needs of the country, and that was in the days of the frontier. The system created bankruptcy and poverty, and the victims moved west and developed the country. It is customary to speak of population pressure as causing the movement west, but that is true only in a limited sense. The east was never too crowded in the pioneer days to support its population insofar as land and raw materials were concerned, but it already had a financial system which automatically created a spread between

---

*The reader need not accept this without proof. Fortunately the records of the period are available in the Washington Archives. See statistics of the Department of Commerce, et al., for those years.

                                        The Author

purchasing power and production, and thereby automatically created an unemployed class, which moved west with the next wagon train to rehabilitate itself in a simpler economy. Oh yes, we had an unemployed class in Andrew Jackson's day, but we called them pioneers!

"So much for the simple fact that in your 1939 economic system over-production or under-consumption or a shortage of purchasing power was a chronic condition. Now let us examine the mathematical nature of purchasing power to discover why this was so. In so doing we shall discover the possible solutions and select the one we like. You see I've done this problem before and can show off how clever I am. You know about Little Jack Horner? I've always suspected that he knew where the plum was before he stuck in his thumb." A grin split Davis' saturnine visage and made him look like a little bald-headed gnome.

"Consider, if you please, two typical units of production, a factory and a farm. Let the factory be large, an employer with many employees; let the farm be small, a one-family affair. These two cases will be typical—insofar as price and purchasing power are concerned—of the entire economic organism. First, the factory: It makes, let us say, shoes. These shoes are placed on the market at a definite price. This price consists of two parts; the cost to the owner of the factory of making the shoes, plus a profit. The cost consists of a number of items, of which the principle are wages to employees, cost of raw materials, depreciation on capital goods, rent of land, interest on invested capital, and taxes. The additional portion of the price is the profit. This is the return to the owner or entrepreneur for his time, personal labor, ingenuity, and so forth, and is the source from which he must support himself and his family. To assume that profit is unnecessary is to assume that employers don't eat. It was popular in your day to attack the 'profit system'. We shall see that profits to an entrepreneur are *not* the cause of unemployment and financial distress. Of course there will arise the question of some entrepreneurs receiving a disproportionate amount of production as their profits, but that is a question of morals to be regulated according to the current customs. It does not in itself cause unemployment, as we shall see. As a matter of fact most persons who undertake the enterprise of new production, or entrepreneurs, did not make an excessive profit; most of them made no profit and went bankrupt. That is a simple matter of record. In your day eighteen out of nineteen businessmen failed in the long run. The groups who attacked the 'profit system' were beating a dead dog.

"Nevertheless, since entrepreneurs must eat, profits are a legitimate part of the cost of production. Henceforth we shall include them as cost charges and consider that the necessary value of an article of production is its total cost, or cost to the entrepreneur plus his necessary profit."

Perry interrupted. "Do you mean to say that the profit system in my day was okay? It seems to me that the profit system was always being attacked as the villain in the piece."

"The profit system was not the villain in the piece. The villain was ignorance of the workings of the economic mechanism, in which the entrepreneurs or industrial leaders were the greatest offenders. At the very least the laborers knew that something was wrong and demanded a change, but the industrial entrepreneurs denied that any change was needed, and stubbornly resisted change with the ignorant willfulness of a Marie Antoinette. Furthermore they possessed the economic and political power to resist change. In that way they were the villains and were responsible for all the tragedy of your era. But let's not condemn them too heartily, as they were ignorant and stupid rather than innately vicious.

"But now let's prove the statements I have made. Let's put this factory into operation and see how a cycle of production and consumption works. I mentioned a shoe factory. That will give us too limited a case to understand the whole industrial system. You understand the mathematical principle of the general case, the one in which all possible factors appear. Consequently any individual problem can be solved if you can solve the general case. Of course you do, very well then, let this factory be the general case of any production unit in the country which employs labor and uses capital. Its raw materials will be the materials it processes even though those materials have previously been processed after leaving mother earth. Thus steel plate or tanned leather may be termed raw material for automobiles factories and luggage factories. The term factory includes buildings and chattels of every sort used in production but which are not themselves the goods produced by the factory. Land includes the sites of buildings, rights of way, and so forth. Do you follow me?"

Perry nodded. "Sure. It's like any algebraic general case, like the general quadratic equation for instance; ax squared plus bx plus c equals zero gives a general solution of x equals negative b plus or minus the quantity the square root of b squared minus four ac all divided by 2a. Substituting the conditions of a particular case gives the answer for that particular case." *

"Exactly. Let's set up the general case of a production-consumption cycle under the rules of your period and work out a few problems. Then perhaps we shall see the principles involved and be able to state a general solution which will answer all our questions about economics."

---

*$ax^2 + bx + c = 0$ $x = \dfrac{-b \quad b^2 - 4ac}{2a}$

The full solution of this general problem of the second degree can be found in any textbook of primary algebra.

The Author

Perry scratched his head. "Look. That's all very well in simple algebra like quadratic equations, but in economics we deal with an indefinite number of unknowns and too many factors. How can we possibly do this?"

"We'll cross that bridge when we come to it. All special cases in the actual world are complex, it is true, even in quadratic equations. But the general case may turn out to have pleasing simplicity. Let's try to formulate it, and see. Have you pen and paper? Let's write down our elements. What are they?"

Perry thought. "A factory."

"Yes."

"The entrepreneur or industrialist."

"Go ahead."

"Raw materials, and labor, and land."

"Continue."

"Consumers."

"That is right, but who are they?"

"Everybody. All of the public."

Davis nodded. "True, but this is the general case. What does that imply?" Perry looked puzzled. "I'll tell you, then. The consumers are the people you mention plus their dependents, and no others. Even retired people enter the picture as capitalists or dependents, as well as consumers."

"Yes, I think I see that."

"Each individual has a dual role, appearing both on the production side and on the consumption side. Even a child appears as a producer through his father and appears as a consumer of goods purchased by his parents. We can disregard dependents from here on as they are represented economically by the head of the family."

"How does a widow living on insurance appear in the set up?"

"As a consumer of earlier production of the deceased head of a family. We'll take that case up later when we are ready to deal with it. Let's get on with our set up. What else do we need?"

"A bank or banks."

"Yes, and bankers, stockholders, bank clerks, and so forth. Will you let me lump them together as a bank and a banker, remembering of course the collective nature of the terms?"

"Okay, I guess."

"Very well, then. Do we need anything else?"

"Not that I can think of."

"Was the United States an anarchy?"

"No, of course not."

"Then we have the government, and all of the subdivisions of government, public servants, taxes, and laws, and the government as a consumer."

"This grows complicated."

"Not too complicated. Let's represent government, and all subdivisions, as 'US', which you can think of as 'United States' or as 'us', for in the United States the government is everybody taken collectively. Public servants work for 'US'. Now do we have all elements?"

"How about farmers and professional men? They are certainly consumers."

"Yes, that's true. The case of the farmer is simple. Economically speaking, he produces in the same fashion as the factory owner, using the same elements; labor, raw material, land, enterprise, and so forth. If he employs no labor but himself and his family, 'profit' should appear as a large item in cost, and labor wages as zero. It becomes simply a special case under the general case. The professional man appears as a different type of laborer when he is hired by a production unit, for example corporation lawyers. Professional men serving the consuming public directly appear in the production-consumption chain in a one-to-one relationship of transfer without destruction of purchasing power. When you pay a medical man ten dollars for advice, your potential power to purchase and consume doughnuts or automobiles is reduced ten dollars and that of the doctor is increased by ten dollars. There is another element we have not named however. Can you guess it?"

"Mmmmmn—no, I'm afraid not. It seems to me we've covered the—Wait a moment. Technique! Knowledge."

"Exactly. Most knowledge is free to all of us. But some things are patented or copyrighted. Let's call the owners of techniques inventors. Now we are ready to roll. If we set up our hypothetical domestic economy so that it is structurally similar in every way to the economy of your period, it should work like your period. If we change the man-made laws to those of this present period, it will work like this present period. The natural laws involved remain the same structurally. If we can distinguish between man-made rules and natural necessity, we will know what we can and what we can't do with an economic system."

"How can we make any such complicated set up in our heads and be sure that it will work out in practice, Master Davis?"

"I shan't ask you to carry all of the moving elements of a complicated function in your head. Let's make a model. I see a set of chess men over there. May I use them? They will do nicely for people. Now have you anything I can use for counters?" Perry rummaged around and produced a box of poker chips. "Gaming chips? That's fine. Now we need something to represent the goods we are to produce and consume. What do you suggest? I'll need a number of units, a hundred or more."

"How about a box of crackers?" suggested Perry.

"A happy thought. Distinctly consumption goods. But we would get crumbs all over the table and they are rather bulky. Do you have any playing cards?"

"Surely." Perry arose and returned with them. "Here are a couple of packs."

"Very well. Let each card represent one unit of production of equal value. They represent all sorts of items; clothing, food, air cars, games, stereo records, books, and so forth. For convenience we split them up into equal-valued units. Now take the chess men and give them their functions. The black king is our entrepreneur, industrialist, or farmer." Davis wrote this on a slip of paper and tucked it under the base of the black king. "There. We will know him when we see him." You will notice that his tag reads 'Entrepreneur-Consumer' to remind us of his dual function. The black queen is his wife. Place her with him. Put a pawn with them as their children. Now another pawn for her father who is dependent on them. He's a crusty old gentleman who hasn't worked since McKinley was shot and thinks the country is going to hell. The white king is the banker. We'll write a tag for him, 'Banker-Consumer'. This box you keep the chess men in will do as a bank, and this book can be a factory. Put tags on them, but don't place the factory on the table yet. It has not yet been built. The black bishop owns the land on which the factory is to rest. He must first be satisfied. The white castle owns a process to be used in our manufacture of playing cards. Now take five or six pawns and mark them 'Laborers-Consumers'. Mark the black horses 'Owners of Raw Materials-Consumers'. Take the white bishops and mark them 'Government Employees-Consumers'. Take a separate tag and mark it 'US' but don't place a chessman on it, as we must not personify the government. 'US' is all of us, acting collectively.*

---

*The reader is urged to make this set up and play it through as he reads. Otherwise the value of the demonstration will be lost. If chessmen are not available; bottles of ink, spools, tin soldiers, and so forth, will serve. Beans, dominoes, or marbles will serve as counters.

The Author

"Now we are ready to run through a typical economic cycle. Call it one eon in length and let it be the time from the building of the factory until it is depreciated in value to zero and is obsolete. Something around twenty years if you must think in definite terms, but it isn't necessary to do so. Suppose you identify yourself with the entrepreneur, Perry, and I'll play the other pieces. You see a demand for playing cards and determine to manufacture them. You have your eye on a suitable site which you can lease at a reasonable price, and you know of a new process that you can buy up. But you haven't the working capital, all of your wealth being tied up in tangible property which you don't want to liquidate. So you go to the banker and ask for a loan of a hundred shekels. You explain your idea and offer security worth quite a bit more than a hundred shekels. From where we sit we see that the bank contains only twenty shekels, the capital reserve required by law. One might think that the banker would say, 'Sorry, Old man. You've got a sound proposition and I'd like to accommodate you, but there isn't that much money in the bank.' But he says nothing of the sort; he lends you the money. How does he do it? You give him a promissory note saying:

> Dear Banker,
> I.O.U. 100 shekels at 10% per eon.
> Signed,
> Entrepreneur

He enters that on the books as a bank asset, credits your account with one hundred shekels, gives you a bank book, and some blank checks, and you thank him for the money, which is new money, monetized by your security and existing only as bookkeeping entries. To symbolize this I hand you these hundred chips, which you must think of as bank credit, or check book money, not as greenbacks, nor metal coin. But you may use them as money in every respect for the banker will cash a few of them from time to time out of the small stock of cash he keeps on hand. He can afford to do this because only on rare occasions will all holders of bank credit ask for cash all at once, placing a run on the bank. Usually cash money paid out by the bank comes back the next day and is re-deposited.

"You have your hundred shekels now and can commence operations. You lease a site for four shekels for the eon. Put four chips by the black bishop. You build your factory, eight shekels for raw materials, eight shekels for labor. Pay out your chips. Now pay the inventor four shekels for the use of his process. Your wages for labor during the eon amount to forty-four shekels. Pay it out. And for raw materials thirty shekels. You will have taxes of ten shekels during the eon."

"I can't pay them. I've only two chips left."

"Never mind. You'll be selling some playing cards soon, and can pay them as you go along. You now manufacture during the eon sixty-three playing cards. Stack them there by the factory. You need eight shekels profit in the course of the eon to support yourself and your family. You figure out what your market price must be for playing cards in order to accomplish this. What would it be?"

Perry set down his expenses and added them up as follows:

Land rent	4 shekels
Factory (labor)	8 "
" (material)	8 "
Production (labor)	44 "
" (material)	30 "
Royalty to Inventor	4 "
Taxes	10 "

Profit   8 shekels
Interest on loan   10 "

                                    ———
                              126 shekels to be recovered
                                      as price.
63 produced units to be sold; therefore price must be 2
shekels each.

Perry looked up. "I get two shekels per card."

"Correct. As you can see, I arranged the figures to give round numbers."

"But I can't possibly sell sixty-three cards at that price. There are only ninety-eight shekels out there to buy my product."

"Don't be in a hurry. Start selling and see what happens. We will assume this time that all these people that received money from you need all the consumption goods they can afford. Sell to them."

Perry dealt out cards to 'Labor', 'Land owner', 'Inventor', and 'Owners of raw materials', and collected two chips for each card.

"How many cards do you have left?"

"Fourteen."

"You have a lot of money on hand. Better pay your taxes."

"Okay." Perry placed ten chips on 'US'.

"Now I'll act for Uncle Sam and pay the public servants four shekels, buy raw materials for four shekels, and use two shekels to buy consumption goods from you."

"Here you are." Perry handed Davis a playing card who placed it on 'US' and gave Perry the remaining two chips.

"Now sell goods to 'Public servants' and 'Owners of raw materials'."

Perry did so, handing out four cards and receiving back eight shekels.

"Now pay the interest on your loan. You'll be doing so in the course of the time period."

"Okay, here's ten shekels."

Davis placed them in the bank. "The banker, with his family, clerks, and so forth, needs some consumption goods. Here are two shekels." Perry solemnly received them and proffered one card to Davis.

"Now pay yourself your profit of eight shekels. Turn it over to your wife. She handles the money in your household. She takes it and spends it for consumption goods." Perry took eight shekels, placed it by the black queen, then picked it up again and placed it by the black king, and placed four cards under the black queen. Davis added a comment. "That operation is symbolic of thousands of wives of entrepreneurs spending their husbands incomes on all manners of goods produced in thousands of factories.

"The eon is over. The cycle is finished. Your factory has depreciated to no value at all. I must remind you that your note is due at the bank."

"Wait a minute. Why do you assume that the factory is now worthless?"

"It isn't necessary. Had you figured for a shorter period, the cost item labeled 'Factory' would have been just the percentage of depreciation during the shorter period. There would have been a smaller number of articles manufactured, smaller items in all respects. The final cost per unit would have been the same, but we decided to run through a full cycle, from the beginning to the end of a producing unit. But come, come, you are stalling for time. What about my note? You owe me one hundred shekels."

Perry counted up his chips and grinned at him. "You'll have to whistle for it. I have only ninety-two shekels. I have four playing cards you can have for the balance."

"I've no use for playing cards. I'm a banker and I have your promise to pay."

Perry shrugged his shoulders and did not reply.

Davis continued. "Very well let's get on with the next stage of the game. You have four units of 'over-production' and can't quite pay your note at the bank. But your banker respects your ability. Your original security is still good, and the banker says that conditions are essentially 'sound'. He re-finances you to go into production again. You sign a new note, this time for one hundred and eight shekels and now have one hundred shekels to your account. But your banker cautions you not to be guilty of 'over-production'. You go away, feeling somewhat confused as you don't see where you made your mistake, but the banker must be right for you certainly were left with four playing cards that you could not sell. You decide that the market only requires fifty-nine cards instead of the sixty-three you produced. So you do it all over again, producing only fifty-five cards which with your carry over of four gives you fifty-nine to sell. What is the result?"

"Why, I come out even I suppose."

"Do you? Last time you spent forty-four shekels on wages and thirty shekels on materials to build sixty-three playing cards. How much do you spend this time?"

"Let me see. Forty-four and thirty is seventy-four. The labor and materials cost per unit is one sixty-third of that." Perry set it up on his slide rule. "It comes to one point one one seven five (1.1175) shekels per card. I'm producing fifty-five cards this time. Fifty-five times one point one seven five is sixty-four and seven-tenths shekels."

"Those people bought thirty-seven cards with their seventy-four shekels last time. What can they buy this time?"

"Thirty-two and a fraction."

"Exactly. You sell your best market five fewer cards than last time. As a result of doing the only reasonable thing, you have more cards left over than before, you've thrown some people out of work, you have created less real wealth for the community to use and you are even farther from being able to pay off your note at the bank for you now owe one hundred and eight shekels and have only ninety-one with which to pay."

"Ninety-one? I figured ninety-two."

"No, ninety-one? Perhaps you forgot that your interest is eleven shekels on a hundred and eight."

"That's right. I figured ten, like last time. Now what happens? It looks like I'm going broke."

"Wait a bit. Do you see what caused the original 'over-production'?"

"Why yes, the banker got money out of me that he didn't turn around and spend with me. Everybody else spent their money as it came in."

"Then what's the trouble?"

"Well, it looks to me as if it was the interest you expected me to pay. If I hadn't had to pay you that interest I'd have come out even."

"Not so fast. They weren't exactly equal and could not therefore have been the same thing. Even bankers have to eat. Why should he run a bank if he isn't paid to do it? Tell me, what would the effect have been if anyone else had saved part of his income instead of spending it?"

"Ohhhoh!" Perry slapped his thigh. "I see! If anyone saves income that he receives from the cycle, it is thrown out of balance and over-production results."

"Exactly. In the problem that we have just gone through I cast the banker as the thrifty villain simply because banks were the worst offenders. They charged as much interest as they could get, and spent very little on consumption, whereas the workers, by and large, had to spend all they got as they went along. But all were guilty of the economic crime of not spending all their purchasing power and thereby saving themselves into bankruptcy, even a father with his life insurance policy and baby with his penny bank."

"Wait a minute, Master Davis. It seems to me that money saved eventually finds its way back into purchasing, even after several years. It all balances out in time. There should have been some consumers spending their savings in that first cycle to make up for those who managed to save."

"There were, of course. If savings are actually tucked away in a sock, it doesn't do much harm. It balances out with just a small carry over of inventories. But most money is not saved that way. Ordinary people invest in life insurance and savings accounts. Industrialists and financiers put it into capital expansion—use it to increase production. In each case it goes into new production."

"But how can that be harmful? We have just shown that money used for production creates new purchasing power to buy the goods produced."

"That's true but you are looking at just one part of the picture. Listen to me carefully. This is the crucial point: Potential purchasing power not spent for consumption but saved and invested for production in a later cycle has appeared as cost in both cycles. When it reappears as purchasing power in the second cycle, it is needed there, and still leaves the first cycle out of balance. For example, if money saved out of your playing card cycle were saved to finance a jelly bean production cycle every shekel of it would appear as cost in the jelly beans and would be needed to purchase jelly beans. It's not available to buy playing cards. To make this exposition rigorous I should mention the possibility that capital funds are occasionally spent on consumption and that money is sometimes taken out of production entirely, but this also produces unemployment and its attendant evils. The Panic of 1907 was of this nature, artificially created by the Morgan Bank and associated interests.

"But let's get back to your playing card factory. It is in trouble. These cycles continue. Each time the bank owns a bigger piece of your business and more of your employees are out of work. Eventually they are in dire distress and private charity cannot carry the load. Congress provides relief. At first Congress tries to pay for relief with new taxes but you business men howl that you are losing money now, which is true. Taxes on everybody—such as the sales tax—rob Peter to pay Paul, and increases purchasing power not a whit. It helps a little to tax the higher bracket incomes but in the long run that inhibits production by striking at a source of capital expansion. Congress is forced to look elsewhere for money to subsidize purchasing power and provide relief, for the spread between production and purchasing power has grown enormous, more than thirty percent in your day, billions of dollars a year. Some congressman from the middle west who cut his teeth on the Bryan campaigns proposes that the government print greenbacks to provide relief for the unemployed, but the bankers condemn this as 'unsound', 'inflationary', 'radical', 'striking at the roots of our institution'. They have great political power and carry their point. There is but one thing left to do and the government does it. It borrows for relief from the banks. True, the banks have very little cash money but the same law that permitted them to lend you money out of the inkwell enables them to lend to the government with the whole United States as security, the security being represented by interest-bearing tax-free bonds. The national debt climbs sky high but the system is held together a few more years, until the banks own practically everything, even the government."

Perry ran his hand through his hair and whistled. "You paint a pretty bleak picture. What is the answer?"

"We undertook to set up a general problem which, when solved, would answer the question in all cases of 'How much money does a country need?' We set up the general production-consumption cycle and worked through some problems under the conditions of your period. We should now be able to work the problem in general terms to arrive at the general answer. I believe you could do it with a little thought, but I will state the general answer for you to inspect and approve or reject. Here it is:

A production cycle creates exactly enough purchasing power for its consumption cycle. If any part of this potential purchasing is not used for consumption but instead is invested in new production, it appears as a cost charge in the new items of production, before it re-appears as new purchasing power. Therefore, it causes a net loss of purchasing power in the earlier cycle. Therefore, an equal amount of new money is required by the country.

"This money must be a new issue, not borrowed from the banks, for there is no way to pay it back. To tax it back from the country as a whole is to destroy necessary purchasing power at a later date. To tax it back from the bondholders is a polite name for cancellation. But that was necessary and was eventually done, in a roundabout manner."

"How?"

"By paying off the bonds with new money, then getting it back with inheritance and income taxes. There are several interesting corollaries to our main proposition. Here is one, 'No economic system can create its own new capital.' That must be done by the fiat of the sovereign state. The banks can't do it, even when they are permitted to create money, as they must recover the money they create and loan, plus a charge for the service, or 'interest'. Furthermore, banks should not be permitted to create money at all, because they are, of necessity, interested only in making a profit. They will inflate or deflate the currency to make a profit regardless of the monetary needs of the country. Their interest rates are a reflection of an artificially created money market with no relation to the cost of the service. No, banks must be required to loan only deposits placed with them for that purpose, that is to say, their reserves must be 100%, not 10% as in your day. They must keep entirely separate the funds left with them for commercial exchange, i.e. commercial checking accounts, funds placed with them to invest or loan, and funds deposited for safe keeping. In such a case the customer pays for the service of checking and exchange, pays for the service of safekeeping, and receives interest on funds deposited for investment. But the banker no longer manipulates the money supply of the nation to suit his convenience.

"Furthermore, from what we defined money to be and from our examination of the production-consumption cycle, we reach the important conclusion that there is no necessary one-to-one relationship between taxes and government expenditure. If a country is expanding industrially as the United States has since it was founded, the government is obliged to put out more money than it receives in amount equal to new capital investment in order to avoid deflation. This is new money never received in taxes. In fact the Federal government need not tax at all, except as a regulatory measure. It needs *no* taxes for revenue. It must *never* tax as much as it spends or gives away, as long as production is rising. This gives the government remarkable freedom. If a new battleship or a new highway was needed in your day, the economically sound thing to do would have been to go ahead and build, paying for it with new currency. Congress should consider only two things: 'Does the country need this battleship, or road.' And 'Is the country rich enough in manpower and materials to produce it?' If both answers are yes, go ahead and issue new money to do it."

"Just a moment, Master Davis. What is this new money worth, if anything?"

"How do you mean that?"

"Well, in my day money could be exchanged for gold, not very easily, but it could be done. How can one be sure that this new money is anything but pieces of paper?"

"As I told you before, the government will accept it for taxes, and for services such as the postal service. But you want to know what it is worth in terms of real wealth, just as the old style dollar was worth so many grains of gold. Very well. If you present a draft for a thousand credit units or dollar bills to any one of several government warehouses, the bursar will give you an assorted group of basic commodities of weights and standards specified by law."

"Where does the government get these commodities?"

"Grows or makes them, buys them in the open market, and may occasionally accept some of them as taxes."

"That seems awfully cumbersome compared with the gold standard."

"It is cumbersome, but it's worthwhile for it gives a much more nearly stable medium of exchange than gold. As a matter of practice the government keeps very small stocks of commodities because with a stable standard for money the public prefers cash or credit at the Bank of the United States to the trouble of handling bulk in commodities. They are satisfied to know that they can get real wealth in specified amounts, if they choose."

"How about foreign trade? This sort of money would be a nuisance there."

"Gold, as well as platinum, silver, and other convenient commodities, is still used in foreign trade exchange. The government buys and sells these commodities in the open market as a convenience to its citizens."

"I guess that clears it up. It still seems complicated."

"It is, Perry, more or less. But it isn't anything to the anarchistic maze that your old money system was. Let's get back the tax problem. The fact that there is no necessary one-to-one relationship between taxes and government expenditure is startling at first, but is evident from the nature of money. Money in the hands of an individual is a token of a debt to one of us owed by all of us. This token in the hands of the government states that all of us, i.e. the government, owe a debt to all of us, i.e. the government—an absurdity. One cannot owe oneself a debt in any but a poetical sense. Money in the hands of the Federal government is a scrap of paper and ink. It is significant only when held by individuals or groups of individuals.

"We recognize nowadays that Federal taxation is a deflating process, and that Federal government spending is an inflating process. Each process has important secondary effects through which it can be used to regulate for the general welfare. Taxation may be used to prevent unwholesome concentration of wealth. It may also be used to prevent too great a difference in the net income of individuals. The issue of new money is an even more powerful instrument in shaping our economic life to suit our wishes. It is a means of ensuring social security for the entire population through the dividend or inheritance checks. It can stimulate production and prevent inflation of prices through the use of the discount. It is used to assure an equal start for every child. In fact the knowledge of how to use money enables us to inhibit or encourage almost anything without coercion. If we desired, we could institute as near complete a socialism in the

United States as we wished, without confiscation and taking over the tools of production. The present set up suits us now. We can change it if we like, when we like, for we understand the economic mechanism. The economic determinism of Marx is an exploded bugaboo, and the American people are the masters, not the slaves, of their economic system."

Davis took a sip of sherry, and looked slightly giddy. "You'll forgive my enthusiasm, I trust. This is my subject and I am sometimes carried away by it."

"I am not surprised," replied Perry. "You have reason. I confess I don't see all those implications just yet, but it sounds amazing."

"You will see," returned Davis, "and by the very method we used. You can set up this game with the chessmen to cover every possible case. For example, throw in some professional men and observe that the cycle is unchanged. Provide a foreign trade with a balance in our favor and see how the cycle can be made to balance. Then a foreign trade in which goods are dumped on us and see how it dislocates our system. Then change the supply to balance it anyhow and observe how we can benefit. Play two tables and let trade flow between the tables. Set up a farm production cycle on one and factory on the other. Throw in corporate organization, trust funds, re-discounted paper, and so forth. Have a labor leader organize the workers and stage a strike. Get a lot of bank credit passed around and then make a run on the bank. Issue stock and watch it fluctuate in market price. Declare war and put industry on a war basis. Inflate the currency. Deflate it. Save your profits to expand your business. Cut prices to meet competition. Get squeezed on your lease. Start out from primitive barter, work up the present system with the dividend, the discount, and the National Account. Do all of those things, but be sure to observe the rule of duplicating the structure of the real world. It's fascinating and you will teach yourself more about money and economics than anyone else can possibly teach you. Bear in mind the fundamental theorem that we formulated about the necessity for new money for capital expansion. If you find any situation which appears to contradict it, or any of our other conclusions, go back and do it over, writing down each step in detail. If you don't find your error, give me a call. But I'm sure you will.*

---

*Several typical problems have been worked out for the benefit of the reader and appear as an appendix at the end of the book. A typical modern cycle is given showing the dividend and discount in operation. Especially interesting are examples of twentieth century economics showing the ridiculous impasses into which our forefathers fell simply through failure to understand the nature of money.

The Author

X

Perry followed Master Davis' advice and spent several days making up problems to play out with his economic tin soldiers. He drafted Olga and Diana into the game, and they solemnly played through various combinations of financial and economic situations. At first the women played simply to be agreeable, but they became fascinated by the strange possibilities of early day finance. Olga developed remarkable skill in stock market and commodity manipulation, and amassed fabulous fortunes on paper. Diana protested this and maintained that it obviously would be illegal for anyone to do such wicked things with the necessities of life. References to history left her only partly convinced. Diana liked to run factories but was a failure as a banker, as she could not see any sense in interest and was reluctant to clamp down on a debtor. Both of them admitted that they had not understood the operations of finance and industry before, and had rather taken the economic regime for granted. Perry found himself in the pleasant position of being able to instruct natives of the new America in the workings of their own environment.

In due course he felt that he understood fully the workings of both economic systems, the old and the new, and felt capable of analyzing correctly any possible economic system. Nevertheless he found growing up inside a curious distaste for the modern system. He now understood the mechanics of it, true, and realized that its mathematical theory was correct, but notwithstanding it did not suit his taste. He decided to call Davis and discuss it with him.

After a decent interval of drink and smoke, Davis opened the conversation.

"What is it, my boy? Found a black swan?"

"Why a black swan?"

"That's the classic example of the fallaciousness of the deductive method. The syllogism ran 'All swans are white. This bird is a swan. Therefore this bird is white.' Along in the nineteenth century somebody found a black swan and the perfect syllogism was wrecked."

"No, I haven't found a black swan, but I do have a problem."

"I don't think you will find a black swan in the conclusions we have reached. You'll find many problems not covered by the Law of Capital Investment. But the law itself is simply a statement of the workings of an invented mathematical entity, money. Sometimes we get into dilemmas through a failure to distinguish between mathematical necessity and objective realism. Marx fell into that error and it vitiated his whole work. For example and in particular, his definition of value. Did you happen to notice that we spoke of cost in money and price in money and never once mentioned value?"

"Now that you speak of it, yes."

"Can you define value?"

"Well, perhaps not. I seem to know what it means."

"Marx defined it as a measure of the number of work-hours required to produce a given article. His definition was meaningless in the real world, and he ran into all sorts of difficulties, which he tried to avoid by patching the definition. But the definition was wrong and his beautiful, monumental, logical structure was invalid. He was important only as an agitator against social injustice and he contributed more error than truth to the art of economics. He made a similar mistake in assuming that a man lives in his belly rather than in his head. Animals do, but not men. They must serve their bellies, it is true, but aside from that, their motives may have nothing to do with economic considerations. Consequently Marx's Economic Determinism was not valid. But I've digressed again. Value in economics is a relationship between an individual and a thing or a service. It is a personal relationship which expresses how much a particular individual *desires* a thing or a service. Economic value of a thing or a service approximates the average of the summation of the personal values placed on the thing or service by the individuals who constitute the consuming public. Value plus purchasing power in the hands of the consuming public constitutes effective demand. Price is a function of supply and demand. Value may be expressed in dollars and cents through this complex functional relationship, but value is not price, and is not a measure of work-hours, it is a word used to express the desire of an individual to possess a thing or a service. I am not giving the word a new definition; I am simply stating explicitly the observed fact that such is what people mean when they speak of value. Sale takes place when the value to the prospective buyer is greater than the value to the owner. Note the difference between Marx's idea of value and that which I have expressed. Marx attempts to measure value by the amount of labor expended. Yet it is an obvious fact in the real world that an inefficient, careless, or unimaginative worker can slave for hours to produce an article practically worthless, that the public won't buy, valueless. An intelligent skillful inventive worker may turn out in a short time an article that the public will snap up at once at a high price. Which has the greater value?"

"The one made by the better workman, of course."

"Of course. There is an old maxim which states it neatly: 'The value of a thing is what that thing will bring.' Even in our present system in which the government ensures the maintenance of sufficient purchasing power, if an entrepreneur is so inefficient that he produces articles of value less than cost, he goes broke. However, I've digressed again. I'm a garrulous old man. What was it you wanted to talk about?"

"Oh no, I enjoyed your digression and it cleared up another point. As to what is bothering me, I believe I understand the present financial system and I see that it works more smoothly than the one in my day, but there are still things about it that I just can't see the justification for. Especially this dividend or inheritance check. Why in the world should everybody in the country be handed money to spend whether they work or not? I concede that it is all right for widows and orphans, the sick and the blind and crippled, but why support in idleness some big overgrown lunk who is too lazy to support himself? Why put a premium on laziness? Here is my idea: let's increase the discount if necessary, and give a big dividend to those who need it but can't support themselves, but if a drone won't work, let him starve. Don't let him live off the rest of us."

"I see your point. It irks you to see anyone at all who is able to work permitted to live without working. But why do you consider work a virtue?"

"Well, these idle persons use up goods that the workers might otherwise enjoy."

"Do you know of anyone who doesn't have everything he wants of the good things of the world?"

"Well, no."

"Then how can you say that the idle are consuming things that rightfully belong to workers?"

"Well, it seems obvious."

"You mean that it seems logical to you. But if you can't find a case in the real world, can your logic be correct? I'm afraid you've encountered a black swan."

"Maybe so. But how can you justify able-bodied men living in idleness?"

Davis pursed his lips. "Ethics is more a matter of opinion than a science. Morals are customs rather than natural law. However if you want a moral argument to justify the situation, I'll give it to you. Did anyone live without working in your day?"

"Oh, those on relief did."

"I'm not speaking of them. They were presumed to be people who wanted to work but couldn't get work, and we have proved mathematically that they couldn't. I mean others who might have worked, but wouldn't, yet lived well."

"Why, no."

"Positive? How about coupon clippers, land owners, owners of capital who were not in management? Idle sons and daughters of the rich? Were there none of those?"

"Oh yes, of course. A few thousand perhaps. But they were entitled to be idle if they chose. Either they or their fathers had earned the money. A man is certainly entitled to provide for his children."

"All the idle today are the rich sons of hard working fathers."

"Are you trying to kid me?"

"I didn't jest, but I did use a figure of speech. Tell me, what are the factors that enter into production of real wealth?"

"Well, there is labor, of course—and raw materials and land."

"What were the factors when we set up our game of production and consumption?"

"Oh yes—and capital, and enterprise or management, and

invention or technique, government came in there too, but I am not sure that it is a factor in production."

"It is, as you will see. Let's examine these factors and attempt to make a rough estimate of their importance. Work is basic, certainly. In any but the most Elysian of South Sea islands, man must work to live. Marx made the mistake of thinking that because it came first, it was the only factor worthy of consideration, even though his writings implied the existence of others. Enterprise is more important than work. Without enterprise, management, directive ability, and imagination, our present highly productive culture would be impossible. It is a form of creative work, more difficult than the imitative work of the laboring men, and absolutely necessary to a high rate of production. Capital or rather capitalization is essentially the willingness of the owner of accumulated wealth to risk it in the hope of acquiring more. Its return is interest. We don't think very highly of it anymore. Capital is plentiful and by direct competition through the Bank of the United States we have driven interest down to a point where the return is commensurate with the risk. Franklin Roosevelt taught us that lesson with the Reconstruction Finance Corporation and the Federal Housing Administration.

"I said that government is a factor. It is, if for no other reason than through its police powers it makes the environment safe to work in. Without it no one could accumulate wealth and the creation of wealth on a large scale would not be feasible. Which is another way of saying that individuals acquire wealth only at the sufferance of the community and the community may require any tribute necessary to promote the general welfare. The government performs many other useful services too numerous to mention, but you see my point.

"Land and raw materials are obvious factors in the production of wealth. In the simplest economy labor must have something to fabricate and some place to stand on in order to produce wealth.

"The last factor is invention or technique. I mean not only new inventions now held by patent, but also all useful accumulation of knowledge from the stone age to date. Although wealth can be created without, or with very little of it, it is the greatest factor of all. You need only consider any common article to be convinced of it. Take a pair of shoes. In a modern shoe factory the production is around six hundred pairs of shoes per man per day. By figuring in raw material and capital costs it drops only to about four hundred pairs per laborer per day. Does one man make four hundred shoes per day? Put him at a cobbler's bench and assume him to be an experienced cobbler, yet he will do well to turn out one pair. Is it management? Management is important, for a poor manager will reduce production by perhaps 50%, yet the factory still turns out enormously more than a number of hand cobblers equal to its employees could do. Obviously the factor which produces this enormous multiplication of wealth is technical knowledge, the contribution of the creative inventor and creative artist. That is why we reward them so highly today. There is one outstanding characteristic of the creator-discoverer. His work lives after him and is cumulative in its effect. We owe more to the unknown genius who invented the wheel and axle than we do to all the workers now on earth. Furthermore, inventors stand on the shoulders of all their predecessors. No modern invention would be possible without the work done by Bacon, Da Vinci, Watt, Faraday, Edison, et cetera without number."

"Yes, that is evident but what of it? I can't see that the work of those men justifies laziness today."

"These men are our forefathers. They have left to each one of us the most valuable inheritance possible, other than the good earth and life itself. To each one of us, mind you, lazy and industrious alike. To refuse your brother who prefers not to work his share in production for moralistic reasons of your own devising is to claim for yourself that which you have not earned and have no right to."

Perry looked baffled but unconvinced. "Granting that what you say is true—it is, I suppose—nevertheless it takes labor to apply this heritage of technical knowledge. Why shouldn't every able-bodied man have to contribute equally to that labor?"

"But surely, Perry, you can see that there is not enough drudgery in this world to go around. The machines have released us from the curse of Adam. How can all of us crowd into the control stations of the machines? We have short hours, naturally, and most machine tenders and such retire at an early age, but it isn't practical to change shifts every fifteen minutes nor to train new men every few weeks. Would you have men dig holes and fill them up again for the sake of work itself? Would you destroy the machines and restore the cobbler's bench? There is always creative work to be done; there is no limit to that, but there is no way to punch time clocks on it either. If a man has creation in his system, all we can do is to give him leisure in which to develop it. Tell me, have you seen very many idle people?"

"No, I haven't as yet."

"You won't. The urge to work exists in more than ninety per cent of the population. Free him from drudgery and he putters in the garden, in a workshop, learns to draw, tries to write poetry, studies, goes into politics, invents, sings, devises salad dressings, climbs mountains, explores the ocean depths, and tries to fly to the moon. Few are those who sit in the sun and whittle."

"Say, are they really trying to reach the moon?"

"Yes, surely. But I want to give you an illustration of the current situation. Suppose in your day seven men own a big car together and all wish to drive from San Francisco to New York. John is crippled and can't drive. Joe is too young to drive. Jack doesn't know how to drive. Jake is a good driver but hates to drive, being of a nervous temperament. Jep is just plain lazy and prefers to watch the scenery, but Jim and George are both good drivers and don't mind doing it. Of course only one person can drive at a time. You propose that they all take turns at the wheel, barring the cripple and the child. Isn't it more reasonable to pay the two drivers for their services and let everyone reach New York in comfort? That is what we do today. Those who perform the drudgery of the nation are paid—and well-paid—in addition to their dividend from their inheritance."

Perry threw up his arms in mock surrender. "Enough. Enough. Frankly, I'm not convinced yet, but you certainly can make out a case."

Davis shrugged his shoulders. "Personally I'm not interested in moralistic reasons. The present system is the one the American people have chosen to serve them at this period of their development. It suits my temperament so I don't try to change it. If you want another you now know how to devise another which will be economically feasible. Then you are free to try to persuade the country to adopt it. You might even try to persuade a state. Several of the states have modifications."

"So I gathered. How do they work?"

"Well, Wisconsin has very high income taxes and pays a state dividend in addition to the Federal dividend. They have a nearly complete socialism with most business run co-operatively. It seems to suit them but I find it a dull pace. However, let me mention the practical advantages of the blanket dividend as compared with your moralistic proposal. In the first place it ensures high wages, because men who are free from economic necessity won't work for sweatshop wages. For the same reason it ensures good working conditions. Unions are no longer necessary. Those that remain have turned into fraternal organizations rather than battalions in class warfare. In the second place it ensures social security for everybody all the time and thereby makes government much simpler. In your day the social service bureaucracy was growing by leaps and bounds. We don't need social service workers where poverty is unknown. And it saves private citizens from the insufferable buttinskyness of social work, the prying catechisms that determine the 'deserving' poor. If for no other reason the dividend is desirable because it ended the incredible red tape and indignities of your old system of relief, and welfare work, and private charity."

"But see here, the dividend will hardly pay for operations and sickness. Suppose the idlers fall sick?"

Davis looked surprised. "Hadn't you gathered that health service is free? It obviously has to be. The community can't afford to let anyone be sick for fear of contagion and unsocial mal-adjustment. If medicine hadn't been socialized we couldn't have stamped out syphilis and gonorrhea for example, and our present social standards couldn't have developed. Medical men are public servants and among the most highly paid in the community."

"Doesn't that tend to make medicine un-enterprising and give it a tendency to fall into a rut?"

"Did it for the army and navy in your day? Before your time they were private professions, you will remember. However, a physician need not be a public servant. He can hang out his shingle if he likes. But with higher returns for public practice, plus every opportunity for research with unlimited facilities and no economic restrictions on the expense of treatment, practically all of the best ones prefer to work for the government."

"That reminds me of another objection. Won't everybody ask to be treated by the best physicians?"

"They ask, but if a physician has more cases than he can handle, he picks the interesting and difficult ones, and mediocre physicians get the commonplace ones. That works out best for everybody. In your day a wealthy hypochondriac could command the services of valuable men who should have been on the difficult cases."

"That's fair enough, I guess. Medicine has always fascinated me."

"You ought to fly up to the United States Medical Academy some day and get them to show you around. It will open your eyes. We've made a lot of progress in the last hundred and fifty years."

"Thanks for the idea. I'll do that someday. But to return to our argument. I'm a die-hard. Everything may appear rosy right now, but I believe that I see the seeds of decay in this system. Doesn't it encourage the reproduction of the unfit in unlimited numbers? Wasn't Malthus right in the long run? Aren't you steadily weakening the race by making life too easy?"

"I don't believe so. I think your fears are groundless. The pathologically unfit are inhibited from breeding by a combination of special economic inducements and the mild coercion of the threat of coventry. The exceptionally brilliant and creative persons are sought after as parents. A famous surgeon, musician, or inventor will receive literally thousands of invitations to impregnate women who desire exceptional children or covet the social honor of bearing the offspring of genius. From a physical standpoint the race is being re-tailored by the development of gland therapy and immunization. A baby born today will never grow excessively fat nor emaciated, and couldn't catch typhoid fever if he slept with a victim of it. Instead of protecting a child from infection we modify the genes of his grandfather so that the baby has ten times the hardihood of a jungle savage. As for

Doctor Malthus, he lived before the day of voluntary conception. If we need to limit the population, we are prepared to do it."

"Well, you've given me a lot to chew over and a lot of new angles to investigate. But I can't help feeling that there's a black swan lurking. Maybe I'll be back at you in a few days."

Davis chuckled. "Go to it, son. You've given me the first real workout I've had in years. Is there any more port in that bottle? That's enough. Thanks."

XI

Olga arrived one morning to find Perry walking the floor, and smoking. A pile of cigarette stubs alongside a barely-touched breakfast showed his state of mind. He flung her a curt greeting. Olga grinned.

"Little Merry Sunshine, no less. What's the matter, dopey? Come down with the Never-Get-Overs?"

Perry ground the butt of his cigarette savagely into a saucer. "All very well for you to joke, but it's serious to me. It's this damned place. I'm sick of it."

Olga's face became serious. "What's the trouble with this place, Perry? Anything wrong? Anything you need? Somebody been unkind to you?"

He scowled. "No. Nothing you can do anything about. The place is swell, and everybody is decent to me. I'm just sick of it, that's all. I know I have to stay here and need to stay here, and I'm not arguing about my sentence, but you can't make me like it. I'm going stir-crazy."

Olga's face cleared. "Why, Perry, you don't have to stay here."

"What? Why don't I? I was sent here for treatment."

"Surely. And you should spend quite a bit of your time here just for our convenience in treating you. But you are free to move around."

"Do you mean that?"

"I always mean what I say."

Perry's face lit up. "Stand clear, boys! Here we go! Say, where can I hire a sky car?"

"Take mine, if you like. I won't be needing it."

"That gives me an idea. Are you busy today? Could you come along? We could have a picnic."

"Why yes, I guess I could go. Sure you wouldn't rather be alone?"

"Hell, no. You're the perfect companion. You don't bother a fellow when he doesn't want to talk."

"Okay. Let's go. I'll see about something to eat."

A short while later Perry pressed back on the stick and they shot into the air at maximum lift. Higher and higher he took them, clear to the ceiling for the little craft. Then he spread his wings and accelerated to maximum speed. They shot along silently except for the muffled whir of the screw. Olga lounged on the cushions and watched him with the half smile of approval with which a mother watches a child at play. Tiring of straight flight, Perry put the machine through its paces, rotor maneuvering, climbing by wing, crashing, quick turns. Presently he leveled off, and spoke. "That was fun. I wish I had my old crate here, though. I'd show you some real acrobatics. Did you ever loop, or fly upside down? Or a power dive in formation? That'll take the enamel off your teeth. This is a grand little boat but it's a baby carriage with shock absorbers compared with our old fighting jobs."

"That sounds exciting, but wasn't it terribly dangerous?"

"Sure it was dangerous, unless you knew your job. Even then it wasn't a tea party. Lots of my pals got theirs from carelessness, or engine failure or something. But it was grand sport. Funny, I never got hurt in the air, but a measly little spill out of an automobile finishes me off. Only it didn't finish me." He grinned boyishly. "Damn funny thing about me popping over all these years. It worried me a lot at first. I was afraid I'd go to sleep and wake up somebody else. You know that Hindu pal of Gordon's. You remember he came to see me. He seems to think that Gordon and I are the same hombre using different memory tracks. I didn't understand it and don't see how he can prove it, but he claims that if Gordon comes back at all I'll simply have two memories. He talked a lot about serial observers and serial time sense. I didn't get it, but he did manage to reassure me."

Olga patted his hand. "That's good. I'm glad."

"The best part about it is that I can go ahead and be a citizen of this world now and not feel like a freak. Say, are you hungry?"

"Not very, but I can usually eat." She patted her soft expanse of tummy.

"I kinda skipped breakfast. Let's drop down somewhere and eat outdoors."

"Okay. Where are we?" They bent over the map screen and Olga glanced out. She placed her finger on the map. "How about it?"

"Twenty minutes more or less. It's an inspiration."

"I'll get lunch ready while you whip up the horses."

Half an hour later they were sitting at the south rim of the Grand Canyon, eating silently while they drank in the ageless wonder of the place. Perry broke the silence. "You know I've seen this many times before, twice since my arrival in this period and several times in my early life. It makes me feel as if the thing that happened to me in time is just a casual incident of no more import than the ten seconds of unconsciousness of a lightly knocked out boxer. Time has moved on here in the past hundred and fifty years, but the change is not perceptible."

Olga nodded but did not answer. She stared out and down. Presently she arose and brushed the crumbs from her coverall. "Let's get going. I have to take this place in small doses." She stepped into the car and loosened the zipper at her throat. Perry followed her, and sealed the door. Once off the ground, coveralls stowed, and cigarettes lighted, Perry inquired,

"Where to?"

"I don't care."

"Aren't we close to the Moon Rocket Experiment Grounds?"

"Yes, it's just east of Flagstaff. Want to see it?"

"Very much."

He leveled off, set his course and clamped the robot. Olga lay back and dozed in the warm contentment of digestion. Perry sat and watched her and mused to himself. This was a very pleasant trip, as much fun as it would have been if Diana were along instead of Olga. Or almost. Olga was a great kid, and a lot of fun to have around. He certainly was fond of her. Not what Master Hedrick suggested of course, he wasn't forming any attachment. He was in love with Diana and was loyal to her, whether such loyalty was customary or not. Could he have fallen in love with Olga if he had met her first? Possibly. She wasn't as beautiful as Diana, nor as young (Perry smiled at this. Time was too scrambled for age to matter.), but she was certainly as seductive in her own way. She didn't dress her hair nor use cosmetics with the consummate artistry of Dian', but she was always meticulously shaven and fastidious about her person to a degree unusual even in 2086. About her character and personality there could be no question; she was tops. Yes, he decided, he could have fallen deeply in love with her—if he hadn't met Diana first. Too bad he couldn't have known her when he was a bachelor. Was he attractive to her? She liked him, he was sure, but Olga seemed to like a lot of people. Did he as a man arouse any response in her as a woman? He would give a lot to know. He wondered what she would do if he were to make a pass at her.

His reverie was broken by the insistent ringing of the alarm gong. The robot checked flight and hovered. He glanced out and saw a series of bright red pylons marching over the rolling plateau. Miles beyond was a group of buildings. Just below was a small landing flat and hangars. The field lights flashed the landing signal and they obeyed. They were received by a wizened weather-beaten desert rat, who showed them where to park their car and indicated with a jerk of his thumb the stairway to the trans-tube. They descended and strapped themselves in the cylinder. Olga touched a button on the remote control panel, relays clicked, and they found themselves almost at once at the field station. They emerged from the stairwell into a large room equipped with a few chairs, a televue control station and some benches. It was almost deserted. A young man was talking to a girl dressed in an asbestos coverall. The hood and visor were pushed back, disclosing a tight mass of copper ringlets. She laughed at something he said and answered in a low tone. An elderly man with a preoccupied look entered from a corridor on the right and shuffled quickly into a side room. No one else was in sight. Olga and Perry stood uncertainly for a moment, then Perry advanced, touched the young man on the arm, and spoke.

"Excuse me."

The young man started, and turned around. "Oh, sorry. I didn't see you. May I do you a service?"

"Service," answered Perry. "We'd like to look around, if it's permitted."

"Certainly. Glad to have you. You'll need a guide though. Joe!"

A blond head appeared from behind the back of a couch, a strapping form followed it. "Yeah?"

"A couple of visitors 'ud like to take a gander around the plant. I've got to handle the controls for Vivian on this test run. Can you do it?"

"I guess so." The youth chucked a magazine into a chair and joined them, long arm and hand outstretched.

Perry thanked him. "Sure this won't put you out?"

"Not at all. Glad to have a little excitement. It's pretty dull around here. Come along. What would you like to see first? The rockets? Most everybody does." He led them into a huge gloomy shed. Dominating the interior was a great sleek metal behemoth that towered over their heads. Perry whistled.

"You've gone further than I thought."

Joe followed his glance. "That? You expect too much. That's just an obsolete strato-rocket. Her top speed won't take her over the heaviside layer. We've got her outfitted to simulate space conditions as far as we can. We've got a crew locked up in there now to see if they can take it without going off their heads. They've been in there six weeks now. Every now and then we give 'em a little surprise like bleeding out half their air pressure." He grinned. "There's another little surprise that they don't expect. One of 'em's under secret orders to go crazy and start trouble."

"Can't they get out?"

"Oh yes, if the skipper loses his nerve. Otherwise not."

Olga clenched her fists. "Why must you do that? It isn't human."

Joe fixed her with a sardonic eye. "Sister, if they can't stand that, what chance have they got in space?"

"Why go out in space? Isn't the earth big enough?"

Joe turned his attention back to Perry. "You can't make a man permanently contented in a nice, pretty, upholstered civilization. We've got to, that's all. There's something out there to be seen, and we're gonna have a look." Perry nodded. Olga held her peace. "But these babies here are what we're working on. Messenger rockets." He indicated a number of metal bodies roughly cylindro-conical in shape. "These are rejected models but they look a lot like ones we've tried. One like this fellow got into a permanent orbit, we think. At least the data showed it making nearly five kilometers when it left."

Olga's lips moved. "That doesn't seem fast; three hundred kilometers per hour."

"Not three hundred; eighteen thousand. It was going five kilometers per second. That ain't enough though. We need a speed of eleven point three kilometers per second to break out of the earth's field entirely."

"That applies to shots rather than rockets, doesn't it?"

"That's right. You know something about ballistics, don't you, bud? Any speed at all will do as long as our accelerating force is greater than gravitational force. The distances are enormous though. Without pretty heavy acceleration you'd grow old waiting to get there."

"Not from here to the moon, surely."

"Oh, no. That's no distance. But if we get there, we'll establish a base there and try some long hops. In a thin gravity field like the moon's we ought to be able to take off for any planet in the system."

"How much acceleration do you figure on using?"

"Two g's is about all that's healthy. I've taken that for ten hours in the centrifuge, but then I'm husky. It's uncomfortable though, and it made me sick to my stomach at first. Of course we can take as high as six or seven g's for a short time in a good corset and braces and a water cushion. I pass out at about five and half."

"What's a 'g'?" Olga whispered to Perry.

"Force of gravity at earth seal level. At two g's you'd feel twice as heavy as you do now."

"Now see this baby," continued Joe, indicating a silver grey torpedo-like body about ten feet long. "We've sent off eight like it towards old Luna. Her pay load is a lot of magnesium ribbon to make a flare. One of 'em got across, at least Flagstaff reported a spark in Mare Imbrium. Pick it up." Perry stooped over and prepared to heave. It came up lightly and he almost fell over backwards. "Light, ain't it? It's a tungsten aluminum alloy, lighter than potassium. Inert, too."

"I should think it would be porous," Perry commented.

"It is, but it's got a mirror surface inside about two molecules thick that would stop the breath of scandal. The only hard metal in it otherwise is the jets themselves."

"Look here," put in Olga, "If you've got a little one across, why not build a bigger one and ride it over?"

"Well, you see all this little fellow has to do is to climb up to the change over point—that's where the attraction of the moon and the earth are equal—then fall down. To get to the moon and back means to climb up, then climb down to the moon, using rocket fuel to break your fall, then climb up again and climb back down to earth again, four stages. We can't do that yet. But we do think that we are well on the way to building one that will do two of those stages; go up, swing in an orbit around the moon, then climb back down to earth again. That's what Vivian, the girl you saw in the lobby, is working on. She's going to ride the ground tests on some new fuel."

"What do the ground tests amount to?"

"They are the nearest thing to flight conditions we can manage on the ground. This stuff has been laboratory tested, and fired in ground jets, and a rocket designed for it which should be strong enough and light enough to do the trick. Today it is tested in a dummy rocket with a full control panel and full size jets, but the whole framework is tied down solid. The rocket reaction produces stress and strain instead of acceleration. We measure the stresses by instrument. If it all checks out the way it should, we'll try the real rocket in flight."

Olga interrupted. "If you've made all those preliminary tests, what can you learn by running a rocket that is tied down? You already have the data on what it will do."

Joe shook his head. "No, not quite. We know what we think it ought to do, but we knew that when the equations of synthesis were for it. But this stuff is all new. Suppose it does something different? We've got to know before a ship leaves the ground."

Perry put in a word. "Why is this girl Vivian running the tests? Isn't it a man's job?"

"It's her right to. She's the molecular synthesist who designed the fuel. This is as far as she can take it though, as she's not a rocket pilot."

A siren howled mournfully from outside the building. Joe moved toward the door. "Come along if you want to see it." They followed him back through the corridor, through the entrance hall and up a spiral staircase which gave into a small observation room. On the side toward the field was a wide shallow window of amber glass. Several persons who were lined up along this window made room for them. Joe spoke to one of the spectators. "How soon do they start?"

"Any minute now. There goes Vivian." Perry looked down and saw a small figure, bunchy in coveralls, climb a ladder to a manhole in the top of a stubby metal shape. The figure hesitated halfway in and turned its helmeted head toward the building. Perry thought he could detect the flash of a smile. An arm waved and the figure disappeared. The manhole cover closed into place from the inside, made a quarter turn and stopped. For a moment all was still in the room and nothing moved on the field. Perry could hear Olga's quick breathing at his ear. Then a little burst of violet flame showed from the stern of the test rocket. Somebody said "There she goes!" and the tension relaxed. The flame shot out again, lightened in color and became a blinding white as solid to the eye as white-hot metal. It fanned a trifle and made a myriad little green sparks where it licked the desert soil. A buzz of conversation spread around the room. "Pretty neat, what?"—"Yeah, she's got it this time."—"Watch it fade. That'ud be clean kinetic in vacuo."—Then charged, the main jet darkened, turned purple and quit. Smaller jets around the waist of the craft lighted one after another, and a nose jet blazed out for an instant. More comment came from around them.—"Pretty as a picture, one-two-three."—"Yeah, but I still like precession. Those fractional controls are too complicated."—"It looks nice though, doesn't it."—The smaller jets cut out and the stern jet cut in again, passing quickly from violet to white. It held steady for several minutes, then trembled and Perry thought that he detected a faint shadow on the under side. The whole flame turned a deep purple and split into two parts. He heard a shout of "Down!" and someone jerked savagely at his arm, unbalancing him. He fell across Olga as a white glare like photographer's flashlight temporarily blinded him. A dumb rumble, a short grinding shock, and then silence. He stumbled to his knees and blinked his eyes. Joe was beside him, already rising. They hurried to the window. Before him still lay the rocket but it had lurched awkwardly toward them and a split had opened for several feet near the stern jet. A cloud of yellowish oily smoke partially obscured the scene. Joe turned and hurried down the stairs. The other spectators were gone. Perry had not noticed when or how. He stared again at the sight, trying to interpret it, when Olga's voice sounded beside him.

"Whatever happened, Perry?"

"I don't know yet. Something went wrong."

"That pretty little redhead—Was she hurt?"

"I can't tell. I don't think so. The rocket doesn't look much damaged."

"Let's go down."

They went back down to the reception room and waited in unease for someone to show up. Presently Joe appeared and Perry caught his eye. "Oh yes, you folks. I'd forgotten you." He stopped by them, apparently annoyed and uneasy. Perry questioned him.

"What happened?"

"Nobody knows yet. Either fuel or the nozzles."

"Anyone hurt?"

"Only the operator."

"Killed?"

"They haven't said so yet. She was burned to a crisp and her right leg's gone. Say, I don't want to be rude but I'm awful busy. Will you excuse me?"

"Oh, of course! Sorry!" And he was gone.

Olga took Perry's arm. "Let's get out of here, please, Perry."

"Right." Neither spoke again until they were back in the sky car.

XII

For the next several days Perry reveled in his new-found freedom. He made a number of trips purely for the pleasure of being out and free. Sometimes one or both of the girls accompanied him, more often he went alone. He made a practice of telling Olga or someone in authority where he was going and when he expected to return, but met with no objection to any of his plans. His trips were varied. By now he had practically complete familiarity with the customs of the country and could get around even in a metropolis without arousing comment. He spent several days in San Francisco just looking around and getting acquainted. He dropped in at Berkeley and looked up Master Cathcart, who appeared glad to see him and showed him around the University. Perry was struck by the un-collegiate quality of the place. There seemed to be few students and little of the ant hill activity that characterized the academic institutions of his day. He asked Cathcart what the enrollment was.

Cathcart answered, "About fifty thousand."

Perry commented that it must be vacation time.

The older man said, no, but that few students were actually in residence at Berkeley. He explained that they made a practice of actually being present only when doing laboratory work, inasmuch as the lecture method had been superseded by the stereoscopic record, such as Perry had used. On the other hand there were close personal relationships between teachers and pupils, as most of the direct instruction was of the seminar rather than the classroom variety. Instruction was characterized by discussion groups and guidance in study rather than the cut-and-dried cram-and-exam methods of 1939.

At this time Cathcart was preparing to leave for a trip to Washington to hear the closing debates of the session of Congress. This was primarily a vacation as he could have heard them as well or better in his home and studied the records at his leisure. But, as he told Perry, he liked to browse around the sessions at Washington and gossip with the officials in order to get the smell of the place. He felt that it helped him when interpreting the current scene to others.

He learned that Perry had not yet been to Washington and invited him to come along. Perry explained somewhat diffidently that he was not entirely a free agent. However a call to Master Hedrick cleared that difficulty and Perry found himself headed for the Bay Rocket Port.

This was Perry's first trip by rocket. He spent the three hours as busy as a small boy with two ice cream cones. A transparent bulkhead separated the passengers' seats from the navigation compartment. Perry placed himself in the first row of seats and tried to figure out the technique of the controls. In place of a stick the principal controls seemed to be a double bank of keys arranged above and below a flange that projected from under the instrument board. Perry asked Cathcart the reason for this peculiar arrangement, but the historian admitted that he had taken it for granted. Cathcart rang for the stewardess and held a short conference with her. She looked dubious but entered the navigation room, and got the ear of one of the pilots, who glanced back through the bulkhead and met Perry's eyes. Then he said something to the stewardess, who nodded and re-entered the passenger compartment. She stopped by Cathcart and reported:

"The Skipper says your friend can ride in the inspector's seat if he's strapped in and keeps quiet during maneuvering."

Perry arose, his face radiant, thanked the young woman and turned to Cathcart. "Sure you don't mind?"

"Not at all. I'd like to catch a nap."

The stewardess let him into the navigation room, and strapped him into a chair just behind and about ten inches higher than the pilot's and navigator's seats. The skipper gave him a curt nod and turned away. Perry followed his glance, saw the field lights turn red, then a light ahead showed green in double flashes. The skipper reached out and pinched a pair of control buttons between thumb and forefinger. A buzzer sounded and a transparency flashed, 'PASENJERS STRAP IN'. Perry felt his own safety belt. The pilot pinched another pair of buttons, then several more in rapid succession. Perry felt heavy and a cloud of white smoke blotted out the view ports. It cleared away almost immediately, and the ground appeared far below. San Francisco vanished beneath them. The pilot's hands moved nervously among the controls. Perry watched the numbers click past on the altigraph, two thousand—three—five—nine—thirteen—up and up. At twenty thousand meters the pilot leveled off and accelerated, faster and faster, until seventeen hundred kilometers per hour was reached. The light in the car had taken on an unreal quality, like the glares and sharp shadows of a welder's arc. Outside the sky was a deep purple and stars shown clearly and without twinkling. Just ahead he saw the sickle of Leo beginning to rise. He twisted around in his seat and attempted to see the sun, but it was obscured by the stern of the ship. He was forced to content himself with imagining what the solar prominences and spots might be like. He recalled the warning printed on his

ticket: 'DANJER! OBTAN DARK GLASES FROM STU-
ARDES BEFORE VUING SON' and he had neglected to
obtain dark glasses from the stewardess. Below the ground
flowed past in plastic miniature, each detail sharp. It looked
remarkably like the illuminated strip map that unrolled on the
instrument board. A glowing red dot floated on the surface of the
map. Perry recognized this as a dead reckoner of some sort and
wondered how the trick was done. Air speed? Hardly. Earth
induction? Possible but difficult, especially in latitude made
good. Radio? More likely, but still a clever trick.

When the pilot was satisfied with his combination, Perry
ventured to speak. "Excuse me." The pilot glanced back and his
grimness relaxed a trifle.

"Oh, it's you. I'd forgotten you were here. Want something?"

"Just one thing. Why are all your controls double?"

"As a matter of fact they are quadruple, in parallel-series
around each pilot's chair. I suppose you mean why the pinch-
buttons."

"Yes, why not ordinary push buttons?"

"Each side *is* an ordinary push button, but you have to pinch
a pair with thumb and forefinger to cause any action. Look." He
ran his finger along the key board, pressing a dozen or more
keys. Nothing happened. "It's a safety device against freezing on
the keyboard at high acceleration. I could pass out and fall face
down on the keyboard and never set off a jet. My partner could
then land by squeezing the keys on his board. For example, if we
had ordinary push buttons and I pressed the combination for
maximum breaking, I'd be pushed hard upon the board by my
own momentum, and I might not be able to release the controls.
With this system I have to will to pinch or nothing happens."

"Thanks. Say, how long does it take to learn to be a rocket
pilot?"

The pilot looked at him curiously but answered his question. "If you are temperamentally fitted, three months should do. There is always more to learn."

The stewardess stuck in her head. "Ready for your tea, Skipper? And you, Jack?" The navigator gave a taciturn nod. The skipper assented, and said to Perry, "I think you'd better have your tea in the passenger compartment."

Perry unstrapped himself and returned to Cathcart, who nodded greeting. "See what you wanted to?"

"Yes, and was dismissed most diplomatically."

Sandwiches, tea, and little cakes brought on sleep. Perry was awakened by the deceleration warning as they circled over Washington. Perry stared out. Here was a place which time had not changed beyond recognition. The Potomac and the tidal basin were below. There stood the Washington Monument and Lincoln still stared into the reflecting pool. The White House still sprawled among the budding trees, serene and cool. And on Capitol Hill the ponderous Greco-Roman majesty of the Capitol still stood, far-flung, solid, and enduring. He choked and sudden tears came to his eyes.

The visit to Washington was amusing but without special incident. The constitutional changes were not apparent on the surface. The city was changed in many details, but the landmarks remained. The streets were unroofed, and, in the absence of surface traffic, constituted popular promenades and lounging places. Perry wandered about them and visited the museums and art galleries. He spent one afternoon in the gallery of the House listening without much interest to the debate Cathcart had come to hear. The president had directed the building of a fleet of fast, unarmed, long-radii patrol vessels, both air and surface, to maintain a constant patrol from the Aleutians through Hawaii and down to Ecuador, and ear-marked a portion of the dividend for that purpose. The President's plan was practically unopposed, but one group wished to enlarge it with a new issue of money to provide more heavy armored short radii rockets for coast defense. The debate dragged on and a compromise seemed likely. As Perry was no longer in the navy this didn't interest him much, especially as the type of armament proposed was obviously unsuited for foreign war. He concluded that the American people were both determined not to fight and determined to let the whole world know that they were prepared to resist invasion.

That night at dinner at the New Mayflower, Cathcart asked him what impressed him most about the Capitol. Perry replied that it was the Congressmen, and explained that they appeared to be a much more able body of men than was commonly reputed to be the case in 1939. Cathcart nodded.

"That was probably the case," he said. "If you got good elective officials in your day, it was a happy accident, better than you deserved."

"To what do you attribute the change?" asked Perry.

"To a number of things. To my mind there is no single answer. The problem involved is the very heart of the political problem and has been plaguing philosophers for thousands of years. Plato and Confucius each took a crack at it and each missed it by a mile. Aesop stated it sardonically in the fable of the convention of the mice, when he inquired gently, 'Who is to bell the cat?'. The present improvement over your period can, I think, be attributed to correcting a number of things which were obviously wrong without worrying too much about theory. In the first place all of our elective officials are well paid nowadays and most of them have full retirement. In the second place, every official makes a full statement of his personal finances on taking office, annually, and again on leaving office. In the third place, public service has gradually been built up as a career of honor, like the military and naval services in your day. A scholarship to the School of Social Science is as sought after as an appointment to West Point was in 1939. Most of our undersecretaries and executives of every sort are graduates. They are recruited for they have the same reputation for efficiency and incorruptability that your West Pointers and Annapolis men have always had.

"Of course you can't teach creative policy making in a school. The top men still come from everywhere. Our complete system of social security makes it possible for any man with a taste for it to enter politics, and several arbitrary changes in the code of customs have encouraged them to do so. Campaign funds and permissible types of campaigning are now restricted enormously, a degree of change comparable to the difference between your day and the elections at the beginning of the nineteenth century when a man announced his vote to a teller at the polls whereupon the favored candidate shook hands with him and gave him a drink of whiskey. Nowadays our object is to ensure that each voter has a chance to know the record, appearance and proposals of each candidate. They must use the franking privilege jointly. They must go on the air together, they must refrain from certain forms of emotional campaigning. The people are better able to judge than they were in 1939 because of the improvement in our educational methods. They are not as subject to word magic, not so easily spellbound.

"Possibly the most important change that has improved the chances of obtaining honesty and efficiency in government was the extension of civil rights after the defeat of the Neo-Puritans. You will recall the new constitutional principle that forbade the state to pass laws forbidding citizens to commit acts which did not in fact damage other citizens. Well, that meant the end of the blue laws, and a grisly unconscious symbiosis between the underworld and the organized churches—for the greatest bulwark of the underworld were always the moral creeds of the churches. You still think that unlikely? Consider this: The churches had great political power. It was almost impossible to be elected to office if the churches disapproved. It is a matter of fact, easily checked, that every public leader of every corrupt political machine was invariably a prominent member of a large, powerful sect. He always contributed heavily to the church, especially to its charities. On the other hand every church stood publicly for honesty in government. At the same time they demanded of the government that there be suppressed all manner of acts, harmless in themselves, but offensive to the creeds of the churches. Churches and the clergy were usually willing to accept the word for the deed. Protestations of integrity, combined with tithing and psalm singing, plus a willingness to enact into law the prejudices of the churches, were usually all that the churches required of a candidate. On the other hand the gang leaders were hardened realists. They cared nothing about a candidate's appearance of pious virtue if he could be depended on to protect from prosecution the gang that supported him. Furthermore they were anxious to have blue laws on the books as long as they were not enforced. Illicitness was the thing that made most of their stock in trade valuable, and they knew it. Where in your 1930's was there a gang leader who urged repeal of the eighteenth amendment? The very blue laws they broke gave them a weapon to destroy competition, for the same machine which gave them protection could be used to destroy an enemy who did not own a piece of the local government. And so it went for years, in every large American city, the gangsters and the preachers, each for his own purpose, supported and elected the same candidates. It was inevitable, because the churches demanded of government things that government cannot or should not perform—things that come under the head of making a man be 'good' for the good of his soul, instead of interfering only to pre-vent him damaging another. The churches had a thousand rationalizations to prove that their nosey-parker interference was necessary for the welfare of all.

"For example, Brown must be stopped from peddling pornog-raphy, because, if he does, he will harm the purchaser, Smith. But note that Smith is to be saved from harm for the good of Smith's soul, as defined by the churches. Sometimes the concatenation is very involved, but in every case you will find at the end the churches attempting to use the state to coerce the citizen into complying with a creed which the churches have been unsuc-cessful in persuading the citizen to accept without coercion. Wherever that occurs you have a condition which inevitably results in the breeding of a powerful underworld which will seize the local government, and frequently, through control of local political machines, seize state and national governments as well.

"One is always asked, 'What about the sweet innocent chil-dren? Are they to have no protection?' Certainly not, but many of the things which were believed to be bad for children were bad only in the unventilated minds of the religious moralists. For example, we now realize that it is not bad for children to be used to naked human bodies—on the contrary it is very *un*healthy for them not to be. We know that knowledge of the objective fact of bisexual procreation is not harmful to children—on the contrary if we satisfy their natural curiosity by telling them lies, we are building trouble for the future. But we do know that nicotine and alcohol do more physical harm to children than to adults and we punish the adult who provides them with such. By the same token we look with disfavor on a church which fills children's minds with sadistic tales of a cruel vengeful tribe of barbarians under the guise of teaching them the revealed word of God. We disapprove of exhibiting pictures and statues of a man spiked to a wooden frame. I say we disapprove—but we do not forbid, for the damage, though probably greater than habit-forming drugs, is hard to prove, but we do insist on some years of instruction through the public development centers to clean their minds of the sadism, phobias, simple misstatements of fact, faulty identifications, and confusion of abstractions that their preachers and priests have labored to instill."

"Is the state actively fighting religion?"

"Of course not. To educate in opposition to particular dogmas of particular sects is not to fight religion. But if a church persists in teaching anti-social doctrine, the state reserves the right to combat those doctrines with argument in rebuttal. It is necessary to remember that head-hunting is a religious rite. Shall we tolerate it? The most popular sects of your day practiced a form of symbolic cannibalism. Is the state obligated to stand in awe of that rather nauseating myth? Our answer is simple. Any religion is free to preach and practice but the state and all individuals have an equal right to combat their doctrines by any peaceful means."

"Haven't some sects attempted to prevent any non-conformist instruction of their children?"

"Yes, some extreme cases have preferred to go to coventry, whole sects. They seceded from us, so instead of fighting, we seceded from them. But we were talking about politics and here we are on religion. What was I saying? Oh yes, why we get better men into office than we used to. I think I've covered most of the reasons. The destruction of the political power of finance capitalism was a big factor, naturally. Required voting helps—only those can draw the dividend who vote, and the franchise calls for a rather stiff course in the details of the mechanics of government."

"Suppose one doesn't pass the examination, does he lose his vote?"

"There is no examination. If there were, the party in power might use it to disenfranchise the opposition, just as such laws were used to disenfranchise the negroes in the South in your day. We just make sure that the citizen has been thoroughly instructed in the machinery of government. All these things help to make a more intelligent electorate and bring out better candidates. In spite of everything we get a certain percentage of stupid, or unqualified, or small-souled men in office. This isn't Utopia, you know. This is just the United States of America in 2086.

XIII

Back in California, Diana paid a call on Master Hedrick. He received her at once and ushered her into his study, his face wreathed in a smile of welcome that managed to make him more birdlike than ever.

"Come in, come in, my dear. May I do you a service? I've missed you lately. But I did see some of your Chicago appearances by telecast. You were magnificent. Lovely! Lovely! Sit you down here by the fire. Something to eat? No? A cigarette? A little glass of wine? Ah, good. I saw your parents when I was up north this past week. Both well and hearty and full of the joy of living."

Diana shifted uneasily in her chair. "Master Hedrick, I'm troubled and need advice."

His face sobered. "I hope that I can help you. Tell me about it."

She drew circles with her toe on the floor, and considered her words. "I hardly know how to begin. You already know a lot about it. You know how Perry got into difficulties and why he was sent here. Well, I am very deeply attached to Perry. I thought and still hope and believe that our association will last throughout our lives and grow and deepen. But the trouble with my dancing partner, Bernard, got us off to a poor start. It worries me that it might happen again and I care so deeply that I find myself willing to do anything to avoid the possibility of anything like it happening again."

"How do you plan to avoid the possibility?"

"I don't know exactly. I could quit dancing with Bernard when this contract expires, and not see him anymore. But this last series we did together went so well that we have been offered a new contract at a considerably higher salary. I know that Bernard expects me to take it. He has even planned what he will do with his additional credit."

"You believe that you might be happier with Perry if you refused to work with Bernard?"

"Well—that is what I've been thinking about. In any case, although Bernard hasn't said anything and apparently the public hasn't noticed it, I know that my work with Bernard isn't as good as it used to be. I am distracted from it by the fear of Perry's opinion. Whenever a dance calls for a love scene, I can't get my mind off Perry. I wonder if he is tuned in, and if he thinks my acting too realistic."

"Do you intend to quit dancing with partners entirely?"

"I hadn't thought that far ahead. I don't know."

"Mightn't you have the same fear about any other partner?"

"I suppose so."

"Do you see that to spend your life guiding your actions by the possible opinions of a person suffering from delusions will become very complicated?"

"Yes, I see you're right. But I'd be willing to try it if I could keep Perry happy and loving me by doing it."

"That does your heart credit, but not your good sense. You are a normal healthy girl and your standards and desires are as sane as can be. But I think that I see the consequences of such a course more clearly than you do. In the first place you won't be helping Perry to get well. You'll make a permanent invalid out of him emotionally. Your whole life will become forced and unnatural. After re-molding yourself to suit his spurious standards, you will then undertake to change the world around you to prevent it from conflicting with his carefully nurtured delusions. Gradually your friends will drop away as they will be made restless by the restraints you will have imposed on their conduct and conversation. Eventually the day will arrive when you will be one of our patients. Tell me, how do you like our friend Olga?"

"Olga? Why, Olga is grand."

"Ever felt any uneasiness about Perry and her?"

"No, not really. Perhaps I have in a way. It sometimes seemed a little unfair to me that he should enjoy her company so much in my absence, when I've been so miserable with Bernard."

"Suppose that you gave up Bernard and all close association with other men on Perry's account and that the two of you were living together. Suppose Perry decides to pay Olga a visit of a few days and you can't go along. Aren't you likely to find yourself fiercely resenting Olga?"

"Maybe I would. It's hard to imagine myself resenting anyone as nice as Olga."

"I see that Perry is becoming very interested in rocketing. Olga tells me that both of you wish he wouldn't because of the physical hazards of the work. Are you going to demand that he give it up?"

Diana looked surprised. "How can I? He must decide for himself and find his self fulfillment in his own way. I must not interfere."

"Yet you plan to give up or greatly modify your own career to fit his delusions. Aren't you likely to tell him someday that, since you have sacrificed the best years of your life for him that the least he can do is to stay out of danger?"

"I'd never say that. It wouldn't be right. Oh dear, perhaps I would. I don't know. It's very difficult."

Hedrick smiled and patted her hand. "Let not your heart be

troubled, my daughter. The situation isn't at all serious. I've just been showing you some of the possibilities in order that you might understand the implications of your decisions. In the first place your young man will have a complete cure. He is doing very well, very well indeed. You can revise your plans accordingly. You are suffering from a slight touch of atavism, a regressive false identification, which you contracted from him. The layman doesn't realize that these non-lesional mental disorders can be as contagious as diphtheria or whooping cough. More so, in fact. In the old days one man sometimes infected a whole nation, particularly after the advent of radio. You have a slight touch. Physically you are well and strong, a beautiful example of a civilized girl, but mentally you have slipped back in part to the stone age woman, squatting on your haunches before the fire and cowering in fear of the unpredictable displeasure of your semi-bestial mate. Now that you know what the trouble is, correct it. Perry will be all right, so you need no longer concern yourself about him. Go ahead. Live your own life. Make your own decisions in your own way. Associate with men and women as freely as you did before you knew Perry, and don't worry."

Diana stood up, smiling, and put out her hand. "Thanks a lot, Master. I'll try it. Anyhow I've decided to take that contract."

"That's fine. If you become worried again, come back and we'll talk it over."

"Thanks again. I can go home and sleep now."

XIV

Perry was very poor company for the next couple of weeks. He threw himself into the study of the arts of rocketry and astronautics, determined to make up quickly his century-and-a-half handicap in technical knowledge. He could easily be persuaded to quit his studies and enter a sky car, but he always insisted on setting the controls for the Moon Rocket Station. This suited neither Diana nor Olga. In time they became reconciled to his single-minded enthusiasm and compromised by insisting that he take regular exercise and eat his meals on time.

Perry found that catching up was not so much of a job as he had feared. In engineering matters he had the simple empirical point of view and consequently was not disturbed by changes in theory. The mathematics of ballistics and astronautics were simpler, rather than more complicated, than the ballistic formulae that he had once used in predicting fall of shot. In particular the Siacci-Vernet method of variable exponents was a much simpler description of the action of a moving body in a gaseous medium than the cumbersome empirical formulae used by Siacci himself. Metallurgic chemistry and explosive chemistry naturally were enormously advanced over his day, but with the advance of knowledge, theory was, as usual, simpler, and he soon found himself able to understand and appreciate the technical publications of the day. He looked for and failed to find any description of the use in rockets of the high explosives of his own day. He made a mental note of this for it seemed possible that he might have some things to teach these latter day engineers.

Late in April Perry received a call from Cathcart. To Perry's surprise, he had a business proposition. Cathcart related that he'd been hired to give technical advice in the recording of an historical adventure drama laid in the United States during Perry's period. Several scenes called for airfighting of the contemporary type and neither Cathcart nor the producer were satisfied with the laboratory process shots. So Cathcart was calling from Hollywood to see if Perry thought he could fly a museum piece airplane. Perry considered, then asked what sort of a plane it was. Cathcart didn't know, but switched to the hangar circuit and let Perry see for himself. It was a Douglas light bomber with a Pratt-Whitney engine, probably 750 horsepower. Perry estimated a top speed of around 250 miles per hour. She'd land pretty hot. He looked the plane over and nodded.

"If she's in shape or can be put in shape, I'll fly her down a rain pipe and out the spout."

A few hours later, he was in Hollywood running loving hands over the controls of the plane. His preliminary inspection had been both pleasing and disappointing. Pleasing, for the craft was in essentially good shape, and disappointing because so much would need to be done before it would fly. Perry condemned the wing fabric and the controls. The metal structures would need to be rayed and tested, and portions would probably need to be replaced. Worst of all no gasoline was available and it was necessary for him to dig out old technical publications and explain what was needed to the young chemical engineer assigned to the job. The Smithsonian Institute, which had lent the plane in the first place, located a parachute which served as a pattern for a new one. Perry packed it himself, there being no one else alive who knew how. Before the plane was ready to fly, Perry had acquired a local reputation as a miracle man, as Cathcart had guarded the secret of the source of Perry's knowledge. The day arrived when he climbed into the cockpit, buckled his safety belt and started his engine. He taxied around the field and, satisfied, pulled back the stick and took off. The roar was startling after the mild whir of a sky car, but it was good to feel the wind pressure burn his cheeks, good to feel the power under the throttle. He turned and passed back over the field, swooping low. Tiny figures ran about and waved. He knew that they were cheering. He took the old crate up a couple of thousand feet and tried her out, loops, inverted flight, flipper turns, spin, falling leaf. She responded like a well trained horse. Finally he returned, landed and taxied back to the hangar. The engine coughed and was quiet. He was pulled out of his seat, pounded on the back and escorted inside by a cheering, red-faced throng.

Two weeks later he made an early start for Tahoe with a pleasant sense of accomplishment. The actual work had been easy and safe as houses in his opinion. Any military pilot of his day performed incredibly harder assignments as a matter of routine. But his associates had regarded his skill as phenomenal and had treated him with great respect. Several rocket pilots had come out from the port to watch him work and he had had the pleasure of taking several of them up on joy hops. The thing that amazed them the most was his admission that he could not pilot rockets. He was assured that he would have no difficulty at all in acquiring the coveted shooting star of a licensed pilot. To add to his general satisfaction he carried a credit draft in his belt that would raise his account to several times its previous level. He thought of the times he had risked his neck in over-sea patrol for ten dollars a day more or less, and chuckled. The law of supply and demand had been in his favor. They had forced the money on him.

The sky car purred along and his thoughts turned to Diana. She would be glad to see him and he to see her. Rehearsals for her new series had prevented them from seeing much of each other while he was in Hollywood, and a stereoscopic televue visit was not the same thing. No, not in several important respects. He smiled to himself. She probably wasn't at Tahoe. However she might be home. Home to Perry was the cottage in the High Sierras. Why not drop in and see?—Surprise her if she was there.

He located their canyon, got his bearings from the waterfall and found the little roof and landing flat. He set the car down gently and proceeded through the hangar and down the steps. He spoke to the door and paused while it glided silently back. He stepped inside and peered around. At first he saw no one, then his eyes adjusted to the gloom. He stood very still for a long moment while his heart pounded and blood throbbed in his ears. Then he backed slowly out, being careful that his sandals made no noise. He tiptoed quickly upstairs and took off at once. Some miles away he hovered in the air and took stock. This was what he had feared. This was what they expected him to tolerate peacefully. Well, at least he had managed not to break his parole and not to make a bloody ass of himself by making a scene. Now what? Where do we go from here? 'Where do we go from here, boys, where do we go from here?' The only dignified thing to do was to go away and not bother Diana further. Fortunately he had enough credit to do as he liked. He'd enter as a cadet at Goddard Field as soon as he was released from Tahoe and in due course he'd have his shooting star and get a job as a rocket pilot. Maybe Hedrick could be persuaded to let him go at once. That was best. It'd be lonely not to see Olga regularly. It'd be twice as lonely not seeing Diana. It'd be just plain awful and he might as well admit it. Not to mention Captain Kidd. Who got the custody of the cat in these cases? He'd never cared much for cats, but he had grown fond of this old scoundrel with his swearing and demands for service. And the way he had of kneading biscuits on your stomach, with his motor running like an electric fan. Yes, he'd miss Captain Kidd. As he mused Perry gradually realized that there was no anger in his heart, no red rage, no black hatred. He didn't even hate Bernard. Not that he ever expected to like the fellow. Men of that artistic sort just weren't his kind. But he realized that he no longer felt any righteous urge to beat up on the beggar. All he felt was a deep regret that a circumstance had come to pass whereby he had to break off matters with Diana. He wished now that he hadn't thought of surprising her. Well, anyhow nobody knew but himself. Say! Nobody knew but him and *he wasn't jealous anymore*. He sat very quietly and considered this amazing fact. Could it be that he had fallen out of love with Diana? He considered this. No. Diana was just as dear to him as ever. She raised his blood pressure just as much. He wanted her here right now, with her arms around him. No, it was simply that he no longer needed to hold her prisoner and snarl at anyone who approached. Somehow he felt even more sure and certain of his love for her, and her love for him.

Then nothing need be changed. He could just ignore the whole thing. A great weight was lifted from his mind. He laughed aloud, then unlocked the controls, and pulled back on the stick.

Twenty minutes later he opened the door of his little cottage at Tahoe. He strode in, whistling merrily, unstrapped his belt and chucked it in a corner. Olga was lying on the couch, reading. She looked up, laid her book aside and spoke.

"Hello, bright eyes. What are you so happy about? Come here. I want to count your arms and legs. Hmm—Seems to be all in place. Perhaps your head is gone, but you wouldn't miss it. Have you had your fill of playing tag with clouds in that outlandish contraption? I've a good mind to recommend you for a restrained ward."

He picked her up, held her in the air, and planted a smacking kiss on her mouth. Then he sat down, swinging her about so that she landed on his lap.

"There now, wench! You and I can talk. Do you miss me?"

She twisted and squirmed. "Perry! Put me down. Is this any way to treat your attending physician?"

He held her tightly. "No side issues, please. I want to talk about you and me. Tell me, strumpet, do you feel hot and bothered when I'm around. Like this for example." He rubbed his cheek against her arm.

"Hot and bothered! What an expression! Perry, what in the world do you mean by this? You're supposed to be in love with Diana."

He grinned at her. "Yes, and suffering from pathological jealousy. Yeah, I know all about that—but you see I've just discovered that I'm cured."

She twisted in his lap and looked at him squarely. "Do you mean that you find you aren't in love with Diana anymore?"

"On the contrary, I love her devotedly, but I just discovered that I no longer suffer from possessive jealousy. That's why I was whistling when I came in. Then I caught sight of you and recalled that I had been wanting to do something for a long time, so I did it. But you haven't answered my question. Fair maid, do I arouse your primitive passions?"

"I'm not a maid and that's a hell of a way to make love."

"You get the idea. How about it? Speak up."

"Well, now that you mention it, it always seems a little warm in your neighborhood."

He kissed her again before replying, "Then come on. What are we waiting for?"

"Perry, you devil, must you be so brash about it?"

"I thought you modern psychiatrists didn't believe in fancy words for simple ideas?"

"Words aren't important, but no woman ever objects to a little tenderness."

"Okay." He proceeded to demonstrate tenderness in caressing. "Is that better?"

"Much better."

He swung her around onto the couch and stretched out beside her. She gave a little gasp. "No, Perry. Be good. It's too soon after breakfast."

"Then hold your breath while I count ten thousand by twos."

"You're incorrigible." She sighed, and her eyes closed.

The next morning Perry awoke feeling crowded and cramped. He discovered that he was hemmed in on a fairly narrow couch by two large objects. When his eyes focused he found that Olga's head rested on his right shoulder and that Diana's head lay on his left. Gently he attempted to disentangle himself. Diana opened her eyes and smiled sleepily, then spoke,

"Hello, darling."

"Hello. If I were back in 1939, I'd light a Murad."

"What does that mean?"

"Never mind. When did you get in?"

It was Olga who answered. "Late last night. I was awake but

you were snoring so beautifully that we decided not to disturb you. So we whispered very discreetly across your manly chest."

Perry decided not to push the matter further. Apparently the girls had settled things in some feminine fashion beyond his comprehension. He decided to let well enough alone.

Diana stretched and yawned. "I'm starved. Anybody want breakfast? I'll order it."

After breakfast Perry announced that he was going to try to locate Master Hedrick. He had told the women about his intention of entering at Goddard Field, and wished to push ahead with his plans.

Hedrick received him with his usual courtesy. Perry recounted what he had been doing, then broached the subject of taking rocket training. Hedrick nodded his approval.

"But you see, sir, if I go to Goddard Field, I'll need to stay there continuously, three months at least. I can't check back here every day or two. Now I feel that I'm cured and fully adjusted to modern life. Certainly I don't suffer from sexual jealousy. Don't you think I'm cured?"

"Certainly you are cured, my boy. The last several association tests you've taken showed it conclusively."

"You've known for some time I was cured?"

"Yes indeed. Yes indeed. In fact I reported to the court that you had been discharged as readjusted over three weeks ago. But I couldn't tell you. You had to find it out for yourself."

"Well, I'll be damned!"

Hedrick smiled. "I think not, son."

XV

"It is implicit in all of our American institutions that there are but two things that every man wants; first, that he should be as secure as possible economically, able to face the future without fear of cold or hunger for himself or his loved ones; and second, the chance to do anything that *he* wants to do, that interests *him*, that seems worthwhile to *him*. The first we could accomplish collectively where no man could accomplish it alone. It's an impossibility alone. So we did it—together—with the dividend. The second is perfectly possible in so far as the things he wants to do don't damage others. Now most people are a pretty good sort, who don't want to damage other people, who would not do it knowingly. Our Code of Customs is designed to prevent such damage, *and for no other purpose*. We take the point of view that, if a man wants to do something and it does not hurt other people—By God, let him do it!"

President Montgomery at the Tri-Centennial
Celebration of the Bill of Rights, 2089.

Diana, Perry, and Olga sat around a table in a small but pleasant living room. Before them were the remains of a gourmet repast. Perry was pouring wine into two tiny cups. He handed them to the women.

"Here's luck. Save the bottle and I'll finish it when I get back." The girls drank and Perry refilled their cups. "We were certainly delighted that you could come, Olga. We haven't seen enough of you this past year."

"You know that I couldn't stay away, Perry."

"Thanks." He arose and stepped to a window. It was night. A gibbous moon rode high to the south and turned the desert soil of Arizona into unearthly fairyland. "I'm glad it's a nice night. Not that it makes any real difference, but it's pleasanter." He glanced at the wall chronometer. "About an hour until meridian. We don't need to leave yet."

Olga fussed with a cigarette and broke it. "How long will you be gone, Perry?"

"A little less than twenty-four hours"

"So short a time? But the moon is so far away!"

"It's far enough, about three hundred and eighty thousand kilometers. My orbit will be about eight hundred thousand kilometers all told. But I'm going to travel pretty fast."

"How fast, Perry?"

"My average speed will be around six hundred kilometers per minute, five eight six point two to be exact. I'll be going faster on the swing around old Luna, but that is because I want to stay down low and take some pictures."

"That seems terribly fast. Won't it crush you to accelerate to such a horrible speed?"

"No, not at all. I could come up to speed in little over half an hour, using only half a 'g'. Except for the first few minutes, though, I won't even use that. I'll get a big shove in the first four minutes, then drop off my first-stage rocket entirely."

"It uses your new fuel, doesn't it?"

"Yes, it uses the picroid. I designed it after a high explosive we used to use, but I've got it controlled. We used to use the stuff it's made from, picric acid, in bombs and shells, but not in guns, because it was too fast and would split a gun wide open. But this stuff I can control and get a tremendous boost with it. When it's gone I drop off its tanks and nozzles, and so forth, and what I've got left is a fairly ordinary little rocket ship."

Diana got up from where she had been sitting and faced him. "Perry, how do you know that stuff won't go off all at once?"

He smiled tenderly. "Don't worry, honey. It hasn't yet on any tests, and it can't, or else I'm no mathematician."

Olga spoke again. "Perry, you are determined to go?"

"What do you think?"

She shook her head. "Oh, you're going all right. Oh Lord, was it for this that we re-made the world? Made it safe to rear babies? Brought sanity into the world?" She walked to the far end of the room and stood with her back to them. Perry followed her, took her by the shoulders and turned her around.

"Olga, look at me. This *is* what men have striven for. Economic systems are nothing, codes of customs are nothing, unless they are the means whereby man can follow his urge to fulfill himself, to search for the meaning of things, to create beauty, to seek out love. Listen to me. If there were a deadly new plague you'd go where it was, wouldn't you?"

"Yes, but that is to save people's lives."

"Don't tell me that. That is your secondary reason, your justification. You'd go in the first place to study something, to find out what made it tick."

"But your trip is so useless."

"Useless? Perhaps. But Pasteur didn't know what use there was in it when he studied one-celled life. Newton thought his calculus was a mathematical toy. I don't care whether it's useful or not, but you've no way of knowing that it won't be. All I know is that there is another face to the moon that we never see, and I'm going out there and seeing. After me someday will come a man in a better ship, who will land and walk on the moon, and come back to tell about it. Then in the next few years and centuries the human race will spread through the planets like bees swarming in the spring time—finding new homes, new ways to live, new and more beautiful things to do. I won't live to see it, but, by God, I can live long enough to show them the way.

"But I won't be killed this trip. At least I don't feel it in my bones. This time tomorrow I'll be back, and we'll all sit down to supper again." He consulted the chronometer. "Come on. It's time to go."

The reception hall of the Moon Rocket Station was crowded with people. Perry was met at the stair by the Director who kept back a crowd of excited visitors. A husky youth in greasy coveralls pushed through the mob. Perry caught his eye.

"All set, Joe?"

"All set, Master Perry." Perry clapped him on the shoulder.

"Cut out the master stuff, kid. It's soon enough when I get back. Besides you go on the next trip."

Joe smiled. "I'll hold you to that, Perry."

"Right. Now, look. You're all through, aren't you? Will you look after the girls here, and see that they get good spots to watch? Thanks." He turned back to Diana and Olga. "I'm going now. It's less than ten minutes to zero. I don't want you out on the field. Give a fellow a kiss and go." He looked around and called out, "Private sphere!" The televue scanners stopped clicking. Then he kissed each of them and they clung to him. He patted them clumsily, arm about each, then gently pulled away. The scanners picked up again. Joe led them to the observatory stairs and Perry stepped through the field lock.

Joe found them places in the observatory tower. They saw Perry in the white flood lights, moving toward his ship with a parade ground swing. The ship itself was silver in the moonlight, huge, uncouth. It rested on a cradle in which it leaned away from vertical and pointed a trifle west of meridian. Perry was climbing a ladder which scaled the framework of the cradle. He reached the manhole in the side of his rocket and slid his legs inside. Then, half seated, he looked back at the buildings and waved his right arm. Diana fancied that she could catch the glint of his smile. Then he slid inside and was gone. The port cover swung into place from inside the rocket, rotated clockwise a quarter turn, and rested.

THE END

you look after the girls here, and see that they get good sp
to watch? Thanks." He turned back to Diana and Olga. I'm
going now. It's less than ten minutes to zero. I don't wan
you out on the field. Give a fellow a kiss and go." He look
around and called out, "Private sphere!" The telphne scanner
stopped clicking. Then he kissed each of them and they clung
him. He patted them clumsily, arm about each, then gently
pulled away. The scanners picked up again. Joe led them to
the observatory stairs and Perry stepped through the field la

Joe found them places in the observatory tower. They sa
Perry in the white flood lights, moving toward his ship with
parade ground swing. The ship itself was silver the moon
light, huge, uncouth. It rested on a cradle in which it lean
away from vertical and pointed a trifle west of meridian. Per
was climbing a ladder which scaled the framework of the cradle
He reached the manhole in the side of his rocket and slid his
legs inside. Then, half seated, he looked back at the buildin
and waved his right arm. She fancied that she could catch t
glint of his smile. Then he slid inside and was gone. The po
cover swung into place from inside the rocket, rotated clockwi,
a quarter turn, and rested.

The End.

APPENDIX
TO CHAPTER IX

NOTE: This need not be read in sequence. It is included to amplify Davis' remarks in order that the reader may understand the causes of economic confusion in the early 20th century.

There is an old tale of five blind men who were taken to "see" an elephant. Each examined it as best he could, and described it in terms of his experience.

One felt a leg and said, "It is like the trunk of a tree."

One had grasped the tail and answered, "How ridiculous! It is a rope."

A third countered, "You are slightly mistaken, brother. It is somewhat like a rope, but is actually a mighty snake." He had touched the trunk.

Another ran his hand across the broad solid side of the beast and exclaimed, "How can you be so deceived? Verily, it is a wall."

The last touched the elephant not at all, but heard him trumpet. He fled, for he thought the Spirit of Death was upon him.

They were all correct insofar as their data went. *Each in grasping a part of the truth had reached a different wrong conclusion.*

Twentieth century economists, of whatever school, almost

unanimously fell into the same sort of error. Illustrations of how they made such errors, through examining some special case of the production-consumption cycle, are set forth below:

RENT TROUBLE (The Single Tax Argument)

Use the same data as used by Perry and Davis, except (1) the banker spends all of his interest, (2) the land owner does not spend his rent. OVER-PRODUCTION: two playing cards.

Nevertheless, title to land frequently results in individuals receiving returns in rent disproportionate to investment. This is Henry George's "un-earned increment." But un-earned increment does not in itself cause over-production, and taxing it away will *not* balance the cycle. On the contrary, it throws it further out of balance. Taxing un-earned increment out of existence is only a means of *social* readjustment.

PROFIT TROUBLE (The Socialist Argument)

Same data except (1) Banker spends his interest (2) Entrepreneur spends only two shekels. OVER-PRODUCTION: 3 playing cards.

Same situation as above. If a concern's profits seem disproportionately high, they may be lowered by punitive taxation, but to do so will not tend to balance the cycle, unless shekel for shekel (or dollar for dollar) an equal amount of money is given away to someone who will spend it.

LABOR TROUBLE (The Conservative Argument)

Using the same data, but with banker spending all the interest, run two cycles side by side. Let the additional cycle suffer from labor trouble, the workers striking for high wages, and winning the strike. Let the additional labor cost be 31.5 shekels. Necessary price of cards will be 2.5 shekels per card in this cycle. But the other cycle can sell to the same market at 2 shekels per card. No matter what the final market price, both cycles will have overproduction, or the second cycle will fail to obtain a return equal to cost, or both.

Results: (a) Market price 2 shekels, 1st cycle balances, 2nd cycle sells all its goods, but is insolvent by 31.5 shekels.

(b) Market price 2 1/2 shekels, combined over-production is 15.75 playing cards.

DUMPING FROM ABROAD (The High Tariff Argument)

Using the same data, place on the market from another cycle with lower costs of any sort, especially labor, playing cards to sell at one shekel. Our entrepreneur is forced to cut prices and goes broke. Orthodox solution, XXth century: protective tariff. Rational solution: Cease to manufacture the type of articles being dumped on us, and pay for them with our currency. We gain the increment in real wealth.

INTEREST (The Anti-Semitic Argument)

There is an element of truth to this argument—that interest not spent as purchasing power unbalances the cycle. The illustration given in the narrative is proof of this. And there were undoubtedly many Jews in the banking business, though by no means a majority. Yet somehow on this slender pedestal, an incredible structure of half-truths and outright falsehoods was constructed many times in history to 'prove' that Jewry was engaged in a conspiracy to enslave the rest of mankind. It is difficult for us, in the enlightened 21st century, to realize that this preposterous myth was the cause of torture, mass murder, and an endless number of vicious acts of racial discrimination.

MONOPOLY (The Trust-Buster's Argument)

This problem should be set up in three ways, monopoly of raw materials, monopoly of technique, and monopoly of a field of enterprise. In each case modify the data to cause the holder of the monopoly to (a) receive too large returns (b) freeze out a competitor.

Monopoly of raw materials is contrary to public interest. The state must exercise its right of control or expropriation to prevent it.

Monopoly of technique is now limited to the royalty rights of the inventor, but in former times the owner of a technique was legally able to monopolize it entirely, even to the extent of neither using it, nor allowing others to use it.

Monopoly of a field of enterprise, where it is not based on the other types of monopoly, usually indicates greater efficiency and should be controlled in the public interest rather than eliminated. We now believe that the interest of the consuming public is paramount. It was formerly held that the interests of the little businessman were paramount. This point of view is roughly equivalent to that of the machine breakers at the beginning of the industrial revolution in the 19th century.

It is obvious that natural causes alone are sufficient to destroy a big business which serves the public less efficiently than a small business, all other things being equal.

The above illustrations, while by no means exhaustive, show the type of error into which our forefathers fell. In each case, the proponents of the above-listed arguments took a special case of the production-consumption equation and treated it as if it were the general case. In each case they were right—as far as they went—but by assuming their special case to be the general case, their conclusions were invariably fallacious.

For comparison with 20th century economies the problem set up by Perry and Davis will now be worked as an illustration of the general case of the production-consumption cycle, applying the modern method of the dividend-discount for balancing the cycle.

Total cost of product:	126 shekels
Number of units (playing cards):	63 shekels

Assume that holders of purchasing power refrain from spending 26 shekels. Therefore, if the government issues a total of 13 shekels as a dividend, and authorizes a discount of 13.126 or approximately 10%, the spread between production and consumption will be eliminated. Capitalization of the country will be increased by 26 shekels and production will be greater in the next fiscal period, thereby increasing the real wealth of the country.

This problem must be worked out with the chessmen, or their equivalent, to be appreciated. This type of problem is worked out in more detail on page 171.

The invention of the discount method of preventing inflation is usually attributed to C.E. Douglas, a Scottish economist of the early 20th century.

AFTERWORD

"A Clean Sweep"

Fifty years before Robert Heinlein's death in 1988, he wrote *For Us, The Living*, his first novel.

Like many writers, Heinlein found himself repeatedly answering the same questions. In particular, "How did you get published?" His polished tale went like this: He had lost a political campaign in 1938, and faced a mortgage and no prospects of employment. He saw a contest in *Thrilling Wonder Stories* offering $50 for science fiction stories from unpublished authors and decided he would give it a try. In four days of April 1939, he wrote his first story, "Life-Line"—and decided it was good enough to submit to the top market of the day, John W. Campbell's *Astounding Science Fiction*. Campbell bought it, and Heinlein never went back to what he called "honest work."

But as James Gifford has pointed out in *Robert A. Heinlein: A Reader's Companion* (Nitrosyncretic Press, 2000), the story is not quite that simple. There was indeed a writing contest, but in the October 1938 *Thrilling Wonder Stories*. However, there was no $50 prize; instead, it was a call for submissions, at the normal word rates. Future great science fiction writer Alfred Bester won that contest and had his first story printed in the April 1939 issue, when Heinlein was just starting "Life-Line"—which shows another flaw in the polished myth: the contest was already publicly won before Heinlein even began his intended submission.

Bester never had a single story rejected by any editor or publisher—but Heinlein did.

In fact, Heinlein faced a number of rejections. His second sale to Campbell, "Misfit," was accepted only with revisions, and Campbell rejected six of his next stories, one right after another. Those six rejections accelerated a learning process into writing the kind of science fiction Campbell *would* buy. And before *Astounding*, even before *For Us, The Living*, Heinlein had tasted literary rejection. When he was in the navy, serving on the aircraft carrier *Lexington*, he had entered a short story in a shipboard writing contest. "Weekend Watch," a little tale of espionage and intrigue at the Naval Academy, still survives in the Heinlein archives at UC Santa Cruz.

Heinlein lost that contest.

Perhaps his most significant rejection came before he wrote "Life-Line." He had already written a complete novel: *For Us, The Living*, which was rejected first by Macmillan, who kept it for some time, and then by Random House, who returned it after only a month in June of 1939.

Precisely when the novel was written is a matter for scholarly conjecture, but the general date is fixed in a letter Heinlein wrote to Campbell on December 18, 1939: "A year ago I wrote a full length novel." That places the window of composition between August 1938, when Heinlein lost his bid for California State Assembly, and April 1939, when he wrote "Life-Line." In August 1934, Heinlein returned to California with his second wife, Leslyn, from a long hospital treatment for the tuberculosis that ended his naval career (Heinlein had a very brief first marriage in the late twenties). He briefly sat in on classes at UCLA—he was never formally enrolled there, nor did he ever audit classes officially—and he soon realized that he would not be able to afford postgraduate study, even if he could surmount the fact that Annapolis granted no undergraduate degrees at that time, making it difficult, if not impossible, to convince UCLA to admit him to graduate school.

Fortunately, in the fall of 1934, Heinlein encountered something far more exciting than running an academic obstacle course. Upton Sinclair is best known today for the 1906 muckraking novel *The Jungle*. In 1934, he was also known for a whole series of novels and books crusading for socialism and radical change—and for running for California governor as a member of the Socialist Party. For the 1934 campaign, he had left the Socialist Party for the Democratic ticket. Sinclair's crusade electrified the nation, and terrorized the Republican Party, which had long been accustomed to controlling California. Robert Heinlein became deeply involved in Sinclair's utopian vision for California: End Poverty in California, better known as EPIC.

EPIC was one of the many plans put forward by various American political figures to solve the problems of the Great Depression, including Franklin Delano Roosevelt and his New Deal; Huey P. Long's Share the Wealth (tax the rich 100 percent after their first million dollars of income, then redistribute the wealth to everyone else); Dr. Francis Townsend's Old Age Revolving Pension Plan (give senior citizens $200 a month); and the Technocracy movement (put engineers and scientists in charge of society). FDR curtailed many of these movements by co-opting their best ideas. He raised the income tax on the rich to disarm Share the Wealth's appeal and instituted Social Security in 1935 to supplant Dr. Townsend.

Sinclair's idea for EPIC can be boiled down to a single phrase:

"production for use"—a phrase which is ridiculed in the 1940 Cary Grant/Rosalind Russell classic, *His Girl Friday*. He suggested that California had two untapped resources: factories and farms that had been closed down, and the unemployed. Why not combine them, so that all the unused land and facilities could be used by the unemployed to produce the goods and services they needed for themselves? They would use scrip to run their economies, and anything left over as surplus could be sold to the general population. On paper, it looked like a simple equation.

In reality, it provoked two responses: one, a wild joy on the part of Sinclair's followers that the problems of the Depression could be solved, and two, a great fear on the part of California's wealthy that the Socialist Revolution had come for their heads—and wallets. The memories of the Russian Revolution were sharp for these wealthy capitalists, who viewed EPIC as a communist plot. The movie industry in particular went to war, producing phony "newsreels" that were far from representative of Sinclair's plans, making it seem as though the communists and the nation's unemployed would turn life in California into a nightmare. The Hearst newspapers and the *Los Angeles Times* went to work as well, destroying Sinclair's hopes for election at every opportunity. FDR hammered the final nail into the coffin when he refused to endorse Sinclair as the Democratic candidate, seeing little reason to spend political capital on a potential rival.

So Upton Sinclair lost the election.

But Robert Heinlein did not give up the fight.

He was a neophyte political volunteer in the 1934 election, although he was quickly given six precincts to run. But after Sinclair's loss, Heinlein began to move up in the Democratic Party, to carry on the EPIC fight over the next four years. Eventually, he helped write and edit the EPIC newsletter (with a circulation of two million in 1934), became a major player in the Democratic Party in Los Angeles, helped write the platform for the state EPIC movement, and served at the state level of the Democratic Party on the California State Central Committee. In 1938, Robert Heinlein moved from behind the scenes and took up the race for political office, running for California State Assembly.

His opponent was the Republican incumbent, corporate attorney Charles Lyons. Their district included Beverly Hills and part of Hollywood, which at that time were not only wealthy, but also conservative and Republican. Heinlein had only a small group of supporters in his campaign, because the Democratic Party believed there was no way to win that seat. He fought the good fight, but because his opponent had cross-filed as a Democrat for the primaries (which eventually became illegal in California), if Heinlein lost the primary, Lyons would automatically win the election—as the only candidate. Heinlein lost, by fewer than five hundred votes.

In many ways, the 1938 election was a triumph for the Democrats—they gained the governor's seat for former EPIC member Culbert Olson and a number of state assembly seats. Although Heinlein's loss stung, it did not end his political involvement. He continued in Democratic politics at least until 1940, when he attended the Democratic National Convention in Chicago as an observer with press credentials.

Still, with his formal education stalled and his political career stymied, where would he turn to pay off the mortgage on his house? His naval disability pension would be enough to keep the Heinleins fed and clothed, but not enough to cope with the mortgage, and in 1938, owing money to a bank was still somewhat shameful.

And how would he continue his efforts to help his country?

EPIC showed every sign of falling apart: the EPIC newsletter ceased publication even before the 1938 primaries were over, and most of the EPIC politicians stopped identifying themselves as such, in order to win elections. Sinclair himself had returned full time to writing.

Sinclair's writings had always harbored social commentary, not to mention social crusades. Heinlein knew Sinclair personally and had worked with him on the EPIC movement. Thus one writer's life and work provided the model for another's incipient career.

Heinlein turned to writing *For Us, The Living*.

Of course, Upton Sinclair was not the first writer to suggest solutions to social problems in the form of fiction—utopias (perfect worlds) and dystopias (nightmare worlds) were well-known literary forms by 1938. Heinlein would have known of the genre's two most famous practitioners: Edward Bellamy and H. G. Wells, both major influences on Upton Sinclair's utopian socialism. Bellamy's 1887 *Looking Backward* remains the most famous utopian novel ever written by an American and may well be the book Heinlein had in mind when writing this first novel. In both novels, the main character awakens in the future to find an ideal society he does not understand. Through a series of Socratic dialogues, the protagonists (and the audience) learn how such a wonderful world can truly exist. Wells, whose "scientific romances" established the paradigms of science fiction for much of the twentieth century, also wrote many novels that portrayed future utopias and dystopias. *When the Sleeper Wakes* was a particular favorite of Heinlein's (the 1910 revision *The Sleeper Awakes* was the book H. G. Wells autographed for Heinlein when they met). The 1936 film *Things to Come*, adapted by

Wells from his earlier novel, *The Shape of Things to Come*, ends with a launch into outer space, as does *For Us, The Living*.

Heinlein was primed by these writers, as well as by the science fiction pulp magazines he read regularly, to trumpet the future as a wonderful opportunity for progress. When he sat down to write *For Us, The Living* he was trying to do what he had done throughout his four years of political activity and would continue to do for much of his writing career—generate change for the better. The title comes from Abraham Lincoln's Gettysburg Address:

> It is for us, the living, rather, to be dedicated to the unfinished work which they who fought here have thus far so nobly advanced. It is rather for us to be here dedicated to the great task remaining before us—that from these honored dead we take increased devotion to that cause for which they gave the last full measure of devotion—that we here highly resolve that these dead shall not have died in vain, that this nation, under God, shall have a new birth of freedom. . . .

If Robert Heinlein could not achieve social change through his political efforts, perhaps he might achieve it through the pen, to gain that "new birth" that is so central to his fiction.

Anybody who has read Robert Heinlein will recognize that he offered provocative commentary on our society and advocated for radical social change. Indeed, his politics have often confused people. How could a man who supported the Socialist Upton Sinclair and the Democrat FDR become a supporter of arch-conservative Republicans Barry Goldwater and Jeanne Kirkpatrick? As Heinlein once explained to Alfred Bester in 1959, "I've simply changed from a soft-headed radical to a hard-headed radical, a pragmatic libertarian. . . ." Heinlein's apparent change in politics makes sense if viewed this way: he saw problems that were not being solved and went to the political forces he believed had the greatest chance of solving them. In 1938, the most dangerous problem he perceived was the Great Depression, and he looked to FDR and Upton Sinclair for results; in 1959, it was nuclear war and communism (a hatred for which Heinlein developed before World War II, not with the Cold War). He supported Barry Goldwater in 1964 because he believed Goldwater would be far more effective against the Soviets than Lyndon Johnson.

Throughout his career, he would suggest solutions to the problems he perceived in society, always implicitly, if not explicitly. Oliver Wendell Holmes said, "Man's mind, once stretched by a new idea, never regains its original dimensions." Heinlein's writing does just that, stretching our minds, teaching us to think and learn, even while entertaining us. If we want to solve persistent problems, we have to think about them in new ways. In criticism of his later works, particularly from the time of *Starship Troopers* on, the most frequent objection is that Heinlein is "lecturing" the reader. If only all of our teachers could hold such wonderful seminars! As is evident in *For Us, The Living*, from the very beginning he wanted to present controversial ideas in his work. In writing for *Astounding*, he learned to produce commercial fiction, focusing on plot and characters and sheer story. Once he built an audience who would read whatever he wrote, he moved the challenging themes back to the forefront, as in this first novel. If readers were outraged by his ideas or by their presentation, so much the better.

Late in life, Robert Heinlein told bookseller Alice Massoglia that he was going to have to change his name and write under a new one. Shocked, she asked, "Why?" His answer: "Because I think I've insulted everybody I can as Robert Heinlein!" Heinlein wanted to provoke response in order to wake up his readers and lead them to really think about the issues at hand.

As Heinlein told Campbell, *For Us, The Living* was "entirely concerned with the origin of certain dominant human thought patterns and how they might change if changes in the economic and social matrix shifted the survival values of these dominant mores. It attempted to show that most ethical standards were relative—that the terms vice and virtue depended on the psychological matrices." In this way, *For Us, The Living* reads more like one of his late novels, rather than one of his earlier works. The more didactic Heinlein of the later novels was always there, subdued in the Heinlein who wrote for *Astounding* and collected those paychecks. With the publication of *For Us, The Living*, the pattern of Heinlein's career takes a completely different shape—the later novels are not an aberration but the completion of a full circle.

So what unusual ideas does Heinlein present in this novel?

Ever hear of the metric system? Clearly, Heinlein felt it was a better standard of measurement, as his future society uses it exclusively.

Heinlein also believed that English spelling needed to be streamlined and made more logical; hence, the use of phonetic spellings such as "Astronomikal Almanak and Efmerides" and "corectiv masaj."

Interesting as well that Heinlein predicts a united Europe, although one different in governing structure and outcome than the one we see today. He also predicted a common European currency, which now exists as the euro.

In 1938, few people considered space travel anything but an insane fantasy. Here, as he so often did, Heinlein advocates rockets and space exploration. He was an avid follower of rocketry, even joining the American Interplanetary Society in 1931 (which became the American Rocket Society, later merged into the American Institute of Aeronautics and Astronautics). After his death, his third wife and widow, Virginia Heinlein, endowed the Robert Anson Heinlein Chair in Aerospace Engineering at the Annapolis Naval Academy.

For today's readers (and for many in 1938), the most unfamiliar idea is that of his proposed economy. The economic program Heinlein advocates is not original to him, and is known by the name of Social Credit. He used the same economic system in *Beyond This Horizon*, where it is referred to as the "Social Dividend" paid to each member of that society.

Heinlein's interpretation of Social Credit Theory was that financial panics and the entire boom and bust cycle are caused by the relationship between production and consumption. Economists recognize that when consumption falls behind production, nothing good can follow. The Great Depression was caused in large part by overproduction in the twenties, followed by layoffs and the resulting decrease in consumption. Farming constantly overproduced, as did other "sick industries" such as textiles and coal mining. FDR's solution was to pay farmers *not* to produce—which we have continued to do, although the recipients are mostly agricultural corporations these days and not individual farmers. As Heinlein looked around him in the thirties, what he saw were failed attempts to restore consumption. He pointed out, in *For Us, The Living*, that FDR had attempted to hand out direct relief and to provide public works, but as we now know, only the massive expenditures of World War II ended the Great Depression—by putting everybody back to work, thus allowing them to consume the goods being offered. Direct relief and public works were simply not enough.

For Heinlein, Social Credit seemed a much better solution. The economist C. H. Douglas had first proposed the idea of

Social Credit in the twenties, and with the onslaught of the Depression, his ideas caught fire in Alberta, Canada. The Alberta Social Credit Party took control of Alberta's government in 1935, and Douglas became their economic adviser. Eventually, Alberta's attempts to implement Social Credit were shut down by the courts. But when Heinlein wrote this novel, there were Social Credit factions in the United States as well, including Los Angeles.

Heinlein's version of Social Credit argues that banks constantly used the power of the fractional reserve to profit by manufacturing money out of thin air, by "fiat." Banks were (and are) required by federal law to keep only a fraction of their total loans on reserve at any time; they could thus manipulate the money supply with impunity. By loaning out money that literally does not exist, and gaining in return actual cash, banks gather enormous profits. Abraham Lincoln once said, "If the American people knew tonight exactly how the monetary and banking system worked, there would be a revolution before tomorrow morning." If you took away that power from the banks by ending the fractional reserve system, and instead let the government do the exact same thing for the good of the people, you could permanently resolve the disparities between production and consumption. By simply giving people the amount of money necessary to spring over the gap between available production and power to consume, you could end the boom and bust business cycle permanently, and free people to pursue their own interests.

Until a society fully implements Social Credit, who can speak to the truth of this argument?

But Heinlein believed in it, as late as 1942 in *Beyond This Horizon*. And Lazarus Long uses the power of the fractional reserve when he works as a banker in *Time Enough for Love*, so

Heinlein clearly hadn't changed his mind about the way banks functioned by the early seventies.

Similarly, he never changed his mind as to the importance of an individual's right to freedom and privacy. Throughout his entire canon, he argues extensively for the need of the government to remain out of the private affairs of individuals; it is most explicit in *For Us, The Living* when he suggests that the cornerstone of his future government is the constitutional recognition of the right to privacy. In this novel, a citizen should be allowed to do whatever he wishes, unless he harms another citizen. What he does in the "private sphere" is simply nobody else's business.

Heinlein's own life was predicated upon this distinction. His marriage to his second wife, Leslyn, was forced to take a dual character. In public, they were the polite couple, genteel, dedicated to public service, "moral" to a fault. In private, they had an open marriage, as Perry and Diana do in this novel, once Perry's jealousy is cured. They also pursued nude photography and actively attended nudist camps, as did several other science fiction writers, including Theodore Sturgeon. Catherine de Camp posed nude for Heinlein, and her picture was shown at a party with the de Camps and Isaac Asimov in attendance. After Heinlein's divorce from Leslyn in 1948, he repeatedly went out of his way to erase their marriage from any public mention. Heinlein's furious insistence on his own privacy, and the shrouding of his past from public inquiry, rests at least in part from a need to protect his public reputation as a political figure and as a writer—and throughout much of the 1950s, his major reputation outside the science fiction community (and most significant income) was that of a writer of children's books.

Yet when he wrote *For Us, The Living*, he crusaded for this revolution in privacy, sexuality, and economic consistency.

When he couldn't get it published, he took up the fight in the science fiction pulps.

These magazines would never have allowed him to write openly about sexual issues. In fact, *Astounding* edited out all sexual references, leading some of its contributors to look for ways to evade the puritanical restrictions, as when one writer inserted a reference to a "ball-bearing mouse trap" (a tomcat) and another used alien names that when pronounced correctly were sexual terms in other languages. But while sex was forbidden, Heinlein would still be able to crusade on issues of privacy, politics, religion—and do so while being paid for it.

Now we return to the matter of rejections. Heinlein's first two submissions to John W. Campbell in April and May of 1939 were accepted. Six of his next stories—"Let There Be Light," "Elsewhen," "Pied Piper," "My Object All Sublime," "Beyond Doubt," and "Lost Legacy"—were rejected. How frustrating for a writer who had already made two sales right out of the starting gate! And his novel, his social revolution, was dead in the publishing waters—by itself, the sexual freedom the novel embraces would have sunk it for mainstream publishers in 1939.

Heinlein, perhaps frustrated, but clearly determined, decided to reshape the material in *For Us, The Living*. The concept of a future history is often cited as Heinlein's greatest contribution to science fiction and remains the core concept of this novel. By lifting, revising, and expanding the most compelling ideas from *For Us, The Living* and turning them into stories, Heinlein found a way to break the dry spell with Campbell. Once he became dominant in the pulps, he was able to stretch the boundaries farther and farther with each tale.

Heinlein always found a way to open up science fiction to wider possibilities. After the war, he was the first science fiction pulp writer to break into the "slicks" of the mainstream. He was the first science fiction writer since H. G. Wells to write a screenplay for a Hollywood movie, the first American film to realistically depict a moon shot: *Destination Moon*. He was the first science fiction writer to begin a series of juveniles that would educate entire generations of readers to love science fiction and outer space. His later novels continually challenged the very definition of science fiction, provoking anger and debate— and, as always, a legion of imitators.

Throughout his career, Heinlein mentored other writers, particularly those just starting out. One of his five rules for writing compiled in "On the Writing of Speculative Fiction" stated, "You must keep it on the market until sold." Not having everything published gnawed at him, and as he once wrote to science fiction editor and writer Frederik Pohl in 1940, the stories "sit here and shame me." The six rejected stories were submitted elsewhere until finally sold—although a story-hungry Campbell actually bought one that he had initially turned down, "Elsewhen."

So why has *For Us, The Living* never been published . . . until now?

Shortly before Heinlein's death, as he and his beloved wife, Virginia, were preparing for his final days, their copies of this unpublished manuscript were destroyed.

By now, having read the novel, longtime fans may have noticed that some of Heinlein's earliest stories (and a few of his later ones) were mined from *For Us, The Living*. In a way, much of this novel has indeed been published, as "If This Goes On—," "The Roads Must Roll," "Coventry," and *Beyond This Horizon*, the most obvious extractions. Perhaps Heinlein thought there was no point in publishing a novel that had already been stripped and resold . . .

but his fans know better. His entire Future History, published primarily in *The Past Through Tomorrow*, uses recurring characters and themes, and the later novels are often a constant blending from previous works. No, there must be another reason.

Robert Heinlein often spoke disparagingly of his writing, rejecting the idea that his work was anything more than just "stories." That posture was a good defense against both the fans who wanted him to be their guru and the few literary critics who chose to write negatively about him. Heinlein showed in *The Number of the Beast* that he had little love for literary critics—he isolated them in an inescapable room, wherein they might practice their vicious and cannibalistic art on one another until they could escape by actually reading the books they were criticizing. The few books published about Heinlein before his death did not give him much reason for respect, given their persistent factual errors and ax-grinding interpretations. So the Heinleins had few expectations that his work would ever receive acceptance outside of the science fiction readership.

Before her death in January 2003, Virginia "Ginny" Heinlein came to realize that her husband's work is now being treated in contexts wider than science fiction. Scholars are beginning to recognize the connections between Heinlein's writing and that of Voltaire, Ralph Waldo Emerson, Mark Twain, Jerome K. Jerome, Rudyard Kipling, and James Branch Cabell, among others. She began to realize that the shroud of privacy surrounding their lives could finally be lifted, in order to help the literary reappraisal now taking hold. She authorized and collaborated on a full biography of Robert Heinlein, which is being written by William Patterson, the editor of the *Heinlein Journal*. She aided many other researchers, including Philip Owenby and Marie Ormes for their doctoral dissertations and me in my own research into the life of Leslyn Heinlein. Ginny helped found and support *The Heinlein Society*, a nonprofit group dedicated to furthering her husband's goals, including education, blood drives, space exploration, and eventually, publishing a scholarly edition of the Heinlein canon (you can join this noble cause at www.heinleinsociety.org).

In short, Ginny decided her husband's work and life should be treated openly and fully.

However, Ginny died before she knew that a single copy of *For Us, The Living* had survived. On Thanksgiving Day, 2002, weakened by a difficult recovery from pneumonia earlier that year, she broke her hip. She seemed to be recovering from her surgery and was to be released the week that I received a copy of *For Us, The Living* in the mail. I was looking forward to discussing my discovery with her when she suddenly passed away in January 2003.

Major writers often leave behind unpublished works. Heinlein himself had two unpublished nonfiction books released posthumously: *How to Be a Politician* (published as *Take Back Your Government!*) and *Tramp Royale*. Hemingway has had no fewer than four major books published after his death. Heinlein's favorite writer, Mark Twain, had several books published after his death, including the masterpiece *The Mysterious Stranger*. Literary scholars treat these works in their proper context, as pieces of the larger puzzle that comprise the writer's entire output.

As the first step in the fifty-year writing career of Robert Heinlein, *For Us, The Living* is like looking at Neil Armstrong's first footprint on the moon—a footprint Robert Heinlein played no small part in making possible, with his fiction glorifying space travel, and his work on *Destination Moon*.

And that is how I believe Ginny would have come to see it; as the beginning, deserving of preservation.

So how did this manuscript survive?

Shortly before his death, Robert Heinlein decided he wanted his biography to be written. Dr. Leon Stover, an expert on H. G. Wells, had written a book on Heinlein that, by and large, Heinlein liked. After his death, Ginny informed Dr. Stover that he was to be the authorized biographer. Dr. Stover immediately began contacting Heinlein's surviving friends with the estate's full approval. One of those friends was the highly decorated Admiral Caleb Laning, Heinlein's best friend at the Naval Academy and his coauthor on two post–World War II nonfiction essays. Cal Laning had kept fifty years' of correspondence with Heinlein intact, and he handed this treasure trove over to Dr. Stover for use in the authorized biography.

But Dr. Stover and Ginny Heinlein soon had a falling out, and she revoked his permission to write the biography.

For the next decade, nothing further happened.

Through my research and contacts with those who knew Leslyn Heinlein, I found myself in possession of a partial manuscript of Dr. Stover's unpublished biography. In the few pages I had, Dr. Stover mentioned his possession of the manuscript of *For Us, The Living*, apparently given to him by Cal Laning.

Attempts to contact Dr. Stover failed, but I had the name of his student assistant, Michael Hunter. Hunter was quite surprised that I had found him, but forthright in discussing his work with Dr. Stover. When Hunter was a senior, Dr. Stover had asked him to read the novel, make a synopsis for use in the biography, and use it in a student project connecting Heinlein's first novel to both H. G. Wells and to Heinlein's later writings. Hunter never did anything with his copy of the manuscript, under the assumption that Dr. Stover's biography would soon be published and Heinlein's first novel revealed to the world. Life went on, and he never heard from Dr. Stover again.

Hunter simply forgot he had a copy of *For Us, The Living*.

At my request, he went digging through his garage and found it, buried in boxes from his college years. He willingly sent me a copy.

After Ginny's unexpected death, I passed the manuscript on to the estate, which decided the novel was well worth publishing.

And now, Robert Heinlein's first and final achievement is in your hands.

"You must keep it on the market until sold."

A clean sweep at last.

Robert James, Ph.D.
Culver City, California
July 2003

ROBERT ANSON HEINLEIN

July 7, 1907–May 8, 1988

Robert Heinlein was born in Butler, Missouri, the third of seven children. He spent the majority of his youth in Kansas City, taking jobs at a young age to supplement his family's income. It was apparent early on that Heinlein was a child prodigy of the sort that sometimes appears in his fiction. He learned chess at the age of four and took an early and abiding interest in astronomy, reading voraciously on the subject and giving lectures as a young student. His 1924 high school yearbook photo caption read, "He thinks in terms of the Fifth dimension, never stopping at the Fourth."

After high school, Heinlein applied to Annapolis—submitting one hundred letters of recommendation to his state senator—and graduated in 1929, twentieth in his class, with the rank of ensign. He was married shortly after graduation, though little is known of that union, which ended after approximately one year. In 1932 he married Leslyn MacDonald, an intelligent and politically radical woman who inspired many of his female characters.

Later that year, while serving aboard the destroyer *Roper*, Heinlein contracted pulmonary tuberculosis and was hospitalized. By 1934, his continual bouts with the disease rendered him disabled and forced his retirement from the military. He went on to study mathematics and physics at the graduate school of the University of California, though recurring illness forced his early withdrawal, and he campaigned unsuccessfully for a district assembly seat in Hollywood.

In 1939, after a failed naval career and a humbling defeat in his political endeavors, Heinlein turned to writing as a way to earn a living. This third career choice proved lucrative. By the early 1940s, he had paid off a large mortgage and was by all accounts a successful writer, having won the respect and admiration of the science fiction community. His first novel, *Rocket Ship Galileo*, was published by Scribner in 1947, and over the next twelve years, he wrote one book a year for Scribner, creating a highly respected and award-winning series of juveniles. During that time, Heinlein also wrote and published short stories, adult novels, and the script for *Destination Moon*, widely considered to be the first science fiction film. The movie was nominated for three Academy Awards and won in the category of Special Effects. During this time he was also divorced from Leslyn and married Virginia "Ginny" Gerstenfeld, a friend and colleague from his Navy days.

The Heinleins spent their marriage traveling, writing, entertaining, and working on behalf of many charitable causes—particularly blood drives, a tradition which is carried on by the Heinlein Society. In 1956 Heinlein won his first Hugo Award, for *Double Star*, and went on to win an unprecedented four Hugos, three Retro Hugos, and in 1975 received the first Grand Master Nebula Award for lifetime achievement from the Science Fiction Writers of America. He earned wide acclaim for novels such as *Stranger in a Strange Land*, *Starship Troopers*, *The Moon Is a Harsh Mistress*, and *The Puppet Masters*. Robert Heinlein continued writing, participating in political debate, and championing the cause of space travel well into the 1980's, when he retired to Carmel, California, with Ginny. His last novel, *To Sail Beyond the Sunset*, was published in 1987, one year before his death.